ADA'S RULES

A Sexy Skinny Novel

Alice Randall

B L O O M S B U R Y
London   New York   Berlin   Sydney

First published in Great Britain 2012

Bloomsbury Publishing, London, Berlin, New York and Sydney

50 Bedford Square, London WC1B 3DP

A CIP catalogue record for this book is available from the British Library

ISBN 978 1 4088 2756 7 (UK edition)
10 9 8 7 6 5 4 3 2 1

ISBN 978 1 4088 3177 9 (export edition)
10 9 8 7 6 5 4 3 2 1

FT
Pbk

Typeset by Westchester Book Group
Printed in Great Britain by Clays Ltd, St Ive plc

www.bloomsbury.com/alicerandall

The Wind D... ...in and the Queen of S...
Rebel Yell

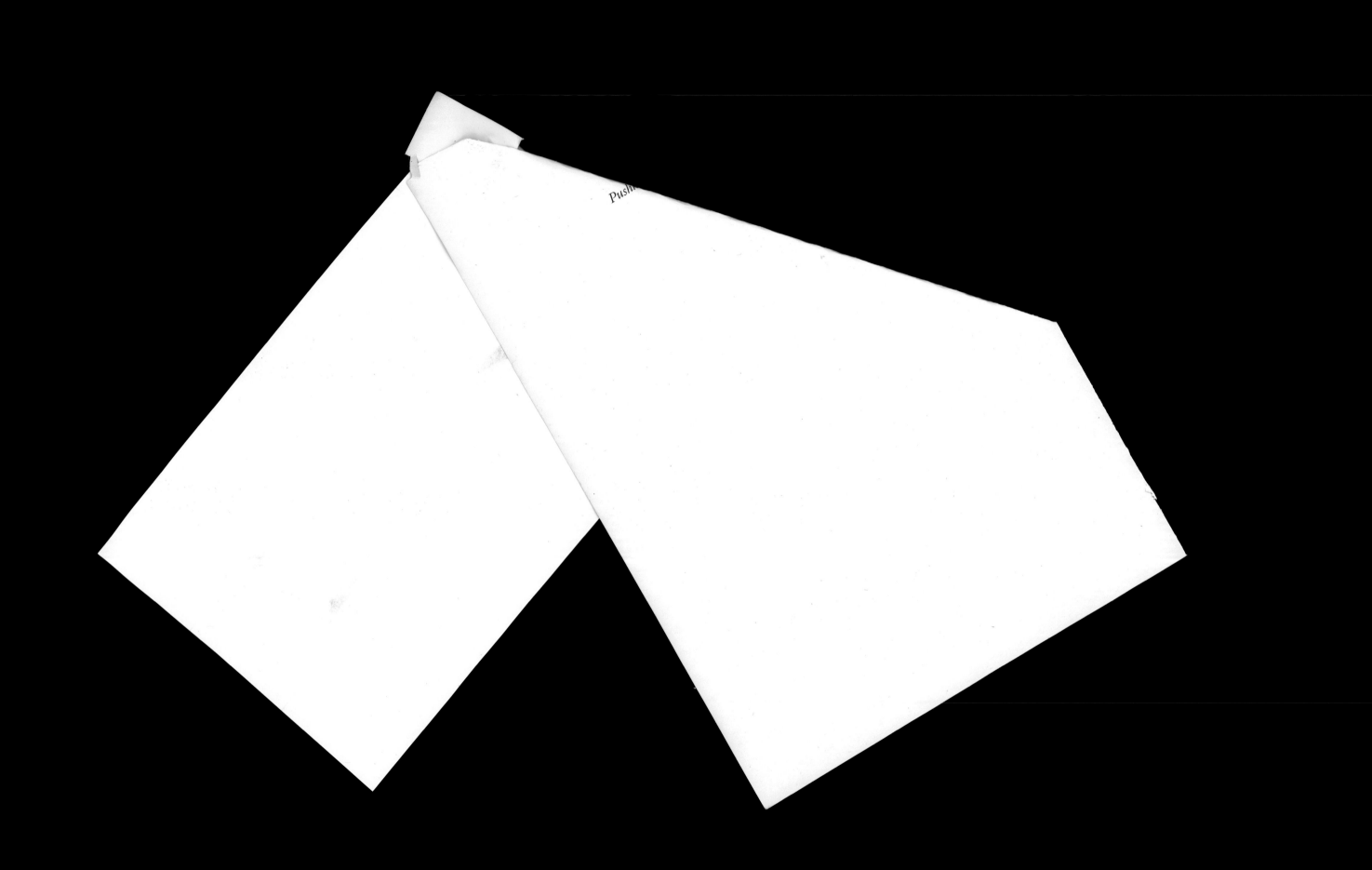

Push

To Fannie Lou Hamer and every big and beautiful black woman who has carried far more than her weight more times than was noticed.

So the very first rule is, If you want to be skinny
easy, pick skinny parents. If you can't pick skinny parents, read
my book. And if you picked skinny parents and you want to stay
skinny in this new fat world—read my book.

Turn to page 329 for how to use my novel as a diet book.

1

DON'T KEEP DOING WHAT YOU'VE ALWAYS BEEN DOING

ADA DEPARTED THE island of fat as she arrived: with little fanfare and for her very own reasons. Edited, she was still luscious. Thin again is not simply thin.

The journey had begun in the usual way. She was approaching a twenty-fifth college reunion, where she would see the man who got away, a man Ada hadn't seen in twenty years.

If that had been all, she might have dieted for a week, then figured out a reason not to go to the reunion. She did not wish to show herself to that particular man a hundred pounds heavier than she had been when they were in love. But that was not all.

She coveted, wanted back, her young brown body, and she mistook that for wanting back her young brown beau. It was a serendipitous mistake, and she went with it.

She began a diet and made an appointment to discuss gastric bypass. She liked backup plans. She didn't exactly want to go under the knife. But truth be told, she wasn't completely repulsed by the idea of being passively sculpted into someone more acceptable. All her other necessary conformity had been achieved by too much hard work.

She had thought she was too tired and too old for hard work. But the invitation had arrived, bringing with it a renewed willingness to go for it, even if she didn't get it, be it a smaller size or a new man.

It startled her to discover hidden within her half-century heart a spirit of conquest. She did not numb herself to that spirit's flutterings. She embraced them. They were all she had to embrace.

Lucius was gone. Lucius was always gone. Lucius was her husband, and he lived at work. If Lucius had been present, she might have embraced him. But he was not. Ada was lonely.

To be different, she had to do different. She knew this. So many times she had warned her daughters, "Crazy means keep doing what you've been doing and expect a different result."

She wasn't crazy. She was ready to work. She called the number in the bariatric surgery ad. She punched in the digits, hoping that she wouldn't need surgery, but wanting to be prepared if the pounds proved unmovable. She left her name and address on a recorder with a request for brochures.

She would be fit and fifty. She would not succumb to mammydom, or mommydom, or husband-come-undonedom. She would have change.

And she would have it in a relative hurry.

The day she committed herself to her goal was in every sense an ordinary day. Just as on every other weekday, she read her mail late in the afternoon, when she first came in from work. Monday, Wednesday, and Thursday, this meant when she came in from KidPlay, the day-care center where she was founder, director, and chief baby changer. Tuesday and Friday, this meant when she came in from tending her increasingly helpless parents. She liked to face the mail before she showered off the germs and finger paint of small children, and the drool and piss of old people.

Most of the mail was bills and pleadings and invitations. She liked to read the bills and begging letters with her out-in-the-world armor on, gray Juicy sweats and a Burberry raincoat. By the time she got to the invitations, her coat was off, she had washed her hands, and she had a sip of cola in her mouth. The trials of her day were over. Tribulations would come again with the sun, but well-earned rest came with the dark. She usually saved the most promising envelope for last. This day, that was a thick navy envelope edged in silver. The colors of her alma mater. Hampton. She tore open the envelope carefully, over-washed hands wielding a tarnished silver knife.

First the announcement of the reunion, then more. With a long, bold stroke, the chairman of the reunion had struck out his typed name and written, in royal blue ink, "Honey Babe" and "It's been too long."

Half an hour later, as the shower water sprayed down on her shoulders, she replayed the moment of opening the letter, seeing then decoding the scrawl over and over again: "Honey Babe, it's been too long."

The words had tickled. Matt Mason didn't talk like that. But he had. Now. After twenty-odd years, a pen-on-paper wink. And it came from her first love. It came from the first man she had shown her body to. A sound between a chuckle and a giggle, a sound she had not made in a decade, had percolated up

3

from her bronze throat and out her plum lips. That gut laugh emboldened her. She laughed again in the shower, remembering.

The shower ended. Old age was coming. Night was coming first. She stood naked before the full-length bathroom mirror. She gazed at the ass in the glass. She didn't want the body she saw.

This body was largely unknown to her. She had never pushed this body to its limits of exertion or its limits of pleasure. She had rarely looked at it. She shivered at the unfamiliarity of her own fat, flesh, and skin.

She had twelve months to get a body she might want to see, want to know, want to show, want to share. Time enough.

She took the first steps as many take them—with high hopes. At the outset of a journey, there is nothing unusual about high hopes. The unusual would come later, after she stayed on the path long enough to discover, when she had walked it to its end, when she wore single-digit sizes again, that journey's end was nowhere near where she thought it would be.

The day she set out, she felt virtuous. There was no one to warn Ada Howard, First Lady of the Full Love Gospel Tabernacle, wife of Preach (otherwise known as Lucius Howard), mother of the twins, Naomi and Ruth, and ninth-generation Nashvillian, that the path she was walking was more dangerous than she could have imagined when she cracked the spine of her new Moleskine journal and wrote, "My Diet Book."

2

MAKE A PLAN: SET CLEAR, MULTIPLE, AND CHANGING GOALS

AFTER THE WORDS "My Diet Book," she wrote: "Rule 1: Don't keep doing what you've always been doing." Then she wrote: "Rule 2: Make a plan." Her immediate plan was to weigh less than 200 pounds. She didn't know how much she weighed, but pushing on the seams of her size 3X sweats, she knew it was something way over 200.

She didn't think she could bear to know the precise number.

Like she couldn't bear to know if Preach was cheating, or with whom. There was some funny—or not-so-funny—stuff going on. He'd bought a new car. He'd lost weight. He had a new haircut. He was gone all the time. He never wanted to have sex. And now he wanted to put a shower in his office, and he wanted the congregation to pay for it. He had to be cheating. And he had to have lost his mind. But she didn't have proof. She had suspicions.

For years he had adored her, and she had adored him. And then they hadn't. She tried to remember the last time she and her husband had had sex. It would have been a holiday. One of the birthdays. Valentine's Day. Their anniversary. There were years they only had sex six times.

And there were years they'd had sex six days a week, sometimes two or three times a day. Twenty-five years of feast and famine.

And every day of them faithful. At least on her part. Always. Good marriages are not open. Good women do not cheat. Ada was a good woman. And she was allowing herself to be inspired, uplifted, pulled forward, by the possibility of flirting with, then doing more than flirting with, Matt Mason.

She wished her sisters were still alive. Glo, and Mag, and Evie weren't with her anymore. If they were, they would be near to seventy. Glo and Mag barely saw fifty-five; Evie, twenty years older than Ada, just made sixty. Her mama said, "Evie went to take care of the babies."

Ada wondered how many lovers, if any at all, her sisters had had. Big and born to boss, Evie had been a man magnet. But not one of her sisters had ever said anything to Ada about tiptoeing into cheating situations, or if they had even known anything about it.

Ada wanted to know something about it. She shocked herself by smiling as she contemplated the fringes of the possibilities.

Ada had never been with another man. It was now or never— this one or no one.

She already had a dispensation—of sorts—for Matt Mason. Preach thought she had slept with Mason before she and Preach had met, and had already "forgiven her for it." Except she hadn't actually slept with Matt Mason. Matt Mason was unfinished business.

Unfortunately, Matt Mason liked the kind of woman she used to be, small with big breasts and a big, but not too big, booty. Truth be told, that was Ada's favorite shape too. Or had been. Till she married Preach and started liking great-big.

Preach thought big was sexy. His for-real drill sergeant daddy was forty the day his only son was born to a country girl who had a little bit of meat on her bones and hailed from a corner of Arkansas time forgot. Even though Preach was born in 1960, just in time to be Queenie's first-anniversary present to Sarge, Preach was old-school.

Matt Mason was something else. He was western. He was international. He was a black man not rooted to the South, not dripping in blues, or blues transported and transformed in the North into sweet soul music. Matt Mason was jazz and funk and hip-hop. He was spare and spacious and modern. He was Miles Davis in Paris, he was Serena Williams at Wimbledon.

Matt Mason was raised in Colorado by his born-Negro parents, black professors, who sent him to nearly lily-white public schools. He took naps beneath a quilt lovingly made from old protest T-shirts featuring Che Guevara and Stokely Carmichael and a raised fist. Matt Mason rocked the New Black Aesthetic. After graduating, with Ada and Preach, from Hampton University, he went to UC Berkeley for graduate school. Having lived most of his adult life in Seattle teaching at one U, he now lived in Los Angeles teaching at another. He practiced capoeira, a Brazilian fighting art developed by slaves, almost like a religion. He liked skinny women.

Preach dismissed Mason as a "colored internet-ual" or a

"wonky black nerd." Ada didn't dismiss Matt Mason. She needed him.

Ada was scared. And Ada was woman enough to know that the only thing that always conquers fear is real good loving.

For years Ada had feared four things: blindness, death, leg loss, and clutter. Mag and Evie and Glo—Ada had lost them all to "the sugar."

"One out of four black women over forty-five has diabetes." Some white woman had spat that statistic at Ada at a cocktail party, and it had terrified her.

Ada didn't want to be one of the afflicted women. And yet somehow she was small the day she buried her first sister, and she was large by the time she buried her third.

Some of it was that her mama went chasing her father down Whisky Road after burying her third daughter, and started pretending she wasn't Ada's mother. Her mother was still alive, but Ada was an orphan.

Ada didn't blame her mother. Ada put on a bit more fat, like she was putting on big-girl clothes, or pulling up her socks, and got on with it. Soon enough, Ada was proud of being one of the large ladies.

Large ladies ran the church. Large ladies ran the neighborhoods. She knew down in her bones part of the reason she was as big as she came to be was that *she wanted to be*. She admired great big women. When she was small, she had coveted their authority, their beauty, and their significance. Then she got some for her own damn self.

Now large worried her—two ways to Sunday, twinned ways to Sunday. If she stayed large, her daughters were more likely to get large. And scared as she was of diabetes, she was six times more scared of her daughters getting diabetes.

For reasons bigger than getting back at your husband, or being afraid of blindness, Ada needed to want a man who liked skinny women.

So she did. She invited herself to want Matt Mason. At fifty, Ada had thirty years behind her of only giving her body to one man, and one man only. Now she had too few or too many, but certainly not the right number, of years of giving her body to that same one man ahead of her. She wanted to stray. Once. At least.

She didn't want to go to her grave not knowing the difference between her man and men. She didn't want to lead her daughters to Sugarland, or Strokeland, or even just Babyand-NoManland.

She would shift herself into a more helpful shape. She had shifted shape before. She was not a complete diet virgin. In the past, she had tried to use her willpower. Ada had a lot of willpower. She would pick a diet, almost at random, and she would stick to it almost perfectly, for a week or maybe two. When it didn't work, she would stop abruptly, eat something to comfort herself in defeat, think about big Botero sculpture-women and Hawaiian princesses, and wonder if society wasn't just conditioning her into thinking she should be smaller when she was meant to be large.

Except she wasn't sure she was meant to be large. And she knew she wasn't meant to be suspicious. But she was both.

She wrote down four names. She knew her husband, and she knew their world. One of the names made her sick. One of the names made her want to jump off the roof. One of the names made her want to cry. And one made her scratch her head and shrug. She inked over the names.

She would use what she had to get what she wanted. She would look like the kind of woman who could find out her husband was cheating and not have half the world believe, even if it wasn't true, that her body was the reason. She'd be somebody the prospect of having to go on a date wouldn't devastate. Be a body less likely to go blind or lose a leg. Be a body that was less likely to orphan or burden her daughters. Capture Matt Mason. Sin. Confess—to God, not her husband. Return to her marriage recommitted.

Ada had a plan. She didn't know the details yet, but she had an intended destination, Fitland, and some good reasons to get there, Naomi and Ruth; and as far as she was concerned, that was a plan.

Having a plan, even a crazy, not fully formed plan, let Ada breathe deeper if not easier.

Reality had Ada flummoxed. Reality had her scared. Reality had her boxed in. She had never had another lover, and she was afraid Preach was cheating. Her girls were getting plump, and she was getting fatter. Her long gaze into the bathroom mirror had revealed a pretty brown and beached whale.

3

WEIGH YOURSELF DAILY

THERE WAS A scale in her bathroom. As she awoke Ada thought about that. She had never stepped on it. She defended herself, to herself, by remembering it was a fairly new scale. Maybe just over a year old.

Her husband got on it every day. He watched his weight. And the congregants watched his muscular body, some of them with tongues hanging out. Just out of his wife's earshot, the congregants called Lucius, Luscious.

Even before she started gaining weight, Ada had cringed when she heard them call him that. Preach tried to get them to call him Lucky instead of Luscious, but Ada suspected he secretly lapped up the praise.

Preach said weighing every day, not once a week or never, was the key to losing weight. He never said it to her—he never talked about weight with Ada or the girls—but she had heard him saying it to male congregants battling midlife bulge. Up to this moment Ada had disbelieved him. It was against the common diet wisdom. Slowly, this day, Ada reluctantly acknowledged the obvious: the common approach wasn't working for the common woman. As her husband's approach was working for him, and clearly whatever she was doing wasn't working for her, she decided to put Rule 1 into practice and change things up.

She laughed out loud. Maybe, she thought, I can just do the opposite of everything I have been doing and lose weight. She liked that idea.

She also liked the idea of following a leader. She would steal a few plays from her husband's book, starting with weighing herself every day and ending with straying. Or not. She pulled a Post-it block off her nightstand and wrote, "Rule 3: Weigh yourself daily."

It was easy to write the rule down. It was hard to even want to get up and walk over to the scale. Easier to whisper the lie that her body screamed how big it was, what she needed to do. She didn't need to see a number.

Right now her bones were telling her—particularly the little ones in her feet and the round ones in her knees and whatever ones there were that made up the small of her back—that she was carrying too much weight. The question was, how much?

It was enough so that she was starting to feel like she had heartburn when she was lying down. Enough so her bra straps were starting to dig into her shoulders, leaving ridges. Enough so she feared getting on a plane because she was worried the belt would not easily get around her. She knew it would, eventually, but the thought of having to tug it and fiddle with it in public kept her grounded.

She wanted to fly up to see her daughter in New Hampshire. She wanted to fit easily behind the steering wheel on the drive to Mississippi. Naomi was in Exeter, New Hampshire, teaching high school; Ruth was near Clarksdale, Mississippi, teaching kindergarten.

Naomi's challenges were dealing with very spoiled, high-strung kids who were overmedicated and self-critical.

Ruth's challenges were dealing with kids who were under-diagnosed, often not given the medicine prescribed, and who best knew how to behave if they were threatened by a beating with a board called a paddle—which Ruth didn't use.

They both wanted their mama to "Come see my class!"

She got out of bed and walked toward the scale. It was on the floor under a towel cabinet. She walked right up to the cabinet and pulled the scale out from under it with her toes. She thought about stepping on it—then she thought of a better idea. She moved toward the toilet.

She emptied herself of all that she could empty herself of in the toilet, then went to the sink and washed her hands. She put on her contact lenses. As she did, she wondered how much her glasses weighed. She went back to the toilet. Remembering something she had once read about high school wrestlers preparing to make weight, she went back to the toilet and spat a few times. It seemed likely every time she spat, she was throwing off at least an ounce. She wasn't sure but she was hopeful. If she had been wearing any jewelry, she would have taken that off. She wasn't, so she didn't. And she was too early-morning tired to shave her legs or armpits, and she didn't think that could make much difference anyway.

All there remained for her to do was pull the white night-gown off from over her head and make herself a promise.

She promised: I'm going to step on this scale every day until I see a number I like. If I ever want to be not stepping on this scale every day, I'm going to have to get down to it. She pulled off her nightgown.

Ada stepped on the scale. It took a moment for the number to show, then it was there: 220. Two hundred and twenty pounds, and she was five foot two. She had a hundred pounds to lose.

At 220 pounds and fifty years old, the future was not a long road. No, sir. If she didn't do something, she would be dead, and not a pretty corpse.

The image of her great big self squeezed into an itty-bitty, ladylike casket made her cackle. She finally understood why her sisters had insisted on being cremated. She had thought it was because they didn't want to waste money. Now, imagining herself squeezed into a black dress and squeezed into a regular coffin, she got it: they were too proud to be squeezed into a regular or lolling about in an extra-wide coffin.

She stepped off the scale and put her nightgown back over her head. Then she took it back off. It was time for her shower. For a moment she thought of taking it with her gown on. A moment later the gown was back off. Then on.

She wondered if this was the beginning of crazy or senility or just another strange day in perimenopause land.

Then she figured out what was wrong. Two hundred and twenty was an unblinding bright light of reality. Everything looked different. She turned off the shower light. Without the electric light her shower was dim even in the daytime. Dim didn't help quite enough. Two-twenty had not just enhanced her vision, it had enhanced all of her perceptions. What she couldn't see, she could feel: she was no longer the firm-feeling woman she had once been.

Ada winced. "Could have been" were the words that killed men. "Used to be" were the words that killed women. I used to be young. I used to be beautiful. I used to be wanted. Soaping her flab, Ada was thinking, I used to be a firm-feeling woman.

Then she stopped thinking about her body and started thinking about *my babies*.

My babies. Not her twins, *my babies*. She had forty-three of them—all the little people enrolled in KidPlay, day care. *My babies*. Some of their mamas were Ada's *my babies*, too. "What will it mean for them if I lose this weight?" Ada wondered out loud as the water whushed down on her round brown bigness.

Most of her my babies called her Ms. Preach. But some of them called her Bigmamada. Wasn't a week went by at KidPlay some child didn't crawl into her lap and make her breasts the crying pillow they could rise from, smiling. Her fat might be missed at KidPlay.

She would prepare the kids to miss her fat. Her fat was going.

Turning off the water and wrapping herself in a towel that didn't quite get all the way round her, Ada wondered who was going to start preparing Preach. Then she got out of the shower and went down in search of her husband before heading out to KidPlay.

4

BE A ROLE MODEL

THE CHURCH WITH its steeple and cross was next door to Ada's house. Separating the buildings were a small basketball court and what had once been a vegetable garden but was now overgrown with an assortment of perennial flowers planted by various Sunday school classes over the years. Immediately surrounding Ada's house—called "the Preacher's House" by most, called the Manse by the oldest members of the church—was a weedy green lawn with an aging play fort and swing set.

Where the grounds of the Preacher's House ended and the grounds of the church began was unclear. On bad days Ada said it was at the paint on the walls of her bedroom. Everything after that belonged to the church. On real bad days Ada said she lived, and loved best she could, in the church. On those days it troubled Ada that she and Preach didn't own even a little tiny home of their own.

Preach's office was on the top floor of the church, above a meeting hall adjacent to the sanctuary. It was originally designed to be a large, open reception area that accommodated three desks, file cabinets, and storage, with a door to an inner, more private office for the minister.

Preach had different ideas. As pastoral counseling was at the center of his ministry and Preach liked to spread out, he replaced two of the three desks with sofas and added a few more soft chairs. He put in a kitchenette, a small refrigerator with freezer, two hot plates, a microwave, and a coffee machine. He used the outer office for meeting with his congregants, and his vestry, and the various groups from the community who were working with the church—from the Boy Scouts to the Nashville Business Alliance.

Preach wrote his sermons on the big desk in the big room. He used the inner office for his most private files, praying, and worrying. Nobody but Ada was allowed in the inner office.

And it was here that Ada expected to find Preach, to start talking a little about the upcoming vestry dinner, to see if he knew if his mother Queenie needed anything special, and to grab a kiss before she set off for work just a little late. Except he wasn't there. It didn't matter anyway. In one corner of the inner office was a door to a small bathroom equipped with sink and toilet. This presumably was where Preach wanted to add the shower. Seeing that door killed the desire for the kiss. Especially after seeing the scale read 220.

She scribbled a tentative menu, a grocery list, and a honey-do list for Preach before remembering she had to pick up Queenie's dry cleaning on her way into KidPlay. She left the honey-do list on his desk, then jumped in the Tahoe.

All the way into work she was biting her bottom lip, thinking about the kiss she didn't want. That and the fact she had
picked the perfect day to be late.

Ada practiced a kind of tough love in her home. At KidPlay she
practiced soft care as she rotated through the classrooms, subbing for teachers taking a planning hour or out sick for the day
in between raising the funds that kept the lights on and filling
out the forms that kept the day care accredited. Between increasing demands for service and decreasing federal funding,
she could afford to pay herself precious little.

A hundred times a day she told herself, My babies are going
to make it. Two hundred times a day the kids did something
that told her for sure she was right: drew a picture, said three
new words, counted to ten, counted to one hundred.

The parents made it harder to hope. Too many just out of jail.
Too many too young to be pregnant again. Too many gang tat-
toos. She wanted to be late to work this day. She wasn't ready to
see any of the big folk with their big mistakes the same day she
saw 220, her big mistake. Expecting drop-off to be over as she
pulled her giant old Tahoe into the KidPlay parking lot, she was
disappointed.

Most of the day at KidPlay, the full-grown women were out-
numbered by small fry. But twice a day, at drop-off and pickup,
mothers, grandmothers, aunties, and female neighbors (paid or
persuaded) swarmed the school. Twice a day the building with
tiny chairs and tiny desks and low shelves and tiny toilets with
pull-up steps turned into an Amazonia.

The profusion of large bodies—some fat, some just tall,

some "grea'big," tall and fat—made all the tiny hands look tinier than they looked during the other hours of the day. There were some skinny and some tiny grown women who came to the school—but they were a distinct minority.

Most days the women who showed up were so large, Ada seemed a woman of less-than-average size. Twice a day Ada got a fix of the lie: I am not so large. I am a smaller-than-normal large black lady.

Today she didn't want a fix of that lie. She got it anyway.

Bunny (one of her two favorite my babies; the other was an actual infant, Jarius) arrived late and immaculately clean—new shoes, hair parted and greased and beaded and perfectly braided—except for the crumbs of Egg McMuffin on her face and an Egg McMuffin in her hand.

Bunny's mother pushed in the door with her behind; her hands were overfilled with a cardboard box top full of cupcakes. Four inches of stiff chocolate frosting was piled tall on each one. Atop the frosting gleamed a cherry.

Ada smiled. Bunny smiled back, proud. Her mother, in pastel green size-4X scrubs, smiled prouder. Usually Bunny's mother's face was wired and smileless at drop-off.

"Looks like it's somebody's birthday," said Ada.

"Yes, Ma'am," said Bunny.

"You're gonna eat those all by yourself?" asked Ada.

"Three or four. Maybe F-I-V-E!" said Bunny.

A wave of nausea struck Ada. Years of close and unpredictable encounters with farts and beating welts had given her a quick-descending, cheerful-yet-serious blank stare. It descended. She put her hand to her face. She held it together.

"Happy Birthday, Bunny. You get to pick the story for nap-time today."

Bunny knew what she wanted. She and her mama had spent Saturday morning at the library.

"*Amazing Grace.*"

The choice put a crook in Ada's smile. Grace was athletic. Her mama called Bunny "Miss Priss."

"Have you read *Amazing Grace*?" asked Ada.

"Saved it for my birthday!" said Bunny.

"I told her about the hymn. My baby loves to hear me sing, how sweet the sound," said Bunny's mother.

"Excellent choice," said Ada.

Bunny's mother, who obviously hadn't actually read the book, looked relieved. She raised her eyebrows and poked the box top of cupcakes toward Ada. Ada nodded, stretched out her hand, and unburdened the woman. Bunny's mother kissed Bunny on the head, then on the cheek.

"I'm gonna be late for work, Miss Priss."

" 'Bye, Mama."

Bunny put the McMuffin in her mouth and pulled her Barbie out of a pocket. She held the doll up to her mother for a kiss. The mother kissed Barbie and headed out the door.

Ada eyed the Barbie suspiciously. After years of working at KidPlay, she had come to blame Barbie for some of the black obesity epidemic. Barbie, born in 1959, was a year older than Ada. Double-dutch, tag, freeze tag, and dodgeball—even picking cotton—all burned off a lot more calories than playing Barbie.

Ada frowned. *Fit feels too close to the fields.* My babies, she thought, poor as they are, suffer from a strange strain of afflu-enza. She let go of the thought; the child was speaking.

"Am I like Amazing Grace?" asked Bunny.

"A lot like Grace," said Ada. She said it like she felt—like she wanted it to be true. She wanted this real girl, Bunny, to fol-low in the fictive Grace's muscularly leaping brown footsteps.

It seemed unlikely. Bunny prided herself on being prissy. Bunny was four years old, but she already knew how to say, "No! Cain't swet my hair" and "No! Cain't break ma nail" when asked to take part in outdoor play.

Bunny preferred, and let everybody at the school know that she preferred, fueled by her mama and aunt and grand-mother's pride in her being prissy, to sit in a corner with her dolls, with a little posse of black Barbies. Which she would never grow up to look anything like if she kept eating cupcakes with four inches of frosting and playing Barbies instead of jumping double-dutch.

Bunny was in a dangerous pudge situation. *My babies are in a pudge predicament.*

Nobody needed to tell Ada there was a health-care crisis in America. She saw it every day.

Looking at Bunny, Ada got it. America can't buy her way out of the health-care crisis, and she can't legislate her way out.

As best as Ada could figure it, too many Democrats believed in throwing money at problems, doing things like making sure people with diabetes get the funds for dialysis, but not doing much about keeping them off dialysis, or realizing that spend-ing on dialysis made many good folk want to spend less money on education. A lot of Republicans wanted to change the laws mandating coverage of treatments they deemed unnecessary like screening mammograms, or home dialysis, or home care for kids with certain ailments, and some proven lifesaving drugs they legislatively defined unnecessary.

Double bullshit. Dem-shit and Repub-shit. Man-shit. Ada was through with all of it.

Looking at Grace hanging from a bar, doing an athletic imitation of an Anasazi spider in the pages of Bunny's picture book, Ada saw a solution: *healthing.* Start living so we get less sick in the first place. Keep everybody's body out of the hands of Democrats and Republicans.

As Ada had not been healthing and wanted to make radical changes in her eating and exercise habits, when she was back in her office (rocking gorgeous baby Jarius while she waited for his twenty-nine-year-old grandma to "rush come get" the fevered infant), Ada phoned for an appointment with her internist. When Jarius's grandma arrived, Ada got back to Bunny's room and on plan.

After announcing to the class that the United States of America needed their help, Ada, huffing and puffing, took fourteen of her babies on a short walk through the neighborhood, their little wrists tied to a clothesline for safety.

In honor of her birthday, Bunny led the row.

5

DON'T ATTACK YOUR OWN TEAM; DON'T LET ANYONE ON YOUR TEAM ATTACK YOU

W HEN ADA LEFT KidPlay, her working day was not over. Twice a week, usually Tuesday afternoons and Friday mornings, depending on when the ever-changing roster of school volunteers scheduled to show up showed up, Ada drove from Nashville, forty minutes on the interstate, to her parents' house out on the lake in Hermitage, Tennessee, to cook and to clean.

The house was a maze. There were piles in every room. Some of the piles were taller than Temple, Ada's father; most of the piles were taller than Bird, Ada's mother. To disappear, all one had to do was dive into the center of any one of the rooms.

The clutter had begun on the perimeters, on the floor near the wall, with stacks of records and boxes of reel-to-reel tapes. When the clutter had wrapped around the walls once, providing a layer of insulation, Bird, who fluttered between the piles in old World War II and Korean War kimonos, had allowed a second wall of "stuff" to arise, three feet in front of the first, then a third.

As floor space vanished, tabletops sprouted piles. When the

tables got littered high—with old stage clothes, boxes of dishes, instrument cases, and boxes of unknown contents taped shut and labeled mysteriously with the word "den" or "bedroom" or some last name that was not Bird's or Temple's—the maze was fully formed.

At the center of each room was hospitable space. In the living room the center was a large sectional couch, upholstered in purple velvet. The pieces could be moved to form an L shape or a square or broken apart to form chairs. Usually Bird had them broken apart and arranged in a little circle, but for reasons only she understood, she moved the furniture about regularly. Whatever shape the sofa took, there would be near it an old acoustic guitar case piled atop another that served as what Bird called her coffee table. Ada called the thing "Mama's medicine chest." The guitar cases were littered with aspirin and Benadryl and Alka-Seltzer and Tums and boxes of Afrin and Astelin, a little bottle of cod liver oil, and a silver spoon that always looked like it needed washing.

Before the house became a maze it had been a modest haven, a four-bedroom, five-bath ranch house with sliding glass doors and picture windows. Every room had a view of the lake or the woods.

Ada had her own key. When she opened the door, she faced a wall of mess that made her blink. Then she closed her eyes and took a breath. *Ganja.*

The muffled sound of talk and coughs passed through the piles to greet her. She called out, "Hey everybody." No one answered. Everybody living in the house was hard of hearing. Years of too loud too good music had damaged her parents'

24

eardrums. She slammed the door hard so they could feel her arrival. She didn't want to scare anybody. After two deep breaths and a prayer she didn't get too strong a contact high, she turned sideways and did her best to squeeze her way into the center of the room without bumping into a pile that might tumble down on her head and knock her out.

When she got to the center, her parents were both on one chair. Bird was on Temple's lap, full-drunk, and he was a little drunk, telling her a story.

The good days were the days they got drunk together. Her father looked up as Ada picked up the dirty spoon, the overfull ashtray. Bird's hand brushed the velour of Ada's sweatpants. This made Ada shiver. Her mother hadn't exactly touched her, but she had almost touched her. It could have been an accident, but it could have been on purpose. It was as good as it got for Bird and Ada in the twenty-first century.

When Temple first came into possession of the house, he had been proud of the fact that it looked out on the same lake and the same kind of trees Johnny Cash's house looked out on. When he saw Cash's big shiny bus parked out on his lawn, he was proud of his own ramshackle bus parked out back.

Temple had bought the house cheap at a foreclosure sale. Dug the cash he had saved (playing country-club dances and betting the occasional number) out of his yard. Because some minor star had shot himself in it, no one else even bid. Temple got it cheap.

When they first moved into the house, Temple and Bird's big girls would tote their laundry in from town to use the new avocado green washer and dryer in the fresh-painted pink garage turned laundry room. But anything red you threw in the wash, no matter how many times you had washed it before, ran onto anything white. And if you tried to get radio reception, the channel would skip itself. And stuff, particularly white towels, seemed to go missing. Mag, Evie, and Glo said the garage was haunted. None of them would go into it. Temple had to move the washer and dryer out of the garage and into the kitchen.

That old washer and that old dryer still stood in the kitchen. There were mink stoles and an old fox coat in the dryer, and mohair and angora sweaters in the washer.

Bird couldn't use the washer and dryer because they reminded her of the daughters she had lost. And she couldn't get rid of the washer and dryer because they reminded her of the daughters she had lost. Bird didn't do wash. Everything, even underwear, went to the dry cleaner—or Ada washed it by hand and hung it on a line to dry. "Waste not, want not," Bird said when she turned appliances into cabinets. When Bird explained this, cheerfully and clearly, it almost made sense.

Bird was still a house-proud woman, though only her husband and her surviving daughter could see it once clutter took hold of the lake house. What remained clear was that Bird was a welcoming woman. There were places to sit and places to rest a glass in each room. If Bird didn't cook much anymore, what she did cook—a platter of fried chicken, a pot of greens, a crown of monkey bread, a skillet of cornbread, a bowl of pasta puttanesca—she cooked well and clean.

Mainly Bird served the casseroles Ada cooked. Ada usually made a dozen at a time, leaving one in the refrigerator and storing eleven in the freezer. Every few months she would spend a whole day at the house just cooking and freezing soups and casseroles. You never knew how many people might want to eat at Bird and Temple's.

Usually Bird was asleep when Ada arrived. Bird kept what she had taught Ada to call "vampire hours." She went down when the sun came up and got out of bed when the sun went down. Usually, Ada found her father alone in the center of the living room when she arrived, or with some of the boarders. When he was alone, she would kiss him on his rough mahogany brown cheek speckled with moles, and he would always say the same thing first: "What you know good, girl, what you know good?"

And while she wondered how he could imagine she could know anything good in this place, she would say, "My mama's rich and my daddy's good-looking," and he would laugh at her joke.

Today Temple was telling Bird about playing Idlewild, reliving seeing "all the rich niggers from 'Cago and Dee-troit sitting at the tables clapping as we looked down from the stage." He was remembering a moment so different from gazing out and trying not to see the rich white folks they saw down in the Delta country clubs.

Days like this, Ada wondered if she couldn't get their house straight again. Days like this, when they could stand to be so close to each other, it seemed they didn't need their house all junked up, that they didn't need the stuff, just needed the memories and the talk, and maybe some of the pictures. Didn't need a thousand boxes to keep them from seeing each other or from forgetting who they were. Days like this, she cleaned their toilets and mopped the kitchen floor and changed the linen on Bird's bed and the linen on Temple's bed and picked up the linen in the boarders' rooms and put fresh towels and sheets on the foot of their beds and washed up the pans on the stove and took out the trash and scrubbed down the refrigerator without interruption. She wondered how it came to be she was this glamorous yellow couple's fat black maid but felt grateful to be near them.

It was getting to be time for Ada to leave, and she still hadn't done everything she needed to do. Bird was sitting at her kitchen window, looking out at the lake. Temple was out fishing.

"What's your name, girl?"

"Ada, Mama, Ada."

"You a big fat girl, you not my daughter. I got four skinny gals."

"I mean, Ada sent me."

"That's good."

"Yes, ma'am."

"Do Ada have the sugar?"

"No, ma'am."

"My first three girls died of the sugar."

"Ada's fine."

"They up and go."

"Who?"

"Daughters."

"Ada doesn't have the sugar."

"You look a lot like her, if she was big and fat."

"I take that as a compliment."

"When you coming back?"

"Next week."

"Good. Ada keep sending you. I ain't finna be nobody's mama no more."

"Don't say that, Mama."

"Don't you call me Mama, gal. What's your name?"

Ada walked out without saying anything. Bird wouldn't remember her rudeness. Or she would, and it would fix her right.

Ada feared Bird's alleged short-term amnesia was a put-on to allow her to say whatever crossed her mind. She feared worse that her mother really didn't know who she was. For months she had told herself she would rather have a mean mama than no mama at all. Today she was tired of mean Mama.

She walked out into the garage. She sat on the floor near to where the ghost stayed. She wondered if her father had really dug up the money for the house from their old yard. And if he had, had he really made it all singing and writing songs he just got paid for and no credit? Maybe it was like that. That's the way her father had told it to her.

Except her father didn't always tell her the truth. Her father lied and ran round with women. Way back when, he gambled. He had gotten away with a lot of stuff—and now it was like all that stuff had come back and got piled up in the house and she was supposed to take care of it while her parents ducked and dodged each other. And some days they found each other and forgot all the ducking and the dodging and the infidelities and the bad Pap smears and the missing breast and missing prostate and just told a story and loved up on each other.

By the time Ada was finished with her work, her parents were sleeping in their separate bedrooms. The door of her mother's room was ajar. She was sleeping in a tailored dress. The old piano lived in Bird's room. The kimono she had been wearing was stretched across the keys. Her dead daughters' clothes were piled high on the piano bench. A bottle of Nyquil was by the bed, along with a joint.

The boarders were out, probably on a road trip to a local farm to score marijuana. It took one to drive, one to navigate, and one to do the talking. They had gotten that decrepit. They paid the rent in pot. Pot and Ecstasy. If someone started dying, or leaving town to live with relatives forever, they would all get together and swallow Ecstasy. Every day of the week they smoked weed.

Ada couldn't tell Preach any of this. Ada couldn't do anything but clean everything up and pray they didn't get busted. It made her sad to realize she was praying as much to the ghost in the garage as she was to the Lord Jesus. She rationalized the choice by reminding herself that *if* there was a ghost in the garage, God had created it—and she wouldn't turn her nose up at anything but evil. What made her sadder was having seen some of her baby clothes on the pile with the dead daughters' stuff. It was the first time she had seen that in the decade she had been cleaning her mother's house.

Ada, who never cried, cried all the way back to Nashville.

6

IDENTIFY AND LEARN FROM ICONIC DIET BOOKS

AFTER SHE GOT back home, after she washed her hands and face in the kitchen sink, after she opened her invites, after she came down from her contact high, after she got the text saying Preach wouldn't be home for dinner, Ada self-medicated with Amazon.

Ada liked to shop online. She particularly liked Amazon. Nobody could see her, but she could see so much. She liked to peek inside dozens of books within the privacy of her room.

She had learned a lot from books. Manners. Cooking. Child rearing. Sex.

Sticking with the principle of using what you have to get what you want, she needed some diet books.

Tucked up in her quilts with her laptop on an online shopping spree, the first one that caught her eye was *The Shangri-La Diet*. *The Shangri-La Diet* was written by a psychologist. It promised radical change without radical change. Smart people endorsed it. Smart people renounced it. *The Shangri-La Diet* was deliciously controversial. Ada had a secret taste for controversy. She had a not-so-simple taste for plain simplicity. Reading the user reviews, she felt this diet would satisfy both. All she had to do was eat two tablespoons of a certain kind of olive oil a day, or two tablespoons of sugar water a day, and somehow this would help her regulate her appetite. In theory she could eat what she wanted, but she wouldn't want. After putting *The Shangri-La Diet* in her cart, she mentally checked off "fun crazy diet" and veered toward the normal diets. Eventually she put *Weight Watchers New Complete Cookbook*, *The South Beach Diet*, and *Atkins for Life* into the cart. She still wasn't ready to check out. She wanted something new. She put *Skinny Bitch* and *The Flexitarian Diet* in the cart. Remembering a few oldie goldies and a few articles that had intrigued her, she searched for a few more diet books and eventually added *The Mediterranean Diet*, *The Sonoma Diet*, *The Big Breakfast Diet*, and *The Mayo Clinic Diet* to the cart.

Ada gorged on purchase till she was sated. Then she checked out with one click and had all the books sent the slowest way possible. She didn't want to change too quickly. She winced when she saw what it added up to, but didn't alter the order. She was half high on consuming.

She took a deep breath. It was strange to be overconsuming to learn how not to overconsume. She exhaled forcefully, blowing out the buyer's remorse. Head clear, she decided in a flash to contribute the books to the church library after she read them. Now the purchase made sense.

And she had a new rule: Identify and learn from iconic diet texts. At the very least, by suggesting how she should eat, each of the books would keep her mindful about eating. She didn't have to follow the plan, but by noting how much she was on or off someone else's plan, she might find her own. And when she didn't have a plan of her own, she could borrow one of someone else's.

Until she could find out what diet worked for her, Ada decided to go on a diet that had worked for multitudes: Weight Watchers Online. The twins had been after her about it for months. She had refused because she thought they were wanting her to go to meetings. Getting together with strangers to chat about intimate things worked for a lot of alcoholics and fatties, but she had suspected it wouldn't work for her. It had been reading *Amazing Grace* to Bunny that had made up her mind to look into it.

She liked what she found. She didn't have to go to meetings, and they were running a special. She signed up. She chose "shrinkingprincess" as her user name. She had a new principle: Do something to further the diet cause every day—even if it's a small thing.

Ada was assigned 22 points for the day, and 35 bonus points she could use over the course of the week. The big problem was, she had no idea in the world how many points there were in anything.

By midnight that was no longer true. By midnight there were things she loved that she would never eat again, and things she would not eat for years. Margaritas, she would never drink again. California rolls, she would not eat for a year. All salads in any chain restaurant she would eye with profound suspicion. Baja Fresh Mexican Grill fajitas carnitas were 25 points more than a day's allotment—never to be eaten. On the other hand, four pieces of red snapper sushi were only 2 points.

Ada needed a drink to process the new information. Except drinks cost points. Lots of points.

Her favorite part of the Web page was 0- to 1-point-value foods. If she wanted to be able to eat three meals and two snacks a day and to have a glass or two or three of wine, she would have to consider sourdough crisp bread an entrée. She decided to tally the points of what it was she had eaten today. The total came to a whopping 36.

She took the 22 points for the day, then borrowed 14 from the 35 bonus points for the week. Which left her with 21, until she realized she had enough points to have a brownie and a glass of red wine. Thinking about starvation was making her hungry.

Or maybe it wasn't thinking about starvation. Or at least maybe it wasn't thinking about *food* starvation. Yes, Ada was hungry. And not just for fajitas carnitas.

Ada was sex-starved.

Her husband had had a late meeting with the vestry, and then he had to make a late visit to a parishioner in home hospice care who wasn't expected to last the week. She believed that was why he still wasn't home—but she suspected something else. In her wilder imaginings she tortured herself with the thought that after he had done his preacherly duty and satisfied the needs of his congregants' souls, he had satisfied the carnal needs of someone else somewhere else.

Those four little names again. This time she didn't cross them out. She wrote question marks beside them.

Three of the names were members of Preach's church. She

rebuked herself for imagining that he was stepping out with one of his flock, but he never saw anyone else but his flock long enough to fall into love, lust, or infatuation.

She liked the word *infatuation*. Particularly right now, because it had the word *fat* in it. *Infatuation* was a wise word, a word you had to have passed through to understand. If you had, you'd know that it wasn't love, but love's cousin. But infatuation had its glories. It was the desire, the aroma of goodwill, that comes from being soaked in the presence of someone you enjoy until you are plumped up to bursting with a kind of confidence that comes from knowing your presence is appreciated. Infatuation is a response to charm, yours and your sweetheart's. It says nothing about honor or perseverance or transcendence or anything high and mighty. Infatuation is sucking the sweet out of the moment and being the sugar tit and thinking for a moment you can be a baby and a grown folk. Once a long time ago she had been that kind of drunk on Preach. Now she wasn't, but she suspected someone else was.

Ada wanted to be infatuated. Again. With Preach. But she wasn't. She was inFATuated. Stuck in a fat situation, and she didn't mean phat, didn't mean good.

She hoped the light she saw in Preach's eyes, which she had not put in his eyes and God had not put in his eyes, came from knowing he was newly adored, not from tasting the adoring one.

She could and would forgive *imagining* the joys of someone else, but she wouldn't forgive him tasting them. She stopped to take note of this and to remind herself she would be anathema to herself if she did in fact cheat. To remind herself it was fine to play with the idea, to inspire herself to lose weight, but she couldn't really indulge in eating the prey she chased. But she could actually chase. At least today.

She wanted to pray again. Truly pray. Down on her brown Episcopal knees, the way Bird and Temple had raised her. She hadn't prayed that way in a very long time. It would have been the last time she went to an Episcopal wedding or funeral. She wasn't even sure she believed in God. That was a break between them—not her uncertainty, but her fear of sharing her uncertainty. If she had told Preach, he would have told her that he had his hours and days of doubt. But she didn't tell him, so he didn't tell her.

She was his wife and his congregant, and though he knew the duty of husband was a profoundly higher standard, he acknowledged his duty as pastor was not to let his doubt become contagious.

If she had told him, she doubted he would have told her, "I plowed that doubt in you, Ada, thrust and kiss." He would have told her, "I am more sure of you than I am of God."

Except year after year, with all the not-telling, it stopped being so.

Ada wanted to create a feast that would bring her husband back to the table of her body. And she wanted to create a feast that would bring herself back to the table of her husband's body. She felt very far from that. And it would be too many Weight Watchers points, anyway.

She giggled, imagining a principle that would be a bald-faced lie: Food eaten in bed during sex is not to be counted as food.

She was happy a kiss had zero points. She wondered if a day would come when the snack she craved was Preach's kisses. Then she started thinking about other ways of eating Preach and stopped herself. She was *the preacher's wife*.

Her mind looped back to less tantalizing Eros. She imagined nibbling on Preach's ear or brown belly instead of on yellow chips and red salsa. With no Preach and no zero-point Wasa bread in the house, she walked down into her kitchen and got herself a brownie and poured herself a glass of wine.

It was oddly like communion. When she had eaten and remembered and prayed, she took herself back to bed. As she drifted off, she heard Preach's key in the front door lock.

7

WALK THIRTY MINUTES
A DAY—EVERY DAY

A DA WOKE UP peculiarly early. She knew it was peculiarly early even before she opened her eyes because Preach was still sleeping beside her.

He was a large man, mahogany colored. Time had been kind. To him. His legs were thin, he had a little belly, and his arms and shoulders were massive. He was bald on the top of his head, but the rest of his body was covered in what she had once called man-fur. He had beautiful hands and beautiful feet.

She wanted to lie atop him, rug and baby. They had played that game Sunday mornings the first years they were married, until they had had the babies. After she began putting the babies on his chest, the space above her husband's waist and below his chin belonged to their daughters. Now that the daughters were ladies, this territory of her husband's body was hers again, but she didn't know how to claim it except by the old game—and she was too big for that. The thought that she would feel like a boulder, not a baby or a lover, lying on her husband's belly got Ada up and looking for walking clothes and walking shoes. Ten thousand steps. She had read and been told ten thousand steps a day was the magic bullet. She had time to take a walk before she went to work. She would do new things. Jump right in it.

Except she couldn't find what she wanted to wear. She didn't know if the items were lost, misplaced, or never existed. It was too early to think, and she hadn't had coffee. She knew she wanted to do something different. She used what she had.

The elastic had come out of an old purple lace bra, giving it a looseness she thought might be comfortable for walking, and it surely was no good anymore for hiking up her bosoms. She cut the underwire out to make sure it was comfortable. She found her old exercise shoes, but not the socks. She decided to go sockless, then thought better of it and put on some black-and-white polka-dotted dress socks. She had some old Umbro shorts, black and white and large, so she put those on. She had a drawer full of big T-shirts to sleep in. She grabbed a clean one and put it on.

She was almost completely sedentary. The walk she had taken the KidPlay kids on was an anomaly. She would start walking a mile a day, a slow mile a day. Even if it took her forty-five minutes. She hoped it would take thirty minutes, feared it would take an hour. Whatever it took, she was doing it.

Sixty minutes later, her feet were roughed up on the top of her toes, her inner thighs were chafed by the seams in the shorts, and her nipples were scratched by the bra.

But she had made a new friend. She had been passed by a very polite plump cyclist, a pretty boy with red hair and what looked like light eyes from the distance and through his helmet. His bike was one of those strange bikes that had been extravagantly customized by local kids that formed a kind of East Nashville gang. She had been surprised to see the east-side bike in her eclectic west-side neighborhood of bungalows and infill and oddities, including her Queen Anne Victorian farmhouse. But the boy doffed his cap to her, and Ada nodded back. When he replaced his cap atop his helmet, she knew her new effort had been saluted.

Then a mosquito bit her. She had forgotten that mosquitoes were out in the early morning. Ignoring the chafing, she double-timed her homeward-bound pace. It was surprising to come upon her house, a cream clapboard farmhouse with wraparound porch and thin spindle columns, not a fancy place but a pretty place, when you came to the break in the shrubs that allowed you to see it from the street of brick rentals and brightly painted cottages. She sighed at the prettiness.

Back in her bedroom, scratching the mosquito bite, for one of the first times in her life she talked to herself, right out loud. "When God invented exercise, he wasn't thinking about me," she said. She was worried that Preach had heard and would think she was crazy. She didn't need to worry. She found a note on her pillow, telling her he had an early meeting and had walked across the yard to the church.

It was still early. Ada made a shopping list:

Running shoes
Sports bra
Running shorts
Running socks
Treadmill

She wondered how much a treadmill would cost. She stopped and grabbed another Post-it—she had a new rule. Budget! Figure out what you will need and how you will pay for it. She needed to distinguish between what she needed and what she wanted, and she didn't think cheap was the way to go. Chafed nipples, chafed thighs, and messed-up feet were not in her plan.

She frowned. She was too poor to get skinny. Or not. She was not too poor if she begged, borrowed, or stole a guitar, or two, from her father. Puzzling over the possibilities, she got in the shower. Three minutes later she was under the spray, doing the Pony, singing loud, in her best imitation of Nancy Sinatra, "Ready steady boots, stay walking."

8

SEE YOUR DOCTOR

THE DOCTOR WAS pleased to see Ada. And Ada was pleased to see the doctor. Willie Angel was a friend, a peer, a Link sister, and, as she was wont to put it with her preferred patients, a "luxuriously large" woman herself. She was also one of the best internists in Nashville.

Willie Angel was pleased with Ada's blood pressure management, and with her last metabolic blood panels. It wasn't that the numbers were perfect, it was that the numbers were not yet too dangerous. Willie Angel was a pragmatist. She wasn't counting on getting Ada off blood pressure medicines, she was counting on keeping the pressure under control and managing the diabetes when it came.

She didn't think there was much to do about Ada's weight except have the surgery or wait for new drugs to be approved. She thought there were two in the pipeline that might really help with weight loss.

Her only other real suggestion was that Ada buy a desk with a built-in treadmill. Ada found that suggestion silly and expensive. Willie knew how much Preach earned. Her husband was on the vestry, and the vestry set Preach's salary. He could not afford to buy his wife a thousand-dollar desk. Besides, Ada didn't work at a desk. She worked on a dingy alphabet carpet. She worked sweeping floors.

Still, she found her doctor's approach reassuring. Dr. Angel reassured Ada with her presence and with her words. And she took the time to say she didn't think Ada should blame herself for her weight.

"It's genes and stress and corn syrup in everything. And food pornography, everywhere we look, creating appetite. Man wasn't built for this much prosperity."

Willie Angel's finger-pointing at everything but Ada gave her patient a measure of relief. Stripped of shame, Ada was better able to carry her part of the blame. And she was able to feel, for once, finally, in a way that motivated her to make a change, her own despair.

"Stick a fork in me, I'm done," Ada said to her doctor. The doctor heard the alarm beneath the humor.

"There's an antidepressant associated with weight loss. Maybe you should talk to a psychiatrist about prescribing it. I could make a referral."

"If I go see a psychiatrist, it'll be to talk. I like my brain chemistry. It's my body that's the problem. I read somewhere fat black women are among the least likely people to kill themselves."

"Are you thinking of killing yourself?"

"I'm thinking of getting fine and fit to go with fifty."

"You're cleared for whatever you want to try. Any normal diet, any normal exercise. And be glad you're not even a little prediabetic."

"It's my big butt and all the coffee I drink."

"That's as good an explanation as any."

"What about you?" Ada asked her doctor who was her friend.

"I'm prediabetic," Willie Angel replied softly.

"One day my butt fat may save an entire Chinese village of diabetes. But you'll get yours first."

"If the diet starts going really well, you might want to lipo some off and freeze it for the advancement of science. There are those mouse studies that say injections of butt fat can prevent the development of type-two."

"You know I haven't had that much luck with frozen body parts," said Ada.

"Fat's different from eggs," said Willie Angel.

"I thought eggs were fat," said Ada.

They laughed till tears were running down both their brown faces. They were crying for their bigness and crying for the third and fourth baby Ada never got to have and crying over the irony of being a physician and a walking advertisement for the problems obesity causes and crying for the joy of fighting the good fight.

Ada liked Willie Angel enough to want to lose weight and be the proof that one of Willie Angel's patients did what couldn't be done.

Willie Angel wanted to be part of Ada's solution. She pulled out her prescription pad. She wanted to give Ada something. She wrote down, "Angel's Rule of Eight—for only the best and biggest patients":

Get eight hours sleep every night.

Drink eight glasses of water a day.

Walk eight miles each week.

Ada took the prescription and sucked her teeth. "You slick, Willie Angel. Very slick." She stood up and hugged the doctor. The doctor hugged her back.

"And count your blessing your husband likes women with a little meat on their bones."

"Don't tell me you know that from firsthand experience."

"I wish."

They shared another big-bellied laugh. Willie was larger and better dressed, Ada was smaller and frumpier, but someone passing the examining room would have thought they were sisters.

9

DO THE DNA TEST

COMING OUT OF the doctor's office, Ada bumped into the president of the Altar Guild and member of the vestry, Inez Whitfield, going in. Inez was another Link sister, and another one of Preach's congregants.

"Hope you're not sick and canceling," Inez greeted Ada.

"Routine stuff. . . . I'm on my way to the grocery, now, hope you're not sick and missing."

"Just picking up a sample of a new med James is trying. I'll be at Altar Guild and may see you at the grocery store."

"You bringing your poached pears?"

"If I get to the store. They got to take my pressure and get me a flu shot too."

Inez buzzed off. In her short black-and-white houndstooth jacket and black pants, with her hair all over her head and wearing big bold black glasses, Inez Whitfield was a decidedly stylish and quirky woman. She was Ada's favorite member of the Altar Guild, and the one person Ada thought she might be able to talk to about marriage and Preach.

The Altar Guild came for lunch the fourth Saturday of the

month. Many of the ladies were eighty or almost eighty. These women had stomped wide paths where before them there had been no paths at all. They didn't just make a way for those who came after; when they could, they made an easy way.

Many of the ladies of the Altar Guild were clubwomen by nature. They liked administration and process; they were Deltas and AKAs and Links and Circle-ets, as well as members of the Altar Guild and sometimes Junior League Sustainers. Some were different. Ada was one of the ones who never saw a meeting or a ledger she didn't have to talk herself into tolerating. A sweet irony of the Altar Guild was that there were a lot of non-clubwomen in the club.

Ada's oldest friend, a singer, Delila Lee was one of the non-clubwomen in the group, and there were two writers; a female farmer, who ran one of Tennessee's last tobacco farms; a retired cateress; a lady who owned a T-shirt and convenience store down on Jefferson Street; and, Nashville being a university town and the home of Meharry Medical College, several college professors and leading doctors.

Inez Whitfield was one of the teaching doctors who was a clubwoman. A retired dermatologist, she still taught at Meharry, lecturing on medical ethics. Inez had a creative streak and a practical streak. She had come from a town in Texas where her family had owned everything: the café, the hairdresser, and the funeral parlor. Now all of that was gone, and they got a gas royalty. Inez was the richest person Ada knew personally, and the largest private donor to KidPlay.

It was the consensus of the club that Inez Whitfield was a woman who had seen more good and bad, more prosperity and more trauma, than a woman should know. She had been at a medical convention in California when her husband had taken her children on a balloon ride. They never came back.

Inez retired. Inez even remarried. Proposing with the words, "No one should carry this much pain alone," she married a man, James Madison Whitfield, who had lost his wife to cancer. Inez doted on his grandchildren and her garden. She worked hard not to think every hour of every day about the children her children would never have. She got down to imagining who they might be only when she encountered something one of her children adored, or excelled at, or hated. She moved out of the house she had lived in with her children. She turned her front and back lawns into a vegetable garden. Her purple hull peas were coveted. Her poached pears, usually served with goat cheese and local honey, were legendary.

Ada was still thinking about Inez as she walked into the grocery store. Five feet away from a tower of sponge cakes, a lady in an apron was offering samples of sausages she was cooking in an electric skillet. The sight and smell of food had Ada crazy hungry.

She grabbed a giant grocery cart, then rolled it back and grabbed a medium cart. If she couldn't be immediately smaller, her grocery cart could be smaller. She could have a skinny woman's cart. It was a small satisfaction. It was not enough satisfaction to distract her from immediate hunger.

She needed something quick to eat that wasn't fattening. No, that wasn't the right idea; she needed something that was useful to her body.

She nibbled on one of her cuticles. Then silently quipped,

Starvation. Quipping to yourself was something a minister's wife had to do. She couldn't risk being snide with anyone else—except the hubby and the girls, and they weren't around. You're it, she said to herself. When am I going to stop thinking about this as an exercise in deprivation, and start thinking about it as an exercise in filling myself up with what is good for me and what I like?

"Probably the day I start losing weight." This last, she said out loud. That was a problem. She was hearing voices and starting to talk too loud out loud, and she looked like a beached brown whale. She needed to hold on to the husband she had and put up with his mess and stop even thinking about running after Matt Mason—except that putting up with the husband she had is what got her to be "the hot mess she was." She prayed she hadn't said this last out loud. It was crazy thinking. This was starvation talking. She pointed her cart at the snack aisle.

She was standing with a bag of Veggie Loot in her hand, munching straight from the bag, when Inez bumped into Ada's butt, gently, with her cart.

Inez sneered at the Veggie Loot. "That's nothing but green Cheezos, cheese puffs, whatever you want to call it."

"One hundred and thirty calories. Low-carb. This is good for you."

"Green air."

"It keeps me from getting too hungry."

"You hungry right now. Unnatural hungry."

"Unnatural hungry?"

"You were not born wanting to eat puffy green air. Puffy green air is not helping you. It's making you hungry. Chewing without filling you up, flavor but not enough flavor. Makes you want to eat. These food companies work together to keep you hungry, and probably they're in it together with the health companies trying to keep us all sick. Fortunes are made on sick folk. I prefer to grow my own vegetables and pay as little money as possible to the drug companies."

"Inez, you are one paranoid woman."

"I am an old rich Negro. I got that way by being cautious. And being curious. I got that way by not doing what everybody else was doing—if I saw everybody else was not doing so good. I see all you young things—and yes, fifty is young, even if you don't know it—drinking Diet Coke and eating Veggie Loot, big as three houses, so I wouldn't be doing none of that now."

"What should I be eating, for a snack?"

"Soul food."

"Fried chicken and monkey bread and collard greens?"

"I mean baked sweet potatoes naked in their jackets, and I mean peanut butter spoons."

"Peanut butter spoons?"

"You get you some organic sugar-free peanut butter and you dip one of your grandma's silver spoons in it and you call that breakfast, lunch, dinner, snack, whatever you want. It got protein and fat, and you won't be hungry an hour after you eat that."

"Sweet potatoes and peanut butter. You want me on the George Washington Carver diet."

"Child, I been on that all my life, and I have never had any problem with my pressure, with my cholesterol, with my knees or with my hip, with my weight or with my sex life. And from what I read in the old folks' magazines and the style magazines, the other oldies like me are having a lot of trouble with their knees, hips, and weight, and the young ones like you are having all kinds of trouble with your sex and your weight and your skin. When I grew up, black girls didn't have bumps all on their faces."

"Next time you hit me with your grocery cart, mine will be piled high with jars of peanut butter and big sweet potatoes."

"Good. Get back to your food roots. Peanuts and sweet potatoes are the mama and daddy of soul food. I love sweet potatoes. You can just throw one in the microwave or the oven."

"Next time the girls come home, I may just serve the entire family peanut butter spoons for breakfast and get myself some rest."

"You could do a lot worse. I don't know why you young people insist on thinking of fried chicken and Kool-Aid and God knows what else as soul food. Soul food may be chicken once a month when the preacher comes, but it ain't fried chicken every day. And it's not anything made with corn syrup or white flour. And it ain't butter neither. Soul food is corn on the cob and peanuts and fish your daddy caught from the pond, or the lake, or the stream. It's simple."

"Amen."

"And you need to get your DNA tested."

"How's that? You see something in my eyes?"

"I think you need more information. Inherent Health dot com. Check it out."

"Inherent Health dot com?"

"They've got a test will tell you what you should be eating and how you should be exercising—according to your genes."

"According to my genes?"

"According to your genes."

For the next three days Ada subsisted on a diet of baked sweet potatoes and peanut butter spoons, and she lost three pounds. That night after the Altar Guild meeting, she scribbled into her journal a new idea that was too funny to be a rule but too useful not to write out in full: Eat like the skinny old folks eat.

10

BUDGET: PLAN TO AFFORD THE FEEDING, EXERCISING, AND DRESSING OF YOU

THE VERY NEXT morning, en route to KidPlay, Ada was back to thinking about stealing guitars, which she knew to be a strange thing for a minister's wife to be thinking about.

Except push had come to shove. Earn and spend, Preach was plain awful with money. He spent too much on his parishioners and would, if he could, let them pay him in homemade cake and great big hugs. This forced Ada to do two things: earn a little money, and get really good at being the frugal housewife. For years now her favorite column in the *Tennessean* newspaper had been the Ms. Cheap column. Doing good while being broke was hard work.

When they first married, Preach had headed up a "regular" church, and Ada had anticipated he would be a well-paid preacher and they would bounce around the country as he advanced. But then the placement came, and it was Iowa. Then they offered Oregon. Preach took the job as the assistant at Full Love.

Stopped at a red light, Ada allowed herself to imagine Preach as a modern-day Sweet Daddy Grace or Father Divine. She saw Preach in front of his independent mega-church. She saw herself driving away from in a white Mercedes-Benz to her giant house way across town where she lay beside her kidney-shaped pool wearing a knit suit with bright brass buttons. The light turned green just as Ada began to wonder if she was going crazy.

She decided to stop at the little black Episcopal church that had been an armory during the Civil War, Holy Trinity. And pray herself back to peace.

Bathed in the light coming through Holy Trinity's stained glass, she tried to clear her mind. Worrying about money was the one thing that really panicked Ada. Growing up in a family that had no salary, that lived by its wits and its instruments, had given Ada a permanent precarious feeling when she had to figure out how to pull together economic ends that wouldn't meet. She hoped the calm of the little church would help.

She wanted a treadmill. She wanted a trainer. She wanted a week at a spa. None of that was happening. Ada knew that.

But she also knew a diet was a war, and a war required a war chest. She would need time and money. She was scared she didn't have the time or the money to make the change she needed.

The real problem with bariatric surgery (aside from Ada being wary of needles and having some superstition that she was more likely to have complications than most people) was that it was just too expensive.

Ada didn't have extra time or money. Ada didn't have great insurance. And she didn't have a heart for any more administrative duties.

Ugh. She hated to write down what checks she wrote out, and never balanced her checking account. That's why she loved debit cards and online banking. And Preach was worse than she was when it came to their personal funds. He carried their tax files to the accountant in ziplock bags and a grocery sack.

She added another item to her shopping list. Buy a Dave Ramsey book. She liked listening to Ramsey, a sort of crazy conservative personal finance guru, on the radio. He talked radical change but made common sense.

Ada wanted to be the Dave Ramsey of weight loss. Somebody who got it all wrong, then got it right and shared the info about The Way. Except she wouldn't charge.

Ada had an idea about what was keeping her—and a lot of folk—from the success they wanted. Ada had her own idea about what was hobbling America by hobbling black America.

Blutter. Black clutter. Blutter was destroying black America—blutter in the bankbooks, blutter in the body, and blutter in the basements and attics. Disorganized finances, disordered eating and exercise, and disorganized homes.

Blutter. There. She had given it a name, and it was still driving her crazy.

She forced herself to keep good books at home. She did manage to look at the numbers, and every so often she would catch a mistake. Usually it was something she had returned that didn't get charged back. She was going to figure out how much money she needed, and she was going to figure out where she could get that money from in her budget.

She was going to spend wisely and exuberantly, as if she was buying a pair of shoes, or a vacation. Well, not like that, because she didn't really spend money on fancy shoes or vacations. Like a new roof for the Manse. No way a house of her own was on the horizon.

The night before she had looked her budget up and down and could hardly get anywhere with it. She ran a fairly tight ship on the domestic financial front, so there wasn't a lot of room for belt tightening.

The care, feeding, exercising, and dressing of her half-century self was an expensive proposition for someone who lived on a combination of a minister's and a day-care director's salaries, especially if the only way you could balance the day-care center's books was to pay yourself eight dollars an hour—less than you paid the man who mopped the floor.

Sometimes all that kept her going on the economic-hope front was her secret project. She was writing a book. *Home Training*. Right now it was just a loose-leaf notebook with forty or so pages. One day her manners guide for urban children whose parents can't be bothered to teach them how to act might land her in O magazine and on *The View* and on *Tavis*— and her book on the bestseller list. *Home Training* was Ada's lottery ticket.

If her number got called, she knew exactly what she would do. After she finished buying the rest of what the little school needed (more books and a playground were at the top of her list) and finished funding a few more scholarships, she hoped there would be enough left over to hire an entourage that would starve her and chase her with a stick, or at least someone to cook and shop for healthy foods for her. But the chances of that happening were Slim and None, and Slim had gone to town.

And Ada was tired of waiting. She waited for Preach to get his money up and his expenditures down. She waited for herself to finish writing *Home Training*. No more. Ada was ready to get the first lick in fast in her anti-blutter budget battle. She would get her arms around a more rather than less accurate prediction of her new expenses. Now.

She had doctor's bills, copays, and lab results. She needed walking shoes. She needed biker pants. She needed spongy socks. That she could remember off the top of her head. She would need to sit down with her checkbook, her bag of receipts, and her journal and try to predict the rest.

The diet books, Weight Watchers Online. That was already spent. A gym membership, exercise classes: All that had to be anticipated, along with exercise equipment for home. She probably wasn't going to have a treadmill in her kitchen, but she needed little dumbbells. She needed a yoga mat. She needed to realize this journey was not just a weight-loss attempt. This journey was something bigger than that. She smiled to know sometimes the biggest thing was the best, even as she planned to shrink, even as she dieted, praying and hoping—not to get thin, but to get to a size that wouldn't hurt so much when she got down on her knees to pray.

She imagined herself back at her home office desk, surrounded by all the tools of administration, ledgers and pencils, and computations that told her she was broke and getting broker by contemplating this war. In the sanctuary of the church she imagined herself staring at her laptop screen with her bank account information pulled up, trying to make the numbers work. Then she stopped imagining and quietly recited Psalm 127. *Except the Lord build the house, they labor in vain that build it . . .* When she came to the last words—*they shall not be ashamed*—Ada still hated administration, but thinking about it in the shelter of the Episcopal church had empowered her. If the Episcopal church was good at one thing, it was managing money.

She didn't want to lose the battle before it began. She feared a death by a thousand little cuts. Each of the nitpicky and not so nitpicky administrative details of the school and the house and her own life were thin slices into her spirit. And now she was telling herself to take on more bureaucracy in the pursuit of beauty in the act of healthing.

God was punishing her. Just like he punished the woman standing on her roof during Katrina, in the joke she couldn't get out of her mind. The woman was praying for God to come save her. Somebody in a rowboat offered to pick her up. She said, "No, thank you, God's coming for me." Then somebody showed up in a motorboat. Again, she said, "No, thank you. God's coming." Finally a helicopter flew over and dropped down a rope. Again, "No, thank you. God's coming." The helicopter flew off, and the woman drowned. When she got to heaven, the lady chastised God: "Why did you let me drown?" God said, "I sent you a rowboat, and a motorboat, and a helicopter!" With that God threw the lady out of purgatory and into hell.

God talked to Ada through cheesy jokes. Ada didn't want to be thrown into hell. But she just didn't see the rowboat, or the motorboat, or the helicopter. Where was she blind to God's helping hand? She had a real sick feeling that beauty, the beauty of her young body and the beauty of her voice, had been her rowboat and her motorboat.

Ada had squandered her prettiness.

She was pretty the day she graduated college. Pretty the day she married. But twenty-five years later, the "stone fox" on a good day was an everyday frump.

She hadn't taken care of her prettiness. Little things like no sunblock. Big things like no exercise. They added up to the erosion and explosion of God-given pretty.

She was by some lights beautiful—truth and passion were carved all over her face and body—but pretty was gone. And maybe gone forever; or maybe she could track down and reclaim at least some of what had been gifted to her by God, and what somehow she had broken into small pieces and thrown away.

She opened her eyes and looked at the altar and the cross above it. She stared at how the priest held the host at the communion table, and she knew that some fragment of that was how she should treasure the living body of herself, but never had, shunning beauty—which was no more or less awful than shunning the helicopter, and the rowboat, and the motorboat and ending up dead, then thrown down to hell.

Ada made a mental note to add money for plain beauty stuff, makeup and clothes and more regular trips to Big Sheba's House of Beauty, to her healthing budget sheet. She didn't know what kind of figure that would be, so she gave herself permission to just put in question marks, but some of the stuff women used to create the illusion of youth and prettiness, the stuff Bird called "powder and smoke," would be a line item. Eventually.

If the church could use "smells and bells," incense and music, to get people into the mood to see God's power and beauty, then Ada shouldn't be above dabbing on some perfume or some makeup base—but she didn't want to bankrupt herself doing it, like some churches bankrupted themselves paying for organs. She would budget, not bankrupt, for beauty.

God was merciful. When she had stopped treasuring her own beauty, he had given her beauty to treasure—the twins.

She chuckled again over the Katrina joke. The twins' young adult beauty was her helicopter and her rope. Ada would climb up and be saved. She saw beauty when she saw her twins. The twins showed her. Beauty is important. Beauty is good. Beauty is not a trivial and vain habit. Beauty is a worthy discipline.

She would embrace ledgers and rouge. She would be Mary and Martha. As she wondered how to balance the books, she realized she had to sell something that didn't involve begging or theft. Iced-tea spoons. She had inherited twelve from each sister, and they had been fortunate; the pattern had been discontinued and had become highly collectible. Forty would fetch a pretty penny. But probably not enough. To buy the time she needed as well as the things, she would sell her car, the great big Tahoe she had kept in perfect condition so she could drive the KidPlay kids, and buy a Mini Cooper. She would have smaller hips and leave a smaller environmental impact.

Or she could find a few dollars out at the lake. *Tell me which, Lord. Amen.*

11

GET EIGHT HOURS OF SLEEP NIGHTLY

A DA CROSSED HERSELF, rushed past the priest, who looked like he wanted to speak but was mercifully tied up with another congregant, and gave four updates on her daughters between the nave door and her car door. All that was easy. All the eyebrows raised silently, asking, Why are you here? was hard.

Deciding next time she needed a shot of smells and bells she would try the white Episcopals, where few if any would recognize her, she got the Tahoe onto the highway, thanking God for three last things: that she had remembered to put the frozen vegetables in a cooler with ice packs; that her mother-in-law lived right around the corner; and that her parents were not out at the lake all by themselves.

That would have left them too lonely, and that would have left her running down the road too often.

Temple and Bird had begun taking lodgers one cold year when the heating bills were high and their friends started losing their houses. They enjoyed helping, and they enjoyed getting a little help. They charged ten dollars a day, and that included all the Frosted Flakes and milk and coffee and sugar and split pea soup you could down.

The lodgers provided their own liquor, but Bird and Temple always kept an extra bottle of Jack Daniel's they were willing to share. And the lodgers provided the marijuana.

Once Temple had a son-in-law who was a preacher, he didn't feel right about buying weed out on the street. He was not a man to disgrace a daughter or a son-in-law. Temple liked the way Preach took care of Ada.

And that made Temple look to others to score for him, which wasn't exactly a godly thing either, but Temple didn't let that one bother him.

The house had become a place where black musicians who had no family, no hits, no membership in the musicians' union, could live large one last time before they died. Some folks stayed a month or two. Some stayed years. When you couldn't walk or change your own adult diapers, you had to leave—unless you had a friend living at the house who could do that for you. Some months there were just three or four lodgers, sometimes the house was overfull.

The men peed in the woods to save the plumbing. Sometimes on a Sunday or a Monday night they would sit around an old phonograph and listen to their dead friends play. Sometimes they would roll the piano out of Bird's bedroom and get up a little acoustic set.

Whether they died in the house or moved on just before death, most of the lodgers left their earthly effects to Bird and to Temple. In that sense almost all the tenancies became permanent.

When somebody passed, Temple would create a monument.

Usually he would sort through the stuff and find someplace to send something to someone. If the person came from a certain town, and that town had a blues museum or a black museum, he might send a photograph or a single. If the person had gone to high school or college, he would find something—a shirt or sweater or tie in the school colors—and send it back to the band office or the school library. Sometimes he remembered something the deceased liked to eat and wrote the recipe into his road cookbook. Whatever he did, he did it grateful Ada had married a man with salary, insurance, and retirement, a man whose job came with a pretty house, a man whose church would bury his daughter when the time came.

Ada and Preach were not rich, but to Temple they were something better than rich; they were secure.

Temple and Bird had been every kind of wild. When they first moved into their lake house, they had been wildflowers blooming by the water.

Temple and Bird had loved this. They loved it so much Temple retired from performing out on the road. Ada, then eight, was the only child who ever lived full-time at the house. Glo, and Mag, and Evie were already on their own. For Temple and Bird, it was like they were eating and sleeping and shitting right in the woods. In a house with few doors, so little stood between them, and they were always on top of each other.

When Ada went off to school, the house became a passion pit. With nothing to do weekdays, they organized their lives around their lovemaking. Bird woke early and got the girl off to school. Then she got back into bed. Eventually Temple awoke and made the coffee and cornbread while Bird showered and brushed her teeth. She drank her coffee in bed while he had a shower. Then he came back to bed, and they rolled around the mattress. This had been their youth, and it was the first of their retirement once the gigs got slow.

They had not expected middle age to be an erotic territory of such flower and flavor. They were surprised to discover that the removed bits, the breast, the prostate, the hip, served to enhance their appreciation of what remained, the inside of the elbow, the back of the knee, the skin just beyond the margins of their most effacing scars.

They kissed, and licked, and bit what remained, but best, they tongue-kissed, and he poked deep into the insides of her lady parts with the same sweet power and fingers with which he thumped the piano keys.

They found pleasure in its hiding places; they invented new pleasures; they applauded themselves with laughter.

Then the daughters died. Glo, Mag, and Evie were wide-hipped good mamas who perfectly performed a hip rock that could calm any fretting child. It was a move they had inherited from their mother, as Bird had in herited it from her mother, MaDear. When that precious part of Bird's legacy vanished with her older daughters into the grave, it took some of Bird's sex with it. Bird had long been the kind of woman who rocked a man like her back had no bone. Then she wasn't.

If sex was death's overture, Bird wanted nothing of it. And she wouldn't acknowledge the fourth child, Ada, as hers. That would mean she had another daughter who could die, and that possibility was too much. Bird drank to drown and kill it. When she wasn't drunk, she thought of jumping into her front-yard lake, the lake she could see from her bedroom window.

Temple went to Preach's church. He sat in the back. He crouched in his pew, head in hands. He prayed for relief. When Bird's fast-descending Alzheimer's arrived, he accepted it as the answer to his prayer. It was not the relief he had wanted, but it was too much relief for him to turn it away.

He prayed more. She forgot more. The house got cluttered. Things were better. She couldn't see the lake from her bedroom. Old friends moved in with them. Things were as good as they were going to be.

When Temple saw Ada sad that her mother did not know her, Temple chastised his last daughter. He said, "Baby, she cain't know you and not know losing them. Ain't no choice. You grown now. You don't need her as much as she needs to not know you. She don't even wanna know me. We got walls inside of walls everywhere in this house."

The piles got higher and more. Eventually Temple and Bird could be in the same room and not see each other. This was a comfort to Bird. When it was not enough comfort, she found her way back to the center of one of her rooms.

Usually she was out in the piles checking the whereabouts of a scrap. She wanted to know where, exactly where, every bit of flotsam and jetsam—which could not get sick, get amputated, get infected, get diabetic retinopathy, go blind, leave behind wailing children that scattered out to California and Oregon—was.

Anything with a ruffle, anything soft as the silk of their hands, any curler or hot iron or little jar of blue grease, any half-used jar of Vaseline or raggedy washcloth she had wiped their noses or butts with, Bird kept and tried to keep track of. Except soon she had too many things to know where anything was. In her drunk fog, she hoped somewhere lost in all the mess her daughters were hiding alive.

Bird listened as Ada cooked. Ada was making the spinach and chicken and noodle casserole. Bird could hear her sautéing the chicken, smell the olive oil and onion. Bird could hear Ada rinse the noodles. Bird knew Ada would mix them with cream cheese. There would be an assembly line on the counter. There would be casseroles in the oven. And in the freezer. There was another good one with wild rice and more chicken. When Ada had the time and everybody was awake, particularly on a Friday, she would fry pork chops or steaks, or fish. Mainly she made casseroles and cleaned the toilets and kept a path clear into each room. She set the mousetraps and collected the dead mice. She was a good daughter. Better than Bird deserved.

Bird wanted to tell Ada that. But they were in the middle of the game where Bird acted like she thought Ada was the maid Ada sent to clean for her. It was easier that way. She didn't want her daughter washing her toilets and picking up dead mice. The mice should be Temple's job, and Bird knew she should be washing the toilets, but after the girls died she couldn't do a single useful thing. Bird left the kitchen, left Ada with the casseroles she was cooking, and made her way to Glo's old room, where Maceo was staying.

"I am tired," Bird said to Maceo.

"Mama love her some Maceo," Temple said all the time,

without jealousy. Maceo had one true woman he loved, and it was Bird. Maceo was dying from lung cancer. He held Bird's hand and coughed.

Bird said, "I want to be a vampire and suck some life out of something or fuck some life into something, I want to be full of life at least for a little, once more, but I ain't. I look like I'm alive, but I ain't. I'm a zombie who needs a face-lift."

Maceo laughed so hard he started coughing. "I'm so way past fucking life into somebody," Maceo said, "or having somebody fuck life into me, but honey I sure would like to suck some life out of somebody one last time. Bring your neck over here, honey."

Bird leaned in close, and she kissed Maceo's cheek and he kissed her neck, then he gummed it. He didn't bother to put his teeth in anymore.

"I'm gonna miss you, Maceo."

"I'm gonna be rolling in Buddy Bolden's arms."

"You crazy, Maceo."

"Crazy as a fox."

"When I get to heaven, I'm gonna see my daughters."

"See Ada this afternoon."

"I ain't seen Ada since her sister's funeral. Ada don't come 'round here. She married a preacher."

"Bird, when I'm gone. You need to do sumpin' fo' me."

"Anything."

"See Ada when she comes."

"I rather be a blind gal than see you walk 'way from me . . ."

"Miss Etta James."

"Used to be I sang it better."

"You sing it better."

Soon Maceo was asleep, and Bird wandered through the maze to the center of the living room and took a Benadryl. She was dozing off when she heard the woman Ada sent to cook and clean arguing with Temple about money. About how she was thinking of selling her car or maybe the silver she had inherited from her sisters. How she needed one of the guitars. The woman's voice sounded so much just like her Ada's, Bird wanted to tell her the records were worth money, and she had some jewelry. But she didn't think she could bear to part with any of it, so she didn't say anything. She wanted to tell Temple that they needed to sell the house with the view and let someone tear it down and they needed to be in a small apartment with help and stop making the gal Ada sent cook and clean.

She tried to remember the day Ada was born. She couldn't. She went into Ada's room to find something to help her remember. Sammy Heart was playing cards with Sonny Dee, sitting on Ada's old coverlet that Bird had sewn herself. Sammy and Sonny paid Bird no mind, and she paid them no mind. She looked through her bookshelves, and she found Ada's diaries. It took her just a few minutes to find the one she was looking for, the one that was pink cloth with flowers. She turned to an entry dated May 10, 1977. Ada talking about the day Ada was born. At her high school graduation lunch, Maceo had told her the whole story, and Ada had written it down that very afternoon.

Holding the diary made Bird know she was right to never let anything go. You never knew what you might forget that a thing might help you remember.

Ada had become some of what she was born to be. According to Bird's reckoning, a preacher's wife was not a complete coming off the stage, wasn't exactly the opposite of being the lead singer's wife, but it was a move in the right direction. It was a far walk from the cotton fields where Ada was born the last weekend Bird ever sang at a Mississippi Delta country club. "Used to be I was Ada's mama," Bird said out loud to herself.

She could smell the aroma of greens boiling on the stove, and she hoped the cleaning lady had put in some side meat.

Next week she might put that diary in the cleaning lady's purse. As Bird went to put the book back where she had hid it, she began to sing, just above a whisper. *This little light of mine, I'm gonna let it shine . . . Won't hide it under no bushel now! I'm gonna let it shine . . . All the time all the time.* Even tired and stoned, Bird knew that she and Preach were bushels, and Ada was a little light. "This Little Light of Mine." It was the very first song she had taught Ada, and it stayed her baby girl's favorite song for a long, long time. And Bird knew she had to take just a little bit more Benadryl, and she wouldn't know it again.

Sonny looked up from his cards, "Come over here, Miss Lady, and take a hit off this, get your mind back quiet." Bird floated over to the bed.

"Deal me in."

After the lake Ada headed to KidPlay. After KidPlay she headed home. Almost home, she made a quick stop. Queenie's.

Preach's mama, Queenie, lived just the other side of Belmont Boulevard from Ada and Preach, in a spotless old house she rarely left.

After she retired from daywork, the week she turned sixty-two and could apply for Social Security, Queenie was home if she could be home. A lifetime of following her enlisted-man husband from army base to army base and supplementing the family income by cleaning the homes of officers left her rooted to her own couch in her own home.

She didn't even go to church on Sunday. When asked about that, Queenie would laugh and say, "I share my son with Ada and the twins—I ain't sharing him with them other women." Not going to church on Sunday was about the only thing the preacher's mama had in common with the preacher's mama-in-law.

If Queenie was sorry Sarge had died before they got to live in a house they owned, not a house assigned to them by the army, or the cheap apartment they rented while getting their down payment together, she didn't say.

Queenie moved on. She'd done it for decades with Sarge, then she did it for decades without him. After moving to Nashville, she did it leaning on Ada and Preach as her sturdy stick.

Soon as Queenie heard Ada's car pull into the drive, she would start making her way to the front door. She tried to be a convenient woman. Queenie would be holding the door wide open by the time Ada was halfway up her front walk. They would start talking before Ada got to the steps. Ada was always rushing, and Queenie knew it.

"Come give me some sugar, baby."

"Hey, Queenie."

Ada plopped a big kiss on Queenie's cheek. Her mother-in-law smacked her one right on the lips.

"Come on in here, chile, I got some charlotte russe in the

refrigerator, and some stuffed crabs in the oven, and baby I got some gumbo on the stove. Fix yo'self a plate."

"Queenie, I'm starting a diet."

"What fo'?"

"Look at me!"

"I am looking at you. Straight at you. You looking good, chile."

"I weigh over two hundred pounds."

"Chile, I weighed two-eighty-five last time I got on a scale. Probably over three hundred now. Don't have diabetes. Don't have but a touch of pressure, and what I got is under control."

"How would you know? You don't go to the doctor."

"'Cause I don't need to go."

"Queenie, you lucky. I don't want to count on luck."

"What we gonna do if we can't eat when you visit?"

"I guess we gonna have to figure that out."

After gossiping more than they had ever gossiped, Ada was out the door with a pot of gumbo in her hands.

Ada was home. Finally. She got on her new biker shorts and one of Preach's T-shirts, but under the T-shirt was a comfortable exercise bra, and on her feet were spongy socks and good, if stiff, shoes. She had made a few extra stops after Queenie's. She had sold the iced-tea spoons to a local fine silver dealer. The dealer had looked a little sad. Ada had made him smile.

"I'm trading the past for the future. That's always a good trade."

And it was. Her first good trade in a long while. Ada knew too much about hard trades.

Sleep for Work was the deal that made her life possible; and Sleep for Work was the deal wrecking her body.

Googling over and over again the words *diet* and *weight loss*, in her nonexistent free time, had left Ada with the distinct impression that one of the reasons she was so fat was she didn't get enough sleep.

The possibility that she could eat what she had been eating and excercise as she had been exercising and lose weight by changing her sleep habits was very attractive. The sleep-more, weigh-less diet sounded downright delightful.

And frustrating. She slept five hours a night, as far as she knew, not because she had trouble falling asleep or trouble staying asleep but because she had nineteen hours of things to do each day.

She usually put in forty hours at the nursery school, at least twenty-one hours a week doing church work, and lately four hours a week sitting with Preach's mother. Another twenty-one hours a week was spent cooking and cleaning, and she wasn't doing enough cooking and cleaning. Half an hour to shower and dress each day and seven hours talking with the girls on the phone, seven hours dining with Preach, twenty-one hours visiting with congregants, and ten hours volunteering—all that added up to too much work to do and not enough hours in a 168-hour week. Schedules were hard.

She multitasked as much as she could. On occasion she was able to convince Queenie they should visit at the Manse while Ada cleaned and cooked. Usually she talked to the girls while she was driving to work. And she would cut back on some of her volunteer hours, but she couldn't cut back too much.

Time was a hurdle. She needed to sleep fifty-six hours a week, eight hours a night, and she needed to spend at least thirty minutes on the treadmill a day. She needed three and a half more hours a day than she had. Add getting in and out of exercise clothes, redoing her hair after she exercised, going to the doctors, doing all the research she needed to be doing, journaling, and her time deficit went from big to huge.

One of the very first changes she was going to have to make was balancing her time budget. She needed to free up some minutes to work on her body.

She couldn't stop visiting Preach's mama. And she didn't want to give up dinner with Preach. Maybe she should cut back on cooking and cleaning and hire someone for out at the lake. If she hired someone, it would be another significant body expense, but it would also be the time she needed for sleep.

She would start looking. It would be easy to find someone who wanted a decently paid part-time job. She could probably get someone to start next week. But she wouldn't. It would be too hard to come up with the money and she couldn't abandon her mother. She had to find the time somewhere else.

She made a little chart.

35 spent sleeping
35 church work
40 nursery school
7 talking to the girls on the phone
14 sitting with Preach's mother
21 cooking and cleaning
7 hours a day dining with Preach

21 visiting with congregants

10 volunteering

Then she wrote down the things she wanted time for and how much time she wanted:

21 more hours of sleep

3½ hours for walking

There was an activity she didn't write down. Sex. Making love. What number to write down? Maybe they didn't have sex because they didn't have time to have sex. Then she noticed that she had written "7 hours a day dining with Preach," instead of "7 hours a week." It made her smile. She did want, though she had forgotten she wanted, seven hours a day with Preach. If they had that kind of long day and long conversation, those unbroken hours, Ada felt certain they would find their way back into bed.

Unfortunately, sorting all that out was just another thing for which Ada didn't have time. She made an executive decision. She called Preach and informed him. She was going to be in bed by ten, and she wanted Preach in bed by the time she was going to bed.

Preach surprised her by saying yes, without argument. Then later that night she surprised herself by learning that she did in fact have trouble falling asleep. She lay in bed feeling achy and awkward and twisting every which way and worrying till near 2:00 A.M., while Preach snored louder than loud. An advantage of falling asleep before Preach was that she didn't hear him snore.

When she finally fell asleep, she had a nightmare.

It was her first pearly gate bad dream ever. She woke up in the middle of the night in a cold sweat. Even awake, she could still see God shaking a bony ebony finger at her before hurrying Ada and Preach toward purgatory. Over and over God said, in a voice that sounded strangely like Dave Chappelle's, "I sent you one God-fearing, family-loving young man, Lucius Howard, finely made, honest, 'umble, ambitious, smart! You done spoiled him rotten! Made that Negro think his shit didn't stink! His mama started it, but that ain't a sin when a mama do it. I made mamas that way. A wife s'posed to keep it real. That's why I gave you all the goodies—two big breasts, a booty, and *everything* in between. What you think you supposed to do with all that? But you don't even tell that Negro you tired. You don't tell him nothing but how sweet he is, and how pretty he is, and how much you love him, except that's starting to be a lie, 'cause he ain't doing enough for you to love him. He's doing it all for his flock. It ain't his flock, it's my flock. And some of them is confused too. Some of them coming to *my* church to flirt with Preach, not to worship me. Y'all are near to ruining one of my best days of work. He need to wean himself off praise if that Negro is gonna grow up! Y'all ain't ever gonna stop giving it to him. Where y'all spoil him rotten, that's where Lucifer gonna sink his teeth in! Even if he is busy doing my work all day, some of it he's doing for the wrong reasons."

"But it gets done. He is busy doing your work."

"See! Getting turned out of Heaven's Door, and you still defending the so-and-so. I made his goodies too good!"

"But I haven't had any lately."

"You in purgatory, chile. You can look. He can look. But

you always gonna be too busy to get together. And all I got to do to turn that into hell is leave you stuck in it forever. You got to woman-up, chile."

"How do I do that?"

"I can't tell you dat! You in purgatory!"

Ada was up at five. Sharing the sink with Preach, as they both tried to wake up by brushing their teeth, was not an unpleasant experience. They could still spit in the same sink at the same time and not be disgusted. This gave her hope for other domestic miracles. Ada asked, gently, if they could try again for an early night. Preached pushed back. He had work to do on the week's sermon. He had family visits to make. Ada pushed back against him. She let the snappishness she felt enter into her voice. "I need more sleep. I need to go to sleep earlier, and"—she stopped and changed her tone, put some sugar on the medicine—"we need to go to sleep together." He stopped buttoning his shirt buttons. Brushed his hand across her bosom by accident. She blushed. Fearing a misunderstanding of what was on offer, she clarified.

"I mean sleep, sleep."

Preach almost looked relieved. Ada shuddered. His expression changed to a clear look of affectionate concern. They parted with a peck.

Hours later, returning home from KidPlay, Ada thought of calling Dr. Willie Angel and asking her for a prescription for Lunesta or one of the drugs she had heard advertised on the television when she was up so late. She hated the idea of being drugged.

The idea she liked was falling asleep to the sound of a storm at the ocean. She didn't punch Willie Angel's seven digits. Instead she told the idea about the water sounds to Preach over dinner, like she was telling him she wanted the moon, like she was confessing she wanted something he would never be able to give her.

He smiled. She thought that was mean. But she knew he wasn't mean, so she wondered what he was thinking about that wasn't her. To stop worrying about that she got up and started clearing the plates. He took the plates from her hands.

"Let me do that. You go take a bath."

By the time she got out of the bathtub, he was already asleep on his side of the bed, snoring loud. On her side of the bed was an old-fashioned boom box. On the top was a Post-it that read "push play." She did, and the sounds of the rain and the storm began. Preach turned over toward her, rousing himself just enough to say, "Sleep is hard."

Ada pressed repeat, slid beneath the sheets, then turned off the television that usually played all night or until one of them remembered to put it on a timer, or woke up enough to turn it off. Then she stretched to reach the light. She fell asleep to sounds of thunder and waves, to fierceness without anger, to God's own intensity.

She woke up eight hours later, half a pound lighter than she had been the day before.

12

EAT BREAKFAST

ONLY SHE DIDN'T know it yet. She hadn't stood on the scale. That would come later. What came the moment she awoke was a desire to roll over and kiss Preach. She rolled over. He was already gone.

He was usually "already gone" when she awoke, so this should not have come as a surprise. But it did. And it pained her. She was almost as surprised by the pang of pain in response to his absence as she was surprised to roll over and want him. Going to sleep together had moved Ada into an emotional neighborhood just next door to optimism. She was no longer living in numb. Optimistic, she wanted to kiss, even before she brushed her teeth. This made her glad Preach was gone. Middle-aged women do not kiss before they brush teeth, at least not lips, or faces. Ada smiled to know that she knew what they could kiss: elbows, knees, bellies, etc.—even if her knowledge was antique.

She got out of bed with a bit of bounce in her step. After her usual pre-scale ablutions, she stepped on the evil measuring square and got the good news. Half a pound down. Her knees bent and her hands went up in the air; her belly shook and her breasts waved; she cried out, loud and proud, "Thank you Jesus." Then she jumped up in the air, landing on the scale with a thunk drowned out by the clap of hands still held high above her head. She grabbed still jiggling breasts with glee. Surprises could still be good. Making changes makes change.

Ada sat her sweet fat ass on the side of her pretty tub. Rested, desirous, she was just starting to wonder what else exhaustion had stripped from her, when some of it started to come back. She thought of her father urging, "Take care of the pennies, and the dollars will take care of themselves."

As she had felt her aged parents emotionally distancing themselves, Ada had moved closer to them, but in the only ways that they, in their grief, would allow: as caretaker, maid, cook, and old-folk tender. She had stopped listening for their advice or remembering the advice they had given. She didn't want to be sorry there was no more of it. Today, "on surprise," as one of her my babies would say, she remembered some advice her father had given her long before.

"Eat breakfast because you don't know if dinner is coming, and we will probably be working through it anyway." He also said, "Eat breakfast like you James Brown, dinner like you Otis Redding, and supper like you me."

By that he meant: eat like a superstar at breakfast, great big, all you want; eat like a just-making-it star at lunch, something medium-size, maybe a sandwich packed by a mama or a girl-friend; and eat an itty-bitty dinner like a road musician would eat, maybe a few sardines and a cracker.

It made her feel like a girl, even thinking about paying heed to her daddy's old saying about food. Made her feel like his girl to know that he called lunch "dinner" and dinner "supper." She would heed her father. Finally. Ada's one concession to wanting to be not-so-big was not eating breakfast. She was going to change it up.

She would stop defying her daddy and start complying with the diet books that had arrived. A precious few rules seemed to be in most of the books and in her family culture. "Eat breakfast" was one. There was even a book called *The Big Breakfast Diet*, which she hadn't ordered but was thinking about ordering, that said breakfast was the key and you could eat almost anything before nine. Then she thought about the kind of breakfast she wanted to eat and the amount of Weight Watchers points she wanted to spend on breakfast. It didn't take a hot second for her to decide she didn't need to send for the *Big Breakfast Diet* book.

Ada's favorite breakfast was French toast and pig candy. Pig candy is bacon microwaved with brown sugar and pepper, and absolutely delicious. None of the diet books she already owned seemed to set out a plan that would allow anything like a full serving of pig candy. That seemed like a principle to follow: Only eat foods that at least three books advise you to eat.

Given pig candy was her favorite breakfast, eating breakfast was probably a bad idea. Unless she changed up her favorite.

She plunged into her newly purchased diet texts, searching for her new favorite breakfast. She settled on a cup of Greek yogurt with six almonds doctored up with cinnamon and nutmeg and clove. A bit of protein, a bit of fat. Some spices to rev up her metabolism and to make the breakfast taste a lot like French toast. Presto, a breakfast all her books and Weight Watchers On-line could endorse. Ada endorsed it too. The almonds made the breakfast crunchy. She liked crunchy.

And she liked that it was a little bit of a healing meditation to eat this breakfast. Traditional Chinese medicine favors the cinnamon stick, and new research highlighted the effect of cinnamon on insulin and on inflammation. Whatever the research came to prove for Ada, this day, the spices were a silent prayer for health. And they tasted good, and it was a breakfast she could make fresh in less than a minute if she mixed the spices together beforehand. And she liked praying silently and deliciously by eating.

She would call her new breakfast "sexy woman candy." She liked that. She really liked it. She went down to get herself a bowlful, singing her new favorite hymn, "Get on the Good Foot."

1 3

SELF-MEDICATE WITH ART: QUASH BOREDOM AND ANXIETY

Between Queenie's and KidPlay, Ada got a call and then a text. It was a good thing she had planned to be at work early. Baby Jarius was home, sick with another cold. The call was a plea from his grandma, Loretha, for Ada to pick up a prescription that had been phoned in. The text was a request from his mama, Dorian, for Ada to call her work and vouch for the legitimacy of her absence later that afternoon. Before Ada walked into the front door of KidPlay, she had done a lot of juggling and was nibbling on a chocolate bar she had hidden in her desk.

After work Ada sped out to the lake and did a quick clean and medicine check with all the doors wide open. She couldn't afford the munchies that came with even a teeny-tiny contact high. Then she came straight home. The package she was hoping for was in the mail. Her DNA test kit.

Ada felt in her bones DNA was the way to go. She knew the jury was out in the medical community about DNA-based diets. From what she could read, many doctors who thought DNA might one day help didn't think that day had come. But

Ada had a lucky feeling about testing her DNA. She had noticed that different diets seemed to work for different people. She had noticed she seemed to get fatter eating things that were not supposed to be fattening, like carrots and corn with no butter on it. After Inez told her about the DNA testing for weight loss, Ada looked it up on the Web. Researchers at Stanford said the DNA testing worked. Or at least they said that when they put people on the diet chosen by the DNA test she was going to take, they were more likely to lose weight and lost more weight than those randomly assigned to diets. Kathie Lee on the *Today* show said the DNA testing could help you find the right diet. The Inherent Health Web site stated something that spoke deeply to Ada: "Don't waste time on the wrong diet." Then it said, "People on the 'right' diet for their genes lost more weight than people on the 'wrong' diet for their genes." It couldn't hurt, it might help, and it was something she had never done, so it was very much following Rule 1. Ada was ready to give DNA testing a try.

The kit was boxed to look like a portfolio. You flipped open the cover, and simple step-by-step instructions were emblazoned on the inside sleeve.

Only the steps were not as easy as she thought they would be. You needed to send them a sample of your bodily tissue, scraped from the inside of your mouth. And you could only take the scrape—they called it a swab—after not eating or drinking anything for two hours. She had a quick cup of coffee, then set a timer for six. She thought of waiting to sample in the morning. She could get up, brush her teeth, drink a bit of coffee, and wait two hours—but there was a seven o'clock pickup at the neighborhood post office, and she wanted to *know*. Soon. Now.

The first half hour she spent waiting to scrape her inner cheek, she spent getting dinner in the oven. When it was in the oven, she spent an hour cleaning.

Ada was a fast cleaner. She got the upstairs and downstairs toilets and the kitchen floor mopped and the front hall stairs swept in just under an hour. That left her half an hour to begin an experiment.

Create emergency kits. Plural. She wanted an "I'm Scared" emergency kit and an "I'm Bored" emergency kit.

She wanted two playlists and a bunch of pictures. She wanted sounds and images she could put in her purse and take with her into battle. She was thinking about flagging will.

First, she needed a playlist of songs that picked her up and made her think about things she liked to think about, especially things she liked to think about, but might have forgotten about. The number-one song she put on her new iPod playlist was Ray Charles, "I Got a Woman." The second song going on the list was Van Morrison's "Brown Eyed Girl." The third song making the cut was James Brown—"I Feel Good." And just thinking about those first songs had got her feeling good. She wondered how many she should have, and she decided on a baker's dozen, thirteen—there was an amusing transgression in having thirteen songs instead of thirteen doughnuts, which nobody in the world would allow themselves to eat, or thirteen cookies, which only a crazy person would eat, or thirteen corn chips, which she ate every time they went out for

Mexican, but couldn't anymore. Thirteen songs that could break through her boredom, thirteen songs she could indulge in anytime she wanted. That was a tonic. And she could change them. Or add another.

That first playlist would be for pulling her up, and then she needed another that would wrap her in bunting and make her feel safe, sheltered. She needed the aural equivalent of fat. She needed a cashmere baby blanket that was always clean and always with her. She needed Billie Holiday.

Ada loved Billie. With all that Billie went through, it was like Ada got the cool of the heroin without the hook when she listened to songs like "Violets for Your Furs." When she listened to Lady Day, it wasn't all going to be all right, it was all right now. She would download the entire *Lady in Satin* album, the one with Billie surrounded by all that string music. Aretha would have to be on this list too. She would put "Respect" and she would put "Stand by Me" and "Michael, Row the Boat Ashore," the Harry Belafonte version.

Both of her new playlists—the pick-me-up and the wrap-me-around—Ada would think of as healthing playlists. They would travel with her everywhere.

Sound was essential, but not enough. Shape-shifting was too much about sight for sound to be enough. Ada needed some eye candy. She would put some beauty in her pocket. Art. Her first choice was easy. Five Rothko postcards. She had seen those Rothkos in college on a visit to the Guggenheim, and she had never forgotten them. Looking at those pictures helped Ada feel nineteen again.

Her spirit had been lifted by those great big gorgeous

canvases. When she first saw them, it was just the colors. Instant inebriation. As she had gotten larger, they had been her proof that big is more. Now she needed proof of the opposite. She needed something that would lift her spirit and give her the confidence to struggle with her body. She found a picture of Josephine Baker. Too intimidating. Ditto Lena Horne. She closed her eyes. What do I want to see when I see me? Van Der Zee. All the way. Those jazzy beautiful black folk. She would get herself some Van Der Zee postcards.

She had calm and confident covered in the emergency kits. But what to put to motivate? Matt Mason, of course. Matt Mason, gorgeous. Unfortunately, the only pictures she had of him were twenty years old. And she wouldn't go poking around on the Internet for pictures of him out of fear he would go poking around for pictures of her. When she thought of Matt Mason, she thought a little like a baby, believing if she couldn't see him, he couldn't see her. The belief gave her comfort.

She wasn't sure comfort was what she needed. She was almost sure it was exactly what she didn't need. The second thing she thought about putting in her emergency kit was a picture of herself now, a naked picture of herself, to remind herself that she was in a state of emergency.

Twenty minutes after the thought crossed her mind, she was naked in front of her MacBook, adjusting the screen to take a picture. First she caught herself front on. Then back on. Then one side and then the other—neither seemed to want to be left out. To soften the effect, she turned the shots to sepia. She wished she knew how to cartoon the drawings, but she didn't. Her daughters could help her, but she didn't want to bother them. She printed up what she had in the privacy of her bedroom.

In bright color the photos had seemed mean and rude. In sepia they offended her less profoundly, but still they offended her. She wondered if her husband liked what he saw when he looked at her. She believed he did, believed it so confidently it surprised her and raised another question. She wondered what her husband saw when he looked at her, and she knew that, whatever it was, what it wasn't was, as she said aloud, "Me, now."

She wrote those words on the back of the picture she printed up, very small, wallet size, and she tucked it in her wallet behind a picture of her as a young mother with baby twins on her lap. She liked wearing her children. She liked the way they cover you up in a picture. It was one of the very few times she had ever used her children as window dressing. She put them in front of her to make prettier pictures of herself than they might have been without them.

People often confuse self-control and self-terror. If I don't do this, that horrible thing will happen. If I am not that, I will hate myself. There were problems with that plan. Threatened people, shamed people, scared people, rarely do their best work. A person could scare herself too bad, too hard, too crazy, if she looked at this new photograph the wrong way. What she wanted to see, and could see if she squinted, was, "This is an emergency and I am a beauty and that is not a contradiction in terms." Since she couldn't see it except when squinting, she squinted.

She couldn't decide if her body looked prettier or just more socially acceptable through squinting eyes. It did look better—less like a body and more like a mural or a map. More like an object she could change, or critique, or embrace without changing or critiquing or even embracing herself.

Something Preach wanted. That was the best part of what Ada saw. But she saw something else too.

She saw a map that could lead her home.

When the timer went off at six, she was startled. She sat down to her dining table and did step one. She registered the test online. That was just a matter of typing in her name, a number on the box, her address, and a few tiny bits of information. Next she filled out a permission form to perform the test. When the paperwork was done, she got herself a bottle of water and went to the sink.

She sipped a bit, swished the water around in her mouth. A doctor friend had suggested that she be pretty vigorous about the swishing and pretty generous with the water, so she went through the whole bottle, working her mouth and cheek muscles hard. She was practically sweating. When the water bottle was empty, she sat down again at the table.

The directions mentioned a drying stand. It took her a moment to realize that the drying stand was two holes on the top of the folio that contained the info. She took out the narrow envelope that contained the brushes. She tore open the top. Being careful not to touch the bristly end, she put the brush in her mouth and began to scrape twenty times against the side of her cheek, moving the brush just a little to make sure it wasn't scraping over and over again in the exact same place. When she got to twenty, she did ten more. She wasn't sure if one scrape down and one scrape up should be counted as one or two scrapes. She put the first brush in the drying stand.

Then she did the other cheek. Thirty brushes. When she put it in the drying stand, she turned on a timer and set it for ten minutes. The first brush would have a little extra drying time.

When the timer went off, she put the brushes in the envelope that they were supposed to go back to the lab in. That envelope sealed, she placed it in the larger envelope provided, along with the paperwork. Finally she sealed that securely. All she had to do was drop that envelope off at the mailbox. That's all she had to do, but it wasn't all she was doing. She was worrying about what other use might be being made of her DNA information. She was worrying about finding out now, or later, that the genes associated with whatever diet destiny or metabolic identity this test revealed would later be associated with some horrible disease. She was parsing a question she had never parsed before: How much medical info is too much medical info? On the way to the mailbox she stopped worrying about all that. She even stopped wondering if Preach was cheating and what her daughters were doing at the exact moment. When she dropped the envelope in the mailbox, all she was thinking was, Please let that be a valid sample. Please let me know what I need to do to be the body I want to be. It was a big enough wish to eclipse other wishes.

Until she knew what she was really supposed to be eating, she would stay on Weight Watchers. She wasn't looking for excuses to fail. And she had already lost more than a few pounds.

14

CONSIDER SURGERY

THE TWINS' BIRTHDAY was on a Saturday, and the girls flew in to celebrate. It was their tradition to eat Mexican food for dinner to mark the occasion, because Ada and Preach had eaten Mexican just before the babies came.

Ada decided to take the girls on a walk around Radnor Lake as part of the festivities. This was not part of the tradition. They wanted to go to the Loveless Café and eat biscuits and bacon and jam and drink Bloody Marys and coffee. Ada offered to feed them sweet potatoes baked in their jackets. The girls agreed—if they could have their birthday presents early, and mani-pedis instead of the walk.

Over breakfast Ada gave each daughter a gym membership for her respective town, tucked into a birthday card.

Ruth and Naomi looked at Ada like she was crazy. Then she handed each a giant dress box wrapped in newspaper and a great big bow. When they opened the boxes, each daughter had a long black party dress. The girls fell out laughing. Ada had recycled their debutante gowns—dyed the white dresses black!

The girls stripped in the kitchen. After tugging, and squeezing, and pulling up of zippers, the dresses were on, and the girls looked fabulous—but they did not look fit.

Seeing them a little too plump but oh so beautiful, watching them let themselves go just a little too much, was hard. Watching them erode some of their beauty, as she had eroded so much of her own, with negligence, with focusing on things that were seemingly more important, was plain painful. It was their birthday. She tried not to let the pain show.

The ache had started at the dry cleaners. There had been the unfortunate incident provoked by her tiny bladder. While Ada was at the cleaners, she got stricken by a need to go, and knowing that the cleaners kept an immaculately clean toilet, she decided to use it.

While she was in the toilet, two old biddies, Melvin and Alfred, arrived to pick up some ties they had dropped off for cleaning. They were taking a very close look at the newly black dresses.

"Girls used to get married in their debutante gowns, not dye them black!"

"Anyone thinking about marrying one of those girls will take one look at the mother and flee."

"Maybe dying them black is right. Those girls won't be getting married and need a second gown."

"Big girls don't."

"Not usually."

"Black girls don't."

"Not much anymore."

"And big black girls with smarts—"

"Never!"

"Back in the forties, I went to a wedding every Saturday in June, sometimes two in a day."

"One weekend in June of 1953 I went to a noon wedding and a six o'clock wedding, then turned around and went to a four o'clock on Sunday wedding. Every one of those girls Phi Beta Kappa, big and brown and brilliant."

"Sure enough."

"This is the era of the skinnywhitedumbgirl."

"Paris Hilton."

"Jessica Simpson."

"Is Nicole Richie black?"

"I don't know."

"Hard to tell."

Just then Ada emerged from the toilet. She had on her blank preacher's-wife smile.

"Melvin, Alfred."

"Ada, your girls were just precious, just precious."

"And those gowns. Exquisite."

"Cut out the picture from the paper. Preach in tails, daughter on each arm. Beautiful."

Ada stared back hard. Her blank KidPlay stare.

"Darling, we didn't know you was in there."

"Of course we did, we just said those things to tease you. You know we know Naomi and Ruth's wedding will be a blowout to end blowouts: Your daddy will get up a band and you'll do the cooking, and everybody will come just to see if Preach walks 'em down the aisle, gives the vows, or both."

"They take after their daddy's side. They're shaped just like his grandmother was shaped at their age. And she was a size eight at eighty-plus."

"Ada, they take after you."

"And you do not need to be as big as you are. Take it from an old queen, as long as you don't end up in jail, pretty makes life easier."

"Let me get these dresses and get home. You a mess. Both of you. And let me see you in church on Sunday and shut your mouths about my girls, unless you want me to snatch you baldhead—oh, you already are."

"Listen at you."

"What."

"Lord have mercy today."

"And—"

"The Lord done done all he can for them gals, the best he can. He gave 'em you. You the best. But you ain't be the best. You is but ain't. But you could be."

"Why you so mean?"

"You were such a pretty bride."

"And?"

"I want you to be pretty again."

"I didn't know I wasn't pretty now."

"You didn't know you were pretty then. First thing you need, child, is an eye for beauty. Till you get you one, let me, or let Melvin, he'p you out."

Ada exited the cleaners carrying a weight heavier than two used debutante gowns: her worry that black marriage was in danger of becoming extinct.

After the dry cleaners incident she had had a nightmare in

which Matt Mason had declared to one of his sons, "Not marrying that woman who turned into a fat pig was dodging a bullet. Avoid those twins like the plague!"

She didn't want to be a giant billboard screaming FAT, OBESE, TOO LARGE, DON'T MARRY THEM. She didn't want Matt Mason to see her too large, because he had the sons and the nephews and she didn't want Matt Mason, or any black man with eligible sons and nephews, or any good man with eligible sons or nephews, to think, This can turn into that, and shudder.

Matt Mason had a son, and he had nephews. It wasn't only that Ada wanted Matt Mason to want her, it was that she didn't want him to regret having once wanted her. She needed Matt Mason to remember wanting her without shame. She had daughters. She needed Matt Mason to be one of the strong black men putting the loud word out: Black women are as good as it gets. Whoever gets one of Ada's girls is getting extraordinary good fortune.

Remembering all of that, as she helped the girls wiggle out of their repurposed finery, Ada reneged on the mani-pedi-instead-of-hike deal. She insisted on the hike. Delighted by their gowns, the girls agreed.

The walk got off to a scandalous start. As they set off on the path, they saw from a distance a friend of Preach's, a woman Ada called Granola Girl, walking the path, flirtatiously bumping into a man who was not her husband. The bumping stopped when Granola Girl, who taught prenatal classes in the church basement, noticed Ada and the twins. The girls and Ada silently lifted their eyebrows and kept stepping after their paths crossed and waves were exchanged. When they got farther away, the girls started laughing. Ada stifled their hilarity by suggesting they tackle Ganier Ridge. The girls grimaced, but when they got to the place where the trail forked, they chose the tough one.

Walking around Radnor Lake with her girls was more fun than she had imagined, even Ganier Ridge—which she usually hated. The girls got behind her and pushed her up the steepest yards of their walk.

Eventually they staggered into the parking lot hand in hand, the mama in the middle. They had walked slowly and laughed, telling stories all the way, but they made it around the lake for the very first time together.

That night at Los Palmas, somewhere between the guacamole (which they ate with cucumber slices brought from home) and her chicken and shrimp fajitas (eaten without the tortillas), the girls told Ada how beautiful she looked. And they meant it. Because they meant it, Ada made herself a promise.

I will lose fifty pounds in the next year, or I will have the surgery.

I will model the health I want my daughters to possess—or I will die trying. Looking at her girls looking at her, and seeing that they believed their mama was beautiful, was complicated.

She wanted her daughters to see her beauty—but she also wanted her daughters to see her differently, to see the limits of her kind of beauty. She wanted them to see her differently because she wanted them to see themselves differently.

Preach was oblivious.

When the birthday flans were served, a lit sparkler atop each, Naomi and Ruth's faces shone brightly in the sputtering light.

Later, when Preach said simply, "Thank you," she knew he was talking about the view from his side of the table, his sight of their daughters. Preach was grateful for the reality of soft round beauty, bronze and cherubic glory. This would make getting the twins skinny harder. But not impossible. Her daughters would follow her anywhere—and she was on her road to fitland.

15

KEEP A FOOD DIARY AND
A BODY JOURNAL

TEMPLE WAS LAID out with a cold. Ada hoped she hadn't brought baby Jarius's bug out to him. As soon as Ada had gotten the toilets cleaned and the soup on the stove, she rubbed her daddy down with a lemon cut in half, then lowered him (wearing purple tighty whities) into a hot bath she had spiked with red pepper flakes and Tabasco. When Temple was up to his shoulders in the water, Ada gave him a shot of whisky.

Then she sat on the toilet and looked out the window into the woods while he soaked. He was too frail to be in the tub alone.

She was having a little tiny period. Being with the girls, who were cycling, had probably brought it on. The flow was so light she barely needed a pad. For the very first time, she hoped this one was the last one. She was ready.

When her father got out of the water, she averted her eyes as he rubbed himself down with a towel. Then she helped slip him into a robe and old silk pajamas. He rested heavily on her as she walked him through the maze to the bed in the center of his bedroom.

"You getting smaller, gal," Temple said.

Ada smiled. "A little. Maybe."

"It's more than a little."

"What you wanna eat, Daddy?"

"Nothing."

"I got some soup on the stove."

"I wanna see the lake."

"It's too much stuff to move just now, Daddy."

"Squeeze in and tell me how it look."

Ada sucked in her breath and edged herself in sideways.

"It's just the way it always is, Daddy. Pretty. Three ducks out on the water. There's a speedboat with some folk drinking . . . sky is blue-gray, and the water is green-gray, and there's a farm across the way that looks like a storybook. I see a silo."

"Pretty, pretty. I love looking at pretty. Seeing you today reminded me of that. Move some of that shit, gal, I gots to see the lake."

"I'll need a wheelbarrow."

"Get one."

"I like that."

"What you gonna do with what you tote outa here?"

"Pitch it in the lake."

"Unh-unh."

"Yes, sir."

"Leave it, then."

"I'll wheel it out to the shed."

"Come here so I can get a good look at you."

"Till you can see the lake?"

"You prettier than the lake."

"Daddy, I'm a old woman."

"You just getting grown, gal, just now getting grown. Two best kinds of women, eighteen years old and fifty. I had 'em both, and I know."

"You ever have an outside woman, Daddy?"

"No."

"You never cheated?"

"They never outside. Always inside. They ain't no outside women. I put a lot of backstreet and backdoor in this house."

"You told Mama?"

"She tasted 'em on me."

"That's disgusting, Daddy."

"When yo' mama kissed me, anything I knew, she knew. Woman could taste how much money I lost on a bet."

"That didn't make you do right?"

"Eventually."

"Eventually?"

"After twenty-three slips, I stopped slipping."

"Or you stopped counting."

On the highway home Ada was hungry for soul food. And she didn't mean collard greens and sweet potatoes and fried catfish. She meant church. She made up her mind to try the white Episcopals.

She needed a place to pray about her body that she didn't

have to worry if it was full of people coveting her husband's body. A place where she wasn't the First Lady, a place she could just be a congregant.

She would go to eleven o'clock at her and her husband's church, and she would go to Wednesday night at her and her husband's church—but she would get up in the morning and go to 7:00 A.M. with the Episcopals after a 5:00 A.M. walk.

It would seem utterly strange to some, but going to St. Bartholomew's would be perfect. She would get a break from congregants wanting to befriend her—most would be too snobby to want her as a friend. And she might learn something; rich white southern women make champion fit freaks.

And Ada had just heard an Episcopal joke that she loved. The one about the middle-aged Episcopal lady who had a heart attack and got rushed to the hospital. On the operating table she had a near-death experience. She saw God, and he told her she had another thirty to forty years to live. Upon recovery she decided to have a face-lift, liposuction, breast augmentation, and a tummy tuck. When she was recovered from all of that, she signed up for a day spa. For twelve weeks she worked out hard. The twelfth week she treated herself to a new haircut and color and a full wax down there. Standing outside the spa, she couldn't wait to get home. She got hit by an ambulance speeding toward the hospital. When she found herself in front of God, she was furious. She told him that he had promised her thirty or forty years. She hadn't even gotten thirty months! To which God replied, "I didn't recognize you."

Ada wanted that kind of change for Ada. She was worshipping with the Episcopals. Surrounded by skinny ladies, she would not forget she was fat.

And she was dividing her diet book into two separate parts: the front would be "The Rules," and a food diary in which she would keep track of every morsel she put in her mouth—even though she also did it on Weight Watchers. And the back half would be a body journal where she vented, and wished, and described, and self-portrayed.

The first time she sat down to write in the back of her journal, she filled pages:

His love of bigness allows me the luxury of laziness. I don't have to do something about this. And even more than that, his beauty testifies that once I was beautiful.

I tell this to darling, and he says I'm beautiful. I hope he actually believes that. I half do. If I'm talking about it in a Hawaiian princess way. Or maybe in a Botero sculpture way. Or getting down to the real nitty-gritty, in a my-grandmother-was-big-as-two-houses-and-she-was-the-most-beautiful-woman-in-my-world way. But MaDear dropped dead a long time ago, and the world has changed.

It's funny how all those naked Rubens women don't look anything but fat anymore. Those hanging bellies scare the bejesus out of me. Bosoms are something else. I love my big pillow breasts. One of the hardest things about losing weight is deflating those giant man and baby cushions. When I look down, I see my big cloud immensities, tipped in chocolate like a present, better than a bow. When I lose more weight, those are going to turn into flat pancakes I need to shove in a bottom-padded push-up bra. But that's okay. When I lose weight, I can find a bra that fits at Victoria's Secret.

MaDear's been shouting out loud to me today. Be careful what you wish for. I always wanted to be a fat old black lady in a flowered dress on a porch, feeding my grandbabies chocolate. But not too soon. And maybe not ever, now.

Me and my body got to find a new way to roll. My new body dance is going to be a three-beat waltz. Sizing, sexing, primping. Oompapa. Can't do the long march stagger another mile. It's oompapa—primping; sexing; sizing. Sizing is eating and exercising and binding it in. Sexing is feeling all the pleasure the body can bring. Primping is decorating and celebrating the body. It's putting the shine on healthing, and that makes the pretty. I can't do all of that—primping, sexing, sizing—every day. For me it seems the deal is, if one of them is not going well, get the other two to kick in. On great days you should work on all three. On bad days one. On no days none, and most days two.

If you can't polish your fingernails, give yourself an orgasm. If you can't do any of that, schedule a mammogram. One of the bad things about getting older is, you can burn a whole lot of time setting up appointments and going to appointments. I have friends who make almost being sick, or checking out that they are not sick, almost a full-time job. I'm not doing that. That's the medicine polka, and it's too herky-jerky for me. I'm sizing, sexing, primping. Oompapa.

One of the things I like about being big is, it makes me feel like I'm not about to die. Too many times that even trumps what I want to do and be for Naomi and Ruth. I need reasons beyond Matt Mason to lose. Or maybe I need a Preach-related non-Preach reason. Maybe I want a pulpit of my own. Or maybe 'cause Preach don't even seem to want me great big, I might as well get smaller.

Hunger's got my mind messed up.

Writing about it helped.

16

ADD A SECOND EXERCISE THREE TIMES A WEEK

HER TEST RESULTS arrived via e-mail on the KidPlay desktop computer. She was a carb restrictor who needed intense exercise three times a week. She loved carbs and liked to exercise moderately daily. No wonder her body was a mess.

There were pages and pages in the report after the summary, but after diligently going through them, she soon concluded all she needed to concern herself with was the first page.

She would be a carb restrictor. And she would up her good fat intake. According to Inherent Health, her meals should be 30 percent fat. That seemed like a lot, but she was going after it. Eating fat to let go of fat. She imagined a little river of fat running through her and out of her, collecting the fat from her blood cells and from her body, a little river of olive oil flowing to and through her, washing everything that did not belong away. These were good thoughts, hippie-dippy, spacey thoughts for sure, but good. And they balanced off the idea that she was about to turn into some kind of cavewoman committed to a diet of meat and veg. She wondered if her ancestors had been Masai warriors, drinking blood from live animals to survive.

Then she wondered if anyone actually did that, or whether it was simply a myth about Africa perpetuated to make black people seem crude and cruel.

Then she stopped wondering. She didn't have time. She had the vestry dinner. She needed to check in with Preach. Get the last tally on who was coming. Remind him to pick up the flowers. Tell him about her results.

Walking across her lawn and through the basketball court, Ada headed to Preach's office. She hoped he would be in, but she also hoped, just a little bit, he wouldn't be. It was a day for new information. Sitting in his desk chair, looking at what he looked at, poking in their files, might give her a little more new information. She walked up the stairs to his office thinking, Bring it on. Whatever it was.

She strode through the young men loitering in Preach's outer office. Preach kept a pot of coffee waiting on a hot plate especially made for the young men of the congregation who had no job or school to go to. He made a pot for them every morning and refreshed it at noon. The morning pot got his posse dressed, out the house, and looking for work. The afternoon pot diluted frustration. Preach, she was quickly informed, wasn't in. Ada kept stepping, making use of First Lady privilege.

Once inside Preach's office, she closed and locked the door. She sat down at his desk. She loved looking at the little gallery of photographs he kept in popsicle-stick frames, made by the girls, on his desktop. There was a picture of Ada on her wedding day. She barely recognized herself. And there were pictures of the girls at all different ages. And there was a picture of

Queenie holding infant Lucius. These pictures made Ada breathe deep and quiet.

The pictures on the wall, ripped out of magazines, then stuck up with tape or pinned with thumbtacks, made Ada uneasy. On the wall Preach mixed portraits of his heroes with his rogues' gallery. A photograph of Sweet Daddy Grace in Washington, D.C., was next to a photograph of Martin Luther King. On the other side of King was a picture of Prophet Jones in Detroit. On the other side of Prophet, who was wearing his full-length mink coat paid for by congregants, was Malcolm X. Just below Malcolm was Father Divine, somewhere in New York. Beside Father Divine was Jesse Jackson. Interspersed throughout were pictures of Preach's father. Ada's favorite was a picture of Sarge in his uniform, near the time of his retirement.

The pictures had puzzled Ada when Preach first put them up. When she asked Preach about it, he said that he had pulled together photographs that would remind himself he would never be as bad as the bad preachers, and never be as big, or good, as the big good preachers. His father had believed preachers picked poor people's pockets. His mother had believed preachers saved them. Preach had put up the most extreme examples he knew of each of their beliefs, to help remind himself to cut his own path. And he had. At his worst he was a low-paid always friend for every member of his congregation; at best he was God's messenger on earth. The photographs reminded Ada of a thing she had begun to take for granted about Preach; he was never boring.

She stood up and looked into one of his file cabinets. She

wanted a peek at their banking account and tax files. She shuddered. Everything was there. Every receipt, every bill, every note about them, so much of everything you couldn't put your hands on anything. A quick glance through two or three drawers of files found six marked "This year's taxes," and they each seemed to contain information on at least three different years. There were eight different files on the girls at Georgetown; loan applications, not in numerical order, mixed in with transcripts; directions on ordering graduation pictures; course catalogs; and bills for presciptions of antibiotics (Naomi) and antidepressants (Ruth, briefly). There were even Ada files. One seemed to be inexpensive gifts he was thinking of buying her. She knew this because he had bought some of them: a flight of wildflower honey, a silk headband, a copy of Paul Laurence Dunbar poems with pretty drawings of brown babies. She closed his files, their files. They were too depressing and too many.

She stared back at his desk. Something was out of place. And most things were not. She touched, for luck, his childhood Bible with his scrawly child handwriting and his crayoned illustrations of his favorite Bible stories. She touched his notes for the next week's sermon. Everything on the desk seemed familiar—except the phone.

She looked at the phone. It looked something like Preach's phone, like the phone Ada knew Preach had, but it wasn't the phone that had sat all the last night on his nightstand. And it wasn't new.

She looked at the speed dial. Ada. Ruth. Naomi. Except he had never called her from this number. He looked at the numbers the phone had called. None were familiar to her, except

Delila's. She put the phone down. She shivered. She wondered if it was his death penalty phone. Some preachers had a special phone for that. Not just for the men on death row, for their families. This could be that.

It was hard being a preacher's wife. You didn't know when you shouldn't be asking questions because you wouldn't want to know the answers and the answers had nothing to do with you and would only invade someone's deserved privacy and perhaps shock you about man's capacity to be inhuman to man. And you didn't know when you should be asking questions, even though you didn't want to know the answer, because the answer had everything to do with your most private life. It was a dilemma.

When it was your husband's job to keep some stuff from you, it was hard to do your wife's job of making sure your husband didn't keep too much stuff from you.

Somewhere along the way Preach and Ada had gotten this all wrong. He told her very little, and she asked him even less. They were both too busy taking care of folk to do any better.

If the truth be told, Ada was too scared of finding out that Preach was too much like Temple to find out who her husband was. And Preach was too scared of being a preacher with his hand out to be the man his wife needed. But there was nobody to tell that truth.

So Ada and Preach both suspected the obvious explanation for why there was less joy in their world—that the one they loved didn't love them, and probably had good reason not to.

As finding out for sure that Preach didn't love her would mean no joy at all, Ada kept on keeping on exactly as before, and so did Preach. Particularly the day the vestry was coming for dinner. But they each did it with rapidly increasing frustration and slowly increasing anger.

Back at the Manse, in her bright kitchen, Ada made soup and baked a caramel cake and spooned pepper jelly onto bread rounds, wondering if there was a way to poison just the portions that would be eaten by the woman she suspected of having an affair with her husband. The other preacher's wife. The one whose husband had died.

Except she couldn't do that. Black women were and will always be spectacularly clean in the kitchen—especially when cooking for somebody who is not family. Black ladies don't play in the kitchen with food. As a people we have been too proud and too poor to do that.

As Ada thought about poisoning her possible rival, she shook her head at the book *The Help*. There is not a self-respecting black woman in the world who would put any part of herself into the food, unless she was doing something hoodoo or voodoo or sacred. We, Ada said silently to herself, don't throw away or give away parts of ourself—even hair or nail clippings— casually. We don't throw parts of ourselves at our enemies. Putting potty stuff in a pie? Never! Anybody hoodoo who has worked one day as a maid knows—a lock of discarded hair, a scrape off a dirty toilet, a drop of blood by a sink, can be used to destroy the one it came from. A certain kind of black woman knows that the detritus of life is powerful.

And you don't poison or desecrate, because it would confirm negative expectations.

A black woman organized enough to get up every morning to take care of her family, who also manages to take care of some other women's families, is not interested in confirming negative expectations. "That Stockett lady lied on us," said Ada, right out loud, shaking her head.

Twenty circles of bread cut later, Ada was sad her emergency kit to ward off boredom could no longer be a sack full of caramel cake slices and pepper jelly sandwiches.

Night was falling as Preach walked into the dining room. He had come to inspect the table. It was just a door on sawhorses, but he had sanded it down good and stained it prettily, and he had made the sawhorses himself twenty years before. It was a solid, sturdy, level table. Like the chairs around it, which he had also made in his basement carpentry shop, the table had given many good years of service and could give many more.

Unfortunately, he wasn't sure how many more vestry dinners the table would be called upon to serve.

His congregants had changed over the years. Some of the vestry lived in big houses with fancy antiques and ten-thousand-dollar rugs. Many no longer fit, or believed they fit, in his handmade, hand-painted chairs.

Preach folded all six foot five, and at least forty more pounds than when he first made the chairs, into the chair at the head of the table. The room looked good in the candlelight. Still. In the dim guests couldn't see the dirt in the creases of the floorboards, the streaks on the now mottled finish of the table, the little chips in the gilt of the good china, or the cobwebs and dust in the corners.

Ada padded into the room and sidled up beside him. He stayed seated but reached around her wide hip to fondle a bit of her belly. She patted his hand until it stopped fondling. Her hand lay flat atop his.

"You right about dinner at six thirty, not five," said Preach.

"You like the flowers, or you think they strange?"

She had filled the girls' old fishbowls with blue colored water and floated the head of a big sunflower, harvested from a neighbor's garden, atop each one.

"I forgot to bring home the roses from the discount place."

"It's good for the vestry to see we broke," said Ada, patting his hand. He took this as permission to fondle a bit more of her belly. When she didn't step away, he took the next second as an opportunity to try to pull her into his lap. Her feet stayed planted. He kissed her arm. She smiled, but she pulled away.

"Considering the topic of the meeting is my raise?"

" 'Xactly."

"Then let's say I forgot the roses on purpose."

"Let's say that."

"I love the sunflowers. They big and bold."

She wanted to drop into his lap when he said this, but before she could, he had stood. He had kissed her on top of the head and hoped that she would turn his face toward her like he was the sun and she was a sunflower, but she didn't. She went into the kitchen to finish getting the dinner ready.

Alone in the candlelight, annoyed by the withheld kiss and anxious about the impending discussion of his salary, Preach began moving the place cards, situating the women with whom he would enjoy flirting, who would lighten the work of the evening, on either side of him, and the two men who would be the hardest to persuade so that they were flanking Ada. Then he changed the cards back. Ada knew best. And the table was small. Everyone would be talking to everyone. Soon enough.

Annoyances flashed then vanished at Ada's dinner table. When the little group—Dr. Willie Angel and her husband, Joel Angel, Esquire; Dr. Inez Whitfield and her husband, James Madison Whitfield; Portia Pierce; and the young attorneys Milton and Susan Hill—got to talking and eating, joy filled the room. Some of it was Ada's fried chicken. Some of it was the sweet tea spiked with bourbon. Some of it was the shared pride in the growth of the church, two jam-packed services on Sundays. Adults and children packed, scrambling for seats, in the Bible study classes. A paid-for church building, a paid-for parsonage, a popular preacher. Vestry dinners, initiated as a time of brainstorming during a difficult transition when the preacher before Preach had to be ousted and Preach, who had come as an assistant, was raised to be the main and only minister, had become a mutual admiration society.

When Preach tapped on his glass with his spoon, just as the fried chicken platter was being passed for the second time, everyone but Ada thought Preach was about to make a toast. Ada thought Preach was about to ask about a raise. He surprised everybody. Possibly even himself.

"I think we need to consider hiring a junior minister."

An awkward silence fell on the group as folk searched each other's eyes and chin sets and mouths for opinions.

Softly and slowly the talk began again. By the time they got to Ada's caramel cake, it was clear Preach had the three of five votes he needed to move the plan from the executive committee of the vestry to the larger body. It was also clear that if he pressed the vote, the two voting against him, Joel Angel, his vestry president, and Milton Hill, the wealthiest black lawyer in town, were going to be truly perturbed.

Preach was not only used to being popular with the vestry; he *liked* being popular with the vestry. He began backing off the proposal and signaling Portia Pierce, the widowed preacher's wife, who had quickly gotten very passionate about the matter, to back off as well. He took another tack. He brought up the issue of a raise. When Joel Angel responded to this second matter, Ada got her second surprise of the evening.

"Preach, we allocated money for your raise, but you insisted we put that money into our elder-care day program."

"That was only supposed to be for this year and last year."

"Folk are joining our church to become eligible for our elder care. You won't let us put in a one-year wait for eligibility. You need to dust off a tithing sermon."

"I don't think he has one," said Milton Hill.

Laughter erupted at the table. Lack of interest in raising money for the church was considered Preach's great and only fault by the vestry. The joke in the neighborhood was that they were the only black church in America that didn't have a building fund. They forgave the fault because he balanced the budget by working so cheap, and without an assistant.

"And I don't think Preach really wants an assistant—then you'd have to share your harem," Portia said, fingering her own snakeskin belt. The bourbon had melted the frost from her.

The table erupted into more laughter. As Ada served coffee, assisted by Susan Hill, Portia intercepted a cup Susan was taking to Preach and handed it to him herself. Preach's fingertips grazed Portia's knuckles in a gesture of thanks before he took the cup. Portia smiled huge and exclaimed, "You so welcome." Susan and Ada caught each other's eyes in a "Did you see that?" moment. Ada smiled bigger and broader, as if she hadn't noticed. Portia, determined to keep Preach's attention, plowed on, looking pointedly from Susan to Milton Hill as she spoke.

"I would like to see some of these young two-career fancy families do a little more," said Portia.

"Give me some time, and I'm going to make that happen. But we want them to be comfortable in the church first."

"Sustained growth, that's the ticket."

"Sustained growth, and we've got that."

"And a paid mortgage . . ."

The talk had returned to the genial babble of a happy church vestry. As Ada cleared away the coffee, she was thinking, No raise, no assistant, no change. She was noting that Milton Hill, the president-elect of the vestry, was inviting Ada and Preach to stay with them in their house down in Seaside, and Preach was saying they would be delighted to join them, *as if* Ada was going to get anywhere near a beach. *As if* Ada owned a bathing suit. Willie Angel's husband, munificent after Preach had backed down so graciously from his play for an assistant, was inviting Preach to come golf with him. They were all so thrilled with their preacher, who always put the church first.

Ada wanted to kill Preach dead, raise him up, and kill him

again. Preferably by strangling him with Portia's purple snake-skin belt.

Instead she stood on the porch and waved as the last car, Preach's, drove off. Then she washed dishes and Swiffered floors, preparing the house for morning, wondering just how hard it would be to tell the twins she was going to divorce their daddy.

17

DRINK EIGHT GLASSES OF
WATER DAILY

ADA FOUND MATT Mason on Facebook.

He was handsome, and he appeared to be divorced. God loved her and was probably Episcopal. She had found Mason on Facebook the very first Sunday she had attended the 7:00 A.M. service at St. Bart's, over a month after the vestry dinner, the day she hit 199 pounds. Twenty-one pounds down.

There was gray in Matt Mason's hair, and he had put on a few pounds, but they had filled him out and made him look prosperous. His fat had not erased anything. Her fat was different.

Her fat is always different. It was an easy decision not to send him a friend request. It was a hard decision to exit his page.

Looking at his face, she remembered her own innocence, her first love, the spirit in which she had given her first passionate kisses to his mouth and his cheeks and his closed eyelids. Then Matt Mason had ridiculed her South with some joke about her daddy's band's suits and their synchronized dancing, and she had fallen out of love with him as quickly as she had fallen in. A few months later she and Preach were arguing about *Their Eyes Were Watching God* in an English seminar, and

Matt Mason, who was still trying to beg back, was kicked to the curb as trash.

She wanted her trash back.

Except Ada couldn't imagine herself beneath her old beau big, and she was every day imagining herself beneath her old lover, as she was every day imagining her husband ducking around corners with members of the choir, or the vestry, or the community at large.

She had read Zadie Smith's *On Beauty*. The twins had given it to her. In it a black woman was married to a white man who wanted her to lose weight. Zadie never seemed to get how delicious big is to the black American woman, pure "d" delicious, not a second best, an exquisite thing.

Now Ada wanted to side with Zadie. Now Ada believed Zadie was onto something after all. Jealousy was rising in Ada's heart, and it was jealousy for smaller women like Portia and even Delila. The jealousy was all mixed up in her heart with love and frustration, desire. This strange cocktail of emotion seemed a useful potion in her search for the pounds below 200.

She had a lot of frustration to work with. Preach's almost-getting-a-raise and almost-getting-an-assistant. Almost getting to a place where they could thrive, not just survive. Preach almost being at home in bed with her, except he had yet *another* congregant sick in the hospital to visit. All that almost-getting left her alone and lonely, trying to calm herself with her emergency kits.

With her iPhone and her iPod, she was ready to take on the world. She wanted a late-night snack. She wanted the comfort of a bowl of ice cream and the excitement of some hot chocolate and crunchy almonds. Instead she put in her earphones, cranked up her diet-comfort playlist, and fell asleep to dream of violets and furs and Billie crooning about cain't nobody say what love is, 'fore they see and taste the blues.

Instead of dreaming of violets and furs and Billie Holiday, Ada dreamed of schoolbuses breaking down in the Mississippi Delta and black kids, little black kids and big black kids, almost getting killed—except they didn't get killed, they got rescued by Ruth, who then drove off laughing in a black Mustang convertible singing loud and off-key a song by the Allman Brothers that had been popular in her high school days, "Ramblin' Man," until they drove off the road toward a gigantic magnolia tree. She woke up before they hit—or avoided—the tree.

She woke up and knew her girls were fine, because she knew if they were not fine, she would feel it in her bones.

Anything big happened to them, she felt it in her body. That's how she knew they were virtuous girls, even if they were not celibates. She suspected Naomi and Ruth already each knew more than one man. As ardently as she hoped they never knew four, she hoped they each knew two or maybe even three. Three or four seemed the right lifetime number.

Five seemed slutty unless you were widowed.

Slut.

She could not decide to what degree her choice to put on pounds had been a choice to put herself beyond sex, or rather beyond sex with anyone other than her husband; had been a choice she made because she was afraid of being a slut.

Had she made use of the fact that he liked largeness to create a chastity belt to which only he had the key? Or was it a movement to accelerate into the future, the wish to be a gunnysack grandma with a lap big enough to ensconce immense broods, which simply arrived too soon in reality?

When she imagined skinny grandmothers, she didn't imagine happy grandbabies. She would try to imagine that. Without a picture of that, she didn't think she would ever make it to skinny.

When she awoke in the morning, she realized she had been dreaming of skinny grandmothers, and she realized her mother was a skinny grandmother, and that Jarius's grandmother was another. She also realized she wanted more than the sound of the water putting her to sleep. She wanted the feel of water waking her up.

She headed to the pool. The Dayani Center at Vanderbilt University Medical Center was only blocks from Ada's house. She only made it to the Dayani treadmill.

Standing between Ada and the pool was a swimsuit she didn't own. Ada hit Vell's during her lunch hour to conquer the obstacle. The obstacle got larger as Ada was approached by a woman who was very, very skinny and blonde and blue-eyed. The woman smiled pleasantly. Ada smiled back.

"Delta Burke."

"Excuse me?"

"Delta Burke, that's the line you need. She knows how to wrap a curve."

The ice-blonde reached in and pulled out a black swimsuit sharply piped in white. Then she grabbed a perfect little swim skirt, also black piped in white.

"Get the boobs up high and cover the thighs."

Ada laughed. "Is that the secret?"

"Only way to go, to the pool, when you're a big girl."

"Is your mama big?"

"Was. And my grandma. I've been a big girl most of my life."

"Did you do the surgery?"

"Bad hepatitis."

"I'm so sorry."

"Enjoy the pounds while you got 'em. I used to hate mine."

As the woman talked, she started looking through the racks like she was looking for something in particular.

"I got hep, hating my body. If you ever wanna get skinny, get skinny the right way. I shot heroin to help me not eat. Wanted to be a singer. Thought I had to be really skinny with big fake boobs and fake hair. Now I'm too skinny to swim, I just sink like a stone. This would look good on you, too."

"I love the first one."

"You want to try it on?"

"Not really."

"It's gonna work. You try it on at home with your underpants on, and if you don't like it, bring it back."

"Thank you, ma'am."

Ada pulled out her credit card. She paid the lady and raced back late to KidPlay. Afterward she went straight to the pool.

In the locker room she pulled off the tags, tugged the suit on, and got in the shower. Slipping tentatively into the water, she swam 1-2-3 laps, doing Ada's version of an Australian crawl, which centered around trying not to get her hair wet. No luck. Her choppy flails had her hair dripping and her arms tired. She considered floating on her back. Her hair would get completely wet, but she would have a little rest. The idea seemed pleasant. She flipped over. Staring at the high, vaulted ceiling, she worried about all the articles she had read that said that somehow swimming caused people to gain weight, not lose. When Ada caught sight of her reflection in the mirror in the dressing room, she wished she hadn't looked. Finally, she paddled back and forth in the pool for an hour. It felt like the sweetest play. It felt like a massage, it felt like being back in the womb. It did not feel like exercise. It felt better than church.

She remembered reading, a thousand years ago, Wally Lamb's hilarious novel about the woman losing weight who swam with her therapist. She remembered that woman losing weight effortlessly, eventually. Ada wanted to get to effortlessly.

She got out of the pool and sat on the side, her legs dangling down. Hair flowed from her shoulders like brown seaweed. In her swim skirt she felt a new kind of appropriate safe, like she was in a little black tennis dress. She liked how the water felt, evaporating on her skin. A younger woman came in from the dressing room and sat a little too near.

"Are you trying to lose weight?"

"Yeah, I guess that's obvious."

"Me too."

"You don't look like you need to."

"Warm water's good for swimming in when you need to lose weight."

"Good to know."

"But what's really important is drinking eight glasses of water a day. I've lost forty pounds drinking water."

Ada wanted to say thank you, but the girl shot into the water and started her laps. Ada was thinking about eight glasses of water and how important it was to cover the basics. And she was thinking there were coaches on every corner.

Looked like God was busy on her behalf, now that she had started looking for healthing miracles.

1 8

EAT SITTING DOWN

THE SCALE SAID 196. One pound up. There was a problem. Ada didn't have time to worry about it. She had a
before-school parent meeting. A volunteer teacher was threatening to quit because one of her parents was threatening to get
her fired. She ate her yogurt with almonds and spices and got a
move on—but it was a disappointed move on.

She was the first to pull into the KidPlay parking lot. She liked
that. She wanted to talk to the irate mama before anyone else arrived. She would wait for her in the parking lot. Walk her into
the building. Close the door of her office. Then they would talk.

Unfortunately the next car to arrive was Loretha's. Loretha
angled herself into a space that provided a bit of shade. In her
rearview mirror Ada could see baby Jarius as he lay curled at
Dorian's breast, sucking on a bottle, wide-eyed.

Ada did not remember sucking closed-eyed at Bird's breast,
though she had seen pictures of it. Seeing pictures of it and
watching her own daughters latch on to her tit with their little plum-flower mouths, she came to imagine that she remembered. What Ada did keenly remember was watching Ruth and

Naomi at her own breast, oblivious to everything but Mama's sweet milk.

Ada couldn't help but be a little sad baby Jarius was robbed of that. There was nothing to do about it. She would have been sadder for Jarius and for his teenage mama if she had dropped out of school to breast-feed him. No fifteen-year-old girl in America was going to pump.

She had just come to the conclusion that wide-eyed could be good when the irate mama pulled in beside her. Ada hustled out of her car and the mama into the building just as the janitor and the lady who helped with the breakfasts arrived.

"What she mean, Keshawn can't have no ice cream fo' his birthday? You need to fire that new teacher. He always has ice cream for his birthday," said Keshawn's mother. The woman had three children under four and no job but collecting welfare, but she kept her kids clean and her apartment up and was trying to work on her GED. Keshawn's mama was a tiny size 4, and Ada wondered if she might not do a midge better if she didn't subsist on Diet Coke and potato chips and keep the babies quiet by feeding them ice cream three meals a day.

"I can't fire a volunteer."

"Keshawn wants peanutbuttychoco—"

"Keshawn is four years old. He hasn't always been doing anything."

"He did it last year."

"And he doesn't know what he wants. He knows what he think he wants! You the mama. You teach him what he wants. That's yo' job. This year he's going to have—"

"She said fruit. What I'm supposed to do? Make some straw-berry shortcake? I don't have time to be thawing out Cool Whip and baking no biscuits! He want ice cream. I want him to want ice cream. It's easy. Grab a box. And it good."

"He can bring plain vanilla. What he can't bring is fake chocolate and nuts and chopped up candy-bar things with five hundred calories and half a dozen chemicals, like he brought last time."

"That's what he likes."

"That's what he knows. How 'bout some little Dixie cups with blueberries in them?"

"Dixie cups with blueberries in 'em. You trippin, Miz Preach."

"Keshawn likes blueberry. He always asking for blueberry Kool-Aid."

"That ain't the same."

"I don't have time to keep talking about this. And you don't have time to keep messin' with that baby's health. These little black boys, they look like they doin' better than our girls, but when they get grown they get sick quicker and sicker—they the ones go from needing dialysis to needing a transplant. You want one of your itty-bitties to grow up and have to loan this one a kidney and walk through life with a scar on her belly, or you gonna start feeding this one right, here and now?"

"I liked you better when you were eating candy bars. Then all you talked about was getting them to read. Getting them to count. Me getting my GED. Now it's all that, and you up in the food too."

"Children are a lot of work."

"They don't even sell blueberries in the store round here."

"Pretend like they a dress you want and get yo'self a ride down to the farmer's market and buy your baby some blueberries and some oranges while you there and tell him that's what big boys eat."

"Is you having ice cream at yo' birthday?"

"We not talkin' 'bout my birthday! My birthday ain't for months. Keshawn's birthday is tomorrow. You got to get off my last nerve. And I got to get to work. I got three begging calls to make this morning. And I got to get to my mama's."

"And I got to go get some blueberries and Dixie cups," said Keshawn's mama. Her nineteen-year-old sassiness had been replaced with a hum of frightened resignation. Ada had managed to put the fear of kidney transplant in her. Thinking about kidney transplants had made Ada think softly of Bird. Bird had given Mag a kidney. It was in Mag when she died.

Ada wondered if having a bit of herself buried was part of what made her mama so sad.

Keshawn's mama stopped at the door.

"I read sumthin' 'bout food deserts."

"Black women been finding water in the desert since Moses tasted salt. Food desert or no food desert, find a way to feed that child right. Or you be snatchin' a kidney out one and begging some doctor to put it in the other one."

Bird was going through a pile of old stage clothes, chiffony dresses with rhinestones. She was squeezing the heavily padded bosoms of the dresses and balling up the dresses, running her hand round the rim of the hems. Every so often she would go at a dress with a scissor.

"I meant to turn these dresses into quilts."

"You starting now?"

"Not now."

"If you give me the dresses, I could start making quilts."

"That's not what I'm giving you."

"Fine, Mama."

"You broke, ain't you?"

"Broke? Not broke, just tired and crazy."

"I mean, you need money."

"*That* kind of broke?"

"You always wear the same clothes."

"I'm fine."

"No, you ain't. But under all that fat and wrinkles, you do favor Ada."

"I am Ada."

"I want you to have something for yourself." Her mother ripped open a seam, and she pulled out a heavy chain of gold. She ripped open another seam, and there were what appeared to be rhinestone or diamond ear bobs.

"This belonged to your great-great grandmother. A woman she worked for gave them to her—in exchange for an abortion. She never wore them or let me wear them. She said the safest thing a black woman could be was ugly. They will bring Ada a pretty penny. Take 'em to her."

"I'm Ada, Mama."

"You don't look like Ada."

"Mama, what else you have buried in here?"

"That's family business."

"Now you're breaking me, Mama."

"But you ain't broke. You go to one of those fancy white lady spas."

"You know I'm Ada."

"I know you take good care of me and Temple."

It was impossible to know what her mother did and didn't know. Ada looked at the shiny things. She wondered if they were real. If they were real, she was going to a spa, she was buying a treadmill, she was building a real playground for the kids at KidPlay.

The jewels were not real. Ada wondered if the old lady had switched them. Or maybe her father had switched them. Somehow what mattered most was, her mother wanted her to have a break, even if she didn't know her name.

Later that week, when Ada went to clean, her mother dropped her old diary in her purse. Reading her birth story made Ada feel spunky. She had forgotten her parents had met the great and great-big civil rights worker Fannie Lou Hamer. She had forgotten the band bus got as far as Mound Bayou, Mississippi, before she plopped out in the parking lot of the Mississippi Delta's only black hospital, Taborian. She had forgotten Maceo pulled a gun when the doctor said they didn't accept dirty babies. She had forget that Delila's mother had delivered her. She had forgotten a lot.

Reading her old diary gave her a thought of rereading her new food diary. Reading over all her pages, it was easy to see exactly where and when the extra calories were coming in—on the run.

The extra almonds she ate going out the back door; the bread she ate running up the stairs; the chai she drank walking down the street on errands.

No more. She had a simple new rule: Eat sitting down.

The very next week she stepped on the scale and was one and three-quarter pounds less round.

This would have been the highlight of the month, except that later that month, Ada got a text from the Hampton alumni office—Matt Mason was passing through town, and wanted to take her to lunch the very next day.

19

EAT SLOWLY

WELL AWARE, FROM years of teaching Sunday school, that a lie of omission is a lie nonetheless, Ada managed to mention, as she headed out her bedroom door toward her morning ramble, that Matt Mason was passing through town on his way to the Mississippi Delta, where he was doing research about bluesmen associated with the Dockery Plantation. Then she started talking about how different the neighborhood looks on foot. That the same redheaded boy on the crazy bike had passed her twice earlier in the week, and the last time he had shouted out, "I'm getting mine, you getting yours." She wondered aloud what he might have meant. She added so many clauses and interesting additional bits of information, she would be able to tell Preach that Matt Mason was passing through town without Preach hearing it. As Preach appeared not to be paying any attention, Ada ventured, "He wants to go out to Mama and Daddy's to interview Maceo. I might ride out there with him."

This would have been a triumph. Safely hidden in her word-cloud, the facts of her day were both told and obscured. She thought. She thought wrong. Preach put his razor down. He had heard something in the tone of Ada's voice that alarmed him.

"Maceo not taking a turn, is he?"

"Won't die today."

"How you know that?"

"Maceo loves," Ada said, dropping into Maceo's voice to quote him, "'settin' the press straight.'"

"He won't croak right before a last bit of spotlight?" said Preach, picking up his razor.

"Exactly."

"Ride out there with Mason. Be good for you."

Ada didn't like getting this permission. It spoiled things. It meant she would have to go a step further to transgress. And she didn't want to go too far. But she did want to transgress. Once. A little. Still. She wanted to poke her toes in the waters of naughtiness without dipping her hips in the waters of nastiness. If she could pull it off, it would be a slick trick. Her one slick trick. And she wanted it. Bad. She was sick of being the virtuous woman, a creature with no mysteries. Just this once she wanted a secret desire. Unvoiced, the wish put a new and faraway smile on Ada's lips.

Startled by the fast-descending distance, Preach blew Ada a soaped-up kiss, a bit of his shaving foam. Ada reached out to catch it with her fingers. They hadn't done that in a long time. Another man's presence, even just on the horizon, was changing things. Walking out the door, Ada was flushing or blushing, she couldn't tell which.

Standing before the steamed-up mirror, Preach was thinking he had a long day and a long week ahead. He was glad for

Ada to have a bit of a diversion. He was glad for Ada to have somebody to go out to the lake house with that wasn't him. He knew Mason wouldn't take a second look at Ada great big, because that wasn't his thing. Except Ada wasn't quite as gorgeously great big as she had been. Every way he looked, sweet stuff was shrinking. Lawd, have mercy today, he murmured to himself. I'm starting to sound like my mama. On the last glide of his razor, he nicked himself.

Back from her walk, Preach gone, Ada hit the shower, and then a final reckoning with what she would wear. She wanted to rush to the mall and buy new clothes. But that would be too crazy, and she already acted crazy enough after getting the text. The day before, she had done something she had never once done in her married life. She had spent time and money on ablutions: she had had her eyebrows waxed, and her lip waxed, and her chin waxed; had her fingernails polished and her roots dyed; and she had bought, on her first trip ever to Sephora, a new foundation, a new mascara, her first nude lipstick, and an old perfume. She hadn't sold the car, and she was dipping to near the bottom of her spoon money. She rushed around and did all this after she got the text, saying HE was passing through.

Over her almonds and yogurt she asked herself, Why? Going to see Mason didn't make sense. She wasn't ready yet. She had lost thirty-four pounds, not seventy, not a hundred. She didn't want him to see her midstream at 186. She had wanted an "aha moment" when he could look at her and say, "Umph, the years have been good to you, girl!" Except he would never say that.

Mason was a black man who had lived all his life among

white people and plastic surgery and diets and prosperity—he would expect her to look good at fifty. And now he lived in Tinseltown, La-La Land, Hollyweird. Every little bit she had fallen away from good would be a disappointment.

The pounds she had lost wouldn't change that. Wouldn't change the tags on her neck, the lines on her forehead; wouldn't vanish the age and time freckles on her cheeks or banish the bags under her eyes. I am going because I don't like pipe dreams, she thought. I am going because there is a possibility he will want me as I am now. And the only way I would have him is if he wanted me now—but it is not a large possibility. There is a large possibility he won't recognize me.

On her morning walk she had concluded she would wear the same ole, same ole: Juicy sweats and Burberry raincoat. In honor of the occasion she would lace on her lucky shoes, her high-top Converse All-Stars. And she would break out the unworn underwear the girls had bought their mama for her last birthday. At long last, she would squeeze into the brown-and-black tiger-striped panties and bra. The point wasn't that Matt Mason would see her tiger stripes. He wouldn't. But he might see the oomph they gave Ada. And she would wear the same perfume she had worn when she had dated Matt Mason, Opium.

Wearing the underwear her daughters had bought her with the perfume Matt Mason had long ago picked out for her seemed just a tad disloyal to Preach. Ada liked that. She hoped it would be significant enough transgression to get transgression out of her system.

Their first and only Valentine's Day together Matt Mason

had bought Opium perfume for her and taken her to eat Chinese food. She would wear Opium and they would go to P.F. Chang's and eat a ridiculously high-calorie, high-carb lunch, and he would see she had turned into an old cow, and this whole thing would be over.

Right. She was ready for over. She was tired of everything. Tired of going out to the lake to see her parents, who didn't see her. Tired of staying married to Preach and not asking the hard questions about what he was doing elsewhere that he wasn't doing at home. Tired of the fantasizing to get through reality. Tired of the diet. Tired of the exercising. Tired of the worrying about the girls. Tired of living in a house they did not own. She was tired of all that, and she wasn't afraid of dying. She wanted to climb up to the top of her green metal roof and jump off—except that would be too exhibitionistic. She wondered if cuddling into a curvy road on a wet night and a tree was not a more dignified way of dealing with exhaustion and unexpressed mourning than feigning amnesia. Whatever. She simply was not pretty enough to see her old beau yet. And the man who thought she was pretty enough, Preach, she was about to wrong. It was all messed up. But there was not a power on earth that would have stopped her from meeting Matt Mason at the P.F. Chang's at eleven o'clock.

For once she was letting herself be impatient. She had to know now. Her beauty clock was ticking down.

She had wanted to get to the restaurant first. She wanted the table to hide some of her blutter. If he didn't see her standing until he had fallen under the spell of nostalgia, she might pull him into her rebound infatuation. Unfortunately, he had arrived before her. She was early. He was earlier. Perhaps he too was eager.

She recognized him, at once, from across the room. She told the hostess she was with a party already seated. The hostess had said she didn't have one. What she meant was, she didn't have one she thought Ada belonged to. Ada silently said, That fixes you fine for thinking about cheating. Out loud she said, "I'll just dash into the bathroom while I'm waiting." Her plan was to veer near Mason's table and get a closer look. If he didn't recognize her, she was leaving. After she was safely in her car, and safely out of the parking lot, and safely back into the center of her boring life, she could call Mason from her cell phone and chirp, "Church emergency, I'm so sorry."

She started her slow walk toward him. He was seated as she had planned to be seated, on the banquette side looking out. His coat, also a Burberry, was neatly folded beside him as she had planned to fold hers. And he was wearing Converse All-Stars, just like hers. She tried to remember if he wore them back then. She didn't think so.

Matt Mason sat at a table with a smile so bright white it had to have been created by a cosmetic dentist. He looked like a cross between a professor and a cowboy, like someone Ada watched on late-night talk television waiting for Preach to come home.

He wore jeans and a blue blazer and a white shirt. His unlined face was tanned a browner shade of chestnut than Ada remembered. She imagined the burnished skin came from the years of practicing his capoeira *ginga* and leg sweeps and knee strikes in public parks beneath the western sun. He looked almost alarmingly young and fit. He didn't seem to recognize her. Proof. Finally she had proof. The years had been too unkind. She decided to risk getting close enough to get a good long gaze at him and perhaps a whiff of his cologne. Then she would walk on. Or maybe her perfume, the old perfume he had bought her years before, would tremble a memory.

It didn't. He was alternating texting and gazing about, but he took no notice of Ada. She had veered away from his table and was almost to the toilets when he called out her name and stood. She had to walk twenty feet with Mason smiling right at every pound of her.

As she approached, he opened his arms wide. She stopped walking. He gave her a "what's this?" shrug, then opened his arms wide again. She didn't run to him, but she got to him quick. He wrapped her in his arms and squeezed. Then he dropped his arms and stepped back so he could stroke her chin with his index finger, just like he had done when they were young and in love and in public. She blushed, and she knew it. This heat on her face was not a flush or a flash.

He took her by the hand, then he kissed that hand. She found herself standing on her tiptoes and giving him a peck on the lips to stop him from kissing the other hand.

"Woman! It is *good* to see you!"

"It is?"

"For sure!"

"I didn't think you'd recognize—"

"I would forget my name before I forgot your face."

"You promised me that once."

"And I keep my promises."

Ada took a half step back from Mason. He immediately closed the distance with a step toward her. They were closer than they had been. She could smell him. He smelled like Lifebuoy soap, and Altoids and smoke, like her college days.

"I didn't think you'd be a promise-keeping man."

"You didn't give me a chance to find out."

"I didn't give you a lot of things."

"Virginity at the top of the list." Ada blushed and hot-flashed at the same moment. She felt a thousand degrees. Mason grinned. "I guess people don't use those kind of words when they talk to the preacher's wife."

He leaned in and kissed her on the cheekbone. He pulled out her chair; she sat down and he sat down. She smiled tentatively. She was trembling.

"It's nice someone can forget I'm 'the preacher's wife.'"

"As long as you don't forget."

"No worry there."

He reached for her hands across the table. She gave them to him for half a second, then squeezed his hands and dropped hers safely into her lap. She told herself he was under a delusion she and Preach had some money to contribute to the alumni fund. She told herself not to believe what she was seeing—that Mason was seeing Ada with old eyes.

"You always be my Baby Boo."

"Boo grown old."

"Boo grown lush."

"I thought you liked skinny little girls."

"A long time ago."

"Your wife is tiny."

"Ex-wife. She got me over itty-bitty women."

"I heard you divorced, I'm so sorry." Ada said this sincerely, said it in her preacher's wife voice.

"Don't be. She turned into one mean skinny hungry heifer."

"I'm still sorry."

"How's Lucius?"

"Wonderful."

"Really?"

"Really."

"Great."

"You had kids."

"And you didn't."

The dangerous moment had passed. It was just behind them. But it was there, a shared giddiness neither had anticipated. The funny way they were wearing the same coat and the same shoes had sparked it. The way he recognized her perfume kept the fire going.

"You know, I've bought so much of that perfume trying to get other ladies to smell like you."

They both ordered lettuce wraps and eggplant and chicken and green peach tea and white rice and a plate of orange slices to be served early. When he opened his chopsticks, she remembered him teaching her how to use chopsticks. That was another dangerous moment. When Ada had mastered the sticks, Mason let her eat rice with chopsticks off his belly.

They had done many kinds of "everything but"—and food had been at the center of the best part. They had played with body paints and bubbles, but they liked the food—from a plastic honey bear, to warm doughnuts, to popsicles, to the rice and chopsticks—best.

Until the moment Mason kissed her cheekbone, Ada had put these memories away. Or rather Preach had pushed them away. After marriage, after feeling Preach push into the center of her, after feeling an orgasm that began in her cervix, a yielding that was not begun on the surface of her—on the tip of her tongue or the pink curve of her most sensitive lady parts—but in her soul, she dismissed all the sex play of earlier days, all sex play begun on her surface, as babyish.

Watching Mason deftly pick up a section of orange with his chopsticks, she was no longer sure. She and Matt Mason had bathed each other, and painted on each other, and licked and bit and wrestled, had cuddled and rocked and dreamed in each other's arms, and they had woken up to kiss for hours. Twenty-five years later she believed she wanted his penis but had been afraid to have it. Even way back then, she knew he'd be a hard dog to keep under the porch.

Now she knew all men were.

Mason was starting to talk about the research he was planning to do in Indianola when the food arrived. Between bites of their shared lettuce wraps she told him that one of her daughters was living down in Cleveland, Mississippi. He said he had a house in Greenville.

"That explains it."

"What?"

"How you got so . . . southern."

"What was I before?"

"Something different."

"I started listening to the blues after you broke my heart."

"You expect me to believe that?"

"It's the truth. All you left me was a stack of records and a record player you didn't want, and I started listening and pretending you were in the next room."

"Western, you were western."

"I'm still western. You are a blues royalty. Your grandfather's people lived on the Dockery Plantation."

"Yep."

"And you were born in a cotton field near Mound Bayou?"

"Yep."

"How did I let you get away?"

"Back then it didn't matter I was blues royalty."

"And . . ."

"You were too aggressive."

"Is that a way of saying too wild?"

"It's a way of saying too *sumthin'*."

"If you were *sumthin'* too, we could ride down to Moorhead, wait for darkness, and do what we didn't do way back when, on the crossroads."

"Now you sound straight Delta crazy."

"Naw, for real, all I'm saying, Lucius is a lucky man."

"You tell him that."

They smiled and got back to eating and smaller talk. He kept her cup full of green peach tea. They picked at the eggplant and the chicken. They were too busy smiling at each other to eat. They were taking the meal real slow. Ada had read that eating slowly helped you lose weight. She had never tried it before. Now she knew. Slow is a good way to eat.

Eventually the waitress brought the check, Mason grabbed it, and the conversation turned back to Memphis Minnie and Mississippi John Hurt and Little Milton and where to find the best tamales in the Delta.

When he finally checked his watch, when she told him there was no time to bop on down to her parents', that he should hit the road, an electric conversation came to an end. He said maybe he'd catch her on the flip-flop when he passed back through Nashville to fly back to Los Angeles.

"Absolutely," Ada lied.

She closed the car door after she hugged Mason good-bye, excited by lying—and taking a new pleasure in her pounds.

The years had not been kind to her, but her almost lover's eyes had been kind. He saw her through the eyes of their history. A female wanting to be coaxed across a line. He saw her as she had been to him at their very beginning. And he let her see that he saw all that. Silently she thanked him for noting she wanted something.

The world might think him a professor, an expert on blues ethnomusicality. She knew he was a frontiersman. She saw him. And he liked what she saw. And now, with more than half a century on her, and her days of passionate gifting rapidly passing, she liked seeing herself in his eyes.

But Ada wished he had not come just then. She had liked sitting with Mason over a Chinese meal wearing the same perfume he had bought her thirty years before too much. She wanted it still ahead of her.

After tugging on her seat belt, she touched both the places he had kissed on her cheek. She let herself feel the echoing tingle at her waist, the place where his fingertips had caught hold of her sweet brown belly, as she wondered how seeing him again, when she had lost the next twenty-five pounds, could possibly get any better.

Then she knew. As she pulled out of the P.F. Chang's parking lot, she imagined Mason gazing at her naked large body and smiling. She imagined him entering it. On her way to KidPlay she stopped at Burger-Up and ate an Olive and Sinclair brownie with homemade ice cream and hot fudge sauce. She would be a blimp before she was a slut.

She knew that too.

20

FIND A SNACK YOU LIKE THAT LIKES YOU

THE GIRLS' RESULTS were in. God loved her and wanted her to be faithful. The family needed her attention. The girl's results were in, and Preach's too, and at once the family was more complicated.

As quickly as she was making new rules, old rules were getting shattered: A family sitting down to eat together should largely be eating the same food. Wrong!

Ada had ordered kits for both daughters and her husband. Naomi and Ruth were not identical twins, but they looked a lot alike, and yet she suspected they would not have the same profile. She wondered if one would be more like her and one would be more like Preach. She truly suspected that Naomi would be more like her and Ruth more like Preach, but she didn't know—and there could be three types between them, not two.

The girls got their test results the very same day, and each immediately called their mother. Naomi was balanced carbs and fat. Ruth was a fat restrictor. A day later they found out Preach was a fat restrictor.

No wonder the whole family was out of shape.

They all needed something different. Preach and Ruth needed big bowls of oatmeal and egg white omelets and lots of fruit and even orange juice. All they had to think about was fat. Naomi needed egg white omelets with spinach and feta but could have strawberries on the side but probably not the orange juice—and she had to watch the calories. Ada needed omelets with the whole egg and turkey bacon and no toast and no tomato and absolutely no oatmeal. She had to watch the carbs.

Ada imagined a breakfast platter she would make for the family. Everyone could have scrambled egg whites with spinach, and she imagined making a big amount of that, and off to one side having grilled tomatoes for Naomi and fruit for Preach and Ruth and turkey bacon for herself. She and Naomi would have coffee; Ruth and Preach would have orange juice.

She tried to think of a perfect snack for all of them and immediately came up with sliced cucumbers—low-carb, low-fat, low-calorie. Cucumbers were the perfect food.

At the other end of the spectrum was the French fry or potato chip—high-fat, high-carb, balanced-nothing. The only one in the family who could possibly touch one was Naomi—if you were balanced carbs and balanced fats, a few wouldn't harm you.

When it came to fruit, Ada realized a peach might be right for Preach and Ruth, an apple for Naomi, and an avocado for Ada.

On the other hand, air-puffed popcorn was perfect for her fat restrictor, and far less perfect for her balanced-diet dieter, and absolutely forbidden for Ada, who in fact could do better eating a chocolate-covered almond than air-puffed popcorn.

Ada wanted to weep for the times she had announced, "I am not a short-order cook," and enticed them all to eat the same breakfast of homemade waffles and bacon. Now she knew she was the only one who should be eating the bacon, and she should have eaten only the bacon; and the waffles needed to be made with fat-free everything for her beloved husband and slightly older daughter.

Ada was no scientist, but she was on fire with scientific questions. Were black people more likely to be fat because our families are more likely to have people who need to eat different food in them? Most black folk Ada knew had a racially mixed background. Black folks come in a lot of colors, even in the same family. That was part of the inheritance of slavery everybody was used to and talked about. Was there something we didn't talk about keeping us fat? Was a black nuclear family in Minneapolis more likely to have members whose dietary needs were different, compared with a white Scandinavian family living in a Swedish community in rural Minnesota? Families who tend to be fit are often families with a positive food culture and a tradition of exercising. Is it also true familes who tend to be fit are families that are lucky enough that their family members need to eat the same things? Have the same, or more similar, weight-related DNA?

Based on what she was seeing in her own family, Ada thought every baby should be tested within the first week of his life, and certainly before he or she got off the breast!

She wanted to give the different types different names—the no-fats would be the oaties, the balanced carbs and fats would be the fruits, and the no-carbs would be the bacons.

Her little family had two oaties, a fruit, and a bacon. She thought lovingly of the poached pears Inez had made for her family and how she loved to serve them with a bit of goat cheese drizzled with honey on the side. Now she knew, the pear was perfect for her oaties, a small amount of both was perfect for her fruit, and she, the bacon, should only be eating the goat cheese. New rule: Don't clean your plate. Eat what's right for you on it.

Ada didn't know if "Don't clean your plate" should be a rule or a principle. Good Link that she was, she was thinking of principles as umbrella concepts—and that she might should have some.

If "Don't clean your plate" was an umbrella principle, under it would be the following rules so far: portion size, the one-bite rule, and "Do the DNA test. "Eat with refinement" was another umbrella principle: "Eat slowly" and "Eat sitting down" were under that. "Eat to be epicurious"—with all the adventuring in it—was an emerging umbrella principle she didn't yet have enough rules for. Her favorite umbrella principle was the one that was making the whole thing work—"Eat abundantly."

Abundantly was the opposite of gluttony.

2 1

ACCESS THE POWER OF
QUICK FIXES: POEMS,
FINGERNAIL POLISH, AND WAXING

ADA WAS ON the treadmill at the Dayani Center, struggling. Not really seeing enough progress had been hard;
seeing progress was harder.

Seeing herself, truly seeing herself, for the first time, in the
mirror at the Dayani Center and realizing that she had not seen
herself before, when she was young and ripe, and firm and tight,
was very hard.

It knocked her to her knees to know this—that she had never
really seen and would not see her body beautiful and young,
because when she had been beautiful and young she had been
effectively blind.

What was harder still was knowing it was Bird's beauty, so
bright, and Mag's and Glo's and Evie's, brighter still, that had
blinded her to her own. Ada, a pretty girl in a house of beauties, had been blinded by their brighter lights to the charms she
had been given. She was so mad that she had been given less
than her sisters and less than her mother, she confused pretty
with ugly. *Lawd! Have mercy, today!*

Minute eleven on the treadmill, Ada's cell phone rang. It

was the older of her twins, Ruth, calling looking for a quick lift. This day Ada had no quick lift to offer.

Fortunately, the younger twin beeped in. Naomi had had a great day before on her diet, an early walk, not a gram of fat all day, and best, she wasn't hungry. Naomi loved her oatmeal. And she had a suggestion for her sister and her mother.

"Fingernail polish."

"Fingernail polish?"

"Instead of eating something delicious like a napoleon, or bruschetta or a fabulous cheese plate with almonds and honey, or—"

"We get the idea!" mother and sister screamed into the phone at the same moment.

"I'm not talking a forty-dollar mani-pedi, I'm talking seven-dollar polish change."

"Polish change?"

"Quick fix."

"Quick fix?"

"Instant high. Legal."

"Mine's getting waxed—what's yours, Mom?"

"Poems. My instant fix is poems."

"You need a fluffing instant fix."

"I heart-fluff. Poems fluff my heart. Keep me keeping on."

"Pamplona Purple keeps me keeping on."

"Waxing, sugaring, and threading do it for me."

"How often can you wax?"

"Between all the places I have waxed, I can get it done every week if I divide it up. One week eyebrows, one week lip, one week bikini."

"Bikini?"

"Don't ask, Mom."

"Prescribe me a poem, Mama."

"What hurts?"

"My kids. Me. Failing them. Trying not to fail them. Watching Christmas come and knowing what they want and what they're going to get."

"Invictus."

Invictus

Out of the night that covers me,
Black as the pit from pole to pole,
I thank whatever gods may be
For my unconquerable soul.

In the fell clutch of circumstance
I have not winced nor cried aloud.
Under the bludgeoning of chance
My head is bloody, but unbowed.

Beyond this place of wrath and tears
Looms but the Horror of the shade,
And yet the menace of the years
Finds, and shall find me, unafraid.

It matters not how strait the gate,
How charged with punishments the scroll.
I am the master of my fate:
I am the captain of my soul.

"That's the poem from that movie about Nelson Mandela."

"Black people in America have been loving that poem since way before Nelson Mandela, but we happy he had it too."

"Did a black man write that?"

"A white man who lost a foot to tuberculosis."

"You see why I prefer Samoan Sand, Mama. That's too black and tragic."

"Honey my child, that is black and happy."

"No, Mama, that's black and transcendent."

"You try my quick fix, I'll try yours, both yours."

"Me too."

"Me three."

"All I know for sure, you girls got your mama through fifty fast minutes on the treadmill."

22

ADD A ZEN EXERCISE: HOOPING, WATER JOGGING, WATSU, AND YOGA

LATER, NOT THAT day but the next week, Ada popped into a salon called Escape. The twins had told her about it, and she listened to her daughters. A nail tech named Nikki put Lincoln Park After Dark on her hands, then changed it to You Don't Know Jacques. Ada left Escape energized.

She had needed it. Ada was exhausted with healthing. She had more to do and less time to do it in. Thinner didn't offset all the hard of that. Some, but not all. What offset a little more was the quick lift of the polish change.

Maybe she was going to like the primping part of healthing. She was staring down at You Don't Know Jacques when she resolved to make healthing more playful, less like a job.

The treadmill and swimming laps couldn't be her only exercise. She headed back to the pool. Something about water jogging appealed.

She had heard somewhere that racehorses with injured legs run in the water, and it made sense to her that something that would be good for a one-ton animal with fragile legs would be good for her. She liked the fact the water took all the weight and stress from her knees and her ankles. She liked doing the same thing over and over again—but she didn't like getting wet. And wearing a swim cap was breaking off her hair. And the chlorine dulled her polish, and she hated strangers seeing any of her body in a bathing suit—even if she had found a perfect little swimming tent dress, black piped with white.

You had to get out of the thing in public or drive home soaking your car seat or remember to put a big black trash bag on the car seat and drive home sitting on it, feeling a little too much like trash.

She was thinking of all of this as she pedaled in the pool. In the middle of Ada's workout a lithe young thing with a black pixie cut and green eyes slipped into the pool and started swimming laps. She had seen the girl before. The girl went fast. Faster than anyone else Ada had seen swim in the Dayani pool. Ada thought once she had probably been on a swim team. She wondered if she had webbed toes like Michael Phelps.

Thirty more minutes passed. The girl was still swimming, but slower, and Ada was jogging faster. One of the things she liked about water jogging was, she could do a lot of it fairly easy. She was worried about the fairly easy part. The nymph was now sitting on the side of the pool, hitting one side then the other of her head, shaking the water out of her ears.

Ada wondered how she looked to the girl. In the middle of the pool, water jogging, she expected she looked like she was stranded and treading water, like she had fallen overboard from some large vessel and was waiting to be rescued. Or that's how she would look if she looked like how she felt, with the green-eyed fit girl staring at her.

Don't be paranoid, Ada said to herself. The green-eyed girl isn't staring at you. But she was.

"You're the twins' mother?"

"Yes." Ada was remembering that she had met the girl. Somewhere, Ada had heard her voice before.

"Ever give lessons?" Ada asked.

"All the time."

"Ever give them to out-of-shape elderly people?"

"Tuesdays and Thursdays at four. But if they stay in my class, they aren't out of shape long."

"Maybe I should try it."

"We're strictly a sixty-five-and-up class. You've got to be old enough to have a grandchild my age, even if you don't have one. I love playing granddaughter. I kick out the young-old. They scare me."

"Scare you?"

"People new to being old are a pill."

"People new to being old?"

"Folks in their fifties, early sixties, they're sad about not being beautiful and scared of being sick and scared of running out of money before dying. Oldie goldies are smug. They beat everybody else out. I like that. They feel lucky, and a lot of them want their luck to rub off on you."

"How do you know so much?"

"I've got a mother and three aunts."

"And no grandparents."

"How did you know that?"

"You idealize old folks."

"Maybe."

"Could you teach me to swim laps?"

"No."

"Because I'm fifty?"

"Because I think you would like hooping."

"Hooping?"

"Like hula-hooping, but with special weighted exercise hoops."

"I've never heard of that."

"A bunch of girls did the whole marathon hooping."

"And you think I would like it?"

"I've got this big, heavy, slow hoop called the White Cadillac. You would love it."

"No one's ever suggested that exercise to me before."

"I saw you at church, in the baby care. The way you had that baby on your hip, rocking it, I said to myself, She is a born hooper."

"You saw me at church?"

"Yeah, C.J. brought me."

"Sweet C.J.! Where would I get a weighted hoop?"

"There's a place in East Nashville called Hoop-a-Rama—they can set you up with a custom hoop and with lessons, and you can do it in your own clothes."

"I am loving this water, but the water isn't loving me. It's hard on my hair, my skin, and my cottage-cheese thighs."

"You were born to hoop, Mamacita."

"Hoop-a-Rama?"

"Find an exercise that makes your soul feel playful."

"What brought you to the church?"

"I'm making a documentary on your husband."

"What brought you to Dayani?"

"Stalking you a little. Can't understand a man without understanding his woman."

All of a sudden Ada was all over goose bumps. This could be her. This sweet girl with firm thighs and green eyes. This adoring thing. But then the girl stood to grab her towel, and Ada saw just how flat her ass was, and she couldn't help but think, Preach would never pick that. And, This child is too sweet to be talking to me if she's sleeping with my husband. Then she thought, I haven't seen my goddaughter, Thea, in a good little while. And except for the accidental meeting at Radnor, I haven't seen C.J. lately. She thought all that and decided to get out of the water.

23

DON'T BE AFRAID TO LOOK
CHEAP—IN RESTAURANTS

T HE LUNCH BUNCH met on the last Friday of the
month. Ada hadn't planned to go, but her encounter earlier in the week with her green-eyed stalker had left her needing a fix of her favorite older women—and they were always
good for a few Black History Month ideas.

Black History Month was always a joy and frequently a trial
at KidPlay. How to tell the story of Harriet Tubman and Fred-
erick Douglass to three-, four-, and five-year-olds without telling the story of slave ships and beatings or, at the other extreme,
making slavery seem like fun in the sun?

Usually Ada settled on talking about Africa before the slave
trade, or modern Africa, and talking about African Americans,
not Afro-America, focusing not on the civil rights workers and
abolitionists who she deeply admired but on artists and athletes.
She had created a little series of paired biographies the five-year-
olds adored: *Before there was, there was.* Like, before there was
Michael Jordan, there was Earl the Pearl. Or before there was
Venus Williams, there was Althea Gibson. Or before there
was Barack Obama, there was Adam Clayton Powell.

With the twos and threes, Ada focused on old playground chants and hand-clapping games and spirituals, "Miss Mary Mack" and "Down Down Baby" and "Wade in the Water" and "This Little Light of Mine"—parts of black history being lost to basketball court reshuffles of the latest hip-hop into jump-rope and hand-clap chants. Ada worked hard, making sure all her my babies had a songbook full of tradition each February.

Just now, outside her window, she could hear Bunny screeching loud enough to be heard through the glass, a gleeful, "I am the sugar in the plum!"

It made Ada happy to hear that. Early in the week Bunny had told Ada, "I ain't pretty." Ada had tried to distract Bunny with a mini grammar lesson, "You ain't ugly or oogly, either. You are pretty. Say it loud, 'I *am* pretty.'"

Bunny just smirked and said, "I am Bunny," leaving Ada to be pricked for the thousandth time by the reality that vision is an assaulted sense for American girls in general and African American girls in big-time particular.

It shamed Ada to recall how ashamed she had been, somehow, every time she looked at angular Marcia Brady from *The Brady Bunch*, with her straight blonde hair.

"I'm not Buffy, from *Family Affair* or *The Vampire Slayer*. I'm not Clarice. I'm not Madonna. I'm not Elly May Clampett. And Bird's not Grace Kelly or Jackie Kennedy. We better," Ada whispered to herself, but it stuck in her throat like a lie.

So many icons of femininity that burned Ada's eyes like lye soap, washing out all appreciation of Ada's beauty and much appreciation of her mother's bronze, well-curved and deeply waved presence.

She had gone over the territory in so many adult Sunday-school classes, in so many book groups, at too many barbecues and fish fries to count. We are taught to think ourselves ugly. Eyes are an assaulted sense. We are taught to behave by spankings and whippings. Touch is an assaulted sense. We are taught we should not smell, or we smell wrong. Smell is an assaulted sense. We listen to songs that call us bitches and 'hos and tell us how to give blow jobs. Hearing is an assaulted sense.

Taste, not so much. This was an Ada idea, and so far she hadn't dared tell it. As far as Ada could figure, taste was the main unassaulted sense. Assaults against the tongue may have been attempted. When you give a family pig intestine to eat, there's a chance you want them to eat shit. When you give a family a pig foot to eat, anybody whose seen a stinky pigpen knows there's a chance you want the family to eat shit. As a woman Ada didn't eat chitterlings and pig feet often, but as a child Ada had loved her some chitterlings and pig feet. Remnant food. And she hadn't eaten shit. Brown ladies know how to clean the intestines and the feet carefully, how to get rid of the shit and turn the offal into a delicacy. Taste is good.

"I am the sugar in the plum!" Bunny called out loud again. Ada stuck her head out the window and yelled, "You go girl." All the other little girls nodded in assent.

The Lunch Bunch could not get over Ada. Watching her week by week, at first, they hadn't noticed the slight changes, but this day, their first lunch at an eco-friendly restaurant on West End Avenue, they noticed.

When they got to the table, they would not let her sit down. Inez made her turn around slowly while they watched.

"What have you been doing?"

"I'm on the Jack Sprat diet."

"The Jack Sprat Diet?"

"Jack Sprat could eat no fat and his wife could eat no lean. Between the two they licked the platter clean. What if both Jack Sprat and his wife were skinny—because each was eating what was right for them? We see the illustrations in children's book of the skinny Jack Sprat and his fat wife. What if they both were skinny? The DNA diet is about figuring out if you're supposed to eat like Jack Sprat or Mrs. Jack Sprat or Goldilocks."

"Goldilocks?"

"Typical European American girl who needs balanced carbs and fats—i.e., plain low calories."

The thinnest woman at the table piped up. "I think the trick is to eat slowly. You young people gobble. You eat so fast, your stomach doesn't have time to tell your mind it isn't hungry. Back in the old days, back in the country, we stretched the meal out, first, seconds, thirds, we didn't pile up plates, we didn't put anything on the plate we didn't know we wanted to eat. The goal was to get everybody full, but just full, and the way to do it was to stretch out the meals, in time, so the stomach could tell the brain when to stop. When my grandmother had big hungry men to feed, and not much to feed them, first she would pass around a plate of biscuits. Then she would wait thirty minutes before she passed anything else, then she would pass some hot soup, maybe chicken and dumplings, and wait thirty more minutes to pass a little ham. All the time we would be laughing and talking and filling up on catching up. By the time she gave us dessert, all we needed was what she had—a loving spoonful."

Being that it was a skinny old-folk rule, Ada adopted it immediately.

"They used to tell us to chew every bite twenty-three times. I could barely get a single bologna sandwich down in a thirty-minute lunch hour, chewing that slow."

"But that bitty sandwich filled you up, didn't it?"

"Yes, indeed, yes indeed."

Ada started to laugh. She really was going a little crazy.

"Do you mean I've got to chew like a cow not to look like a cow?"

"You must chew like a cow to look like a heifer, just so."

The body was full of little ironies that Ada was starting to love a little. She loved them particularly well in the company of such a diverse group of black female bodies.

Ada had only been a member since her twins left for college, but she truly believed membership in the informal club of about thirty rather interesting and down-to-earth black women, most of whom did not attend her husband's church, whose children were not friends with her children, was a soul-sustaining association.

She needed those. She loved the Links and the Altar Guild, but she grooved on the Lunch Bunch. The Lunch Bunch was a Joan Elliot (Nashville's straight black Gertrude Stein) legacy, and it was a segregation legacy. When restaurants really became desegregated in Nashville in the 1970s, the Lunch Bunch was, in part, a way to buffer the fear of checking out restaurants where, as any of the members would have put it, "*We* didn't know if *we* were welcome."

The format was simple. The hostess picked a venue and issued an invitation. Everyone paid for themselves.

And there lay a problem. Ada did not want to appear cheap, but she wanted to portion control. She wanted, for the sake of diet, to order an appetizer for her main course, and she wanted to drink plain tap water because it had less salt. And she didn't want an appetizer or a dessert. And she knew if she ordered like that, everyone would think she was broke. That it was in bad taste. That she was acting like some black person who did not know how to act when she went out.

The Lunch Bunch ordered three courses. And drinks. The Lunch Bunch was sharp, was bon vivant, was anything but frugal. The bold Creole cry, *Laissez les bons temps rouler*—Let the good times roll—was the Lunch Bunch motto.

The Lunch Bunch went to new restaurants, or to old restaurants offering something new. This day they chose a new eco-friendly place. The tables were made out of bamboo. All the fish was fresh catch. As much as possible, things were literally and figuratively green. Ada was impressed and distracted.

As the waiter went around the table, taking orders, Ada listened as women ordered appetizers and main courses and drinks, even though most were staying away from the very tasty bread basket.

When she had eaten with a group of white women at the same table, once pleading the cause of KidPlay and another time against food deserts, many had asked for sauces on the side and dressings on the side; many had split plates, proudly, or without thinking; many had ordered just one course, all in maintenance of great figures and great checkbooks.

When the waiter approached, she had made her decision: an appetizer portion of scallops as her main course, and a small salad without dressing before.

"Will that be all?"

"Yes."

"When would you like me to serve the scallops?"

"With the main courses."

"Certainly."

Just before turning to the next customer, the waiter winked at her. Ada didn't think it could be so, but it seemed his pale face and dark lashes winked and flashed a smile—and if she read it right, it was a smile of encouragement.

One of the older ladies near her sucked her teeth and glared, implying that while Ada might have had *some* home training, she did not have the sense God gave her to know how to go out into the luxury world as a black woman wanting respect.

Ada lifted her chin higher and pretended she was talking to Joan Elliot. "I see no reason in the world I need to order food I can't afford to eat, from a caloric perspective, to prove to white people I don't know that I can afford to order anything I want, from an economic perspective. If rich white women can come here and order green salad without dressing and the governor's water, I can too. We can too. I just did it. And some of you look like you need to be doing it with me. Being afraid to look cheap in restaurants is making us fat, and I don't want to be fat.

Anymore. I don't want to pay for food I'm not going to eat, or eat food just because I paid for it." Then she silenced herself by sipping water.

It was a vast improvement over silencing herself with a buttered roll.

The woman who had glared at Ada looked shocked. Ada herself looked shocked. If she had been nibbling on one of the excellent flatbread sticks or sipping on the herbal tea, she might have swallowed back down all these truths more politely. It occurred to her that eating and drinking was a soft muzzle.

The dowager dragon who served as club president had put the glass of sweet tea she had held to her lips during Ada's outburst back down on the table. The table went silent.

"I've been waiting ten years for you to say something that wasn't what the preacher's wife, what the First Lady, was s'posed to say. Next meetin' sit by me," said Madame President.

"She's going to keep sitting by me!" said Inez.

"Another polite black woman found her voice," said the vice president, seconding the emotion.

"We've spent a quarter century celebrating that we could spend money in white restaurants; let's spend the next twenty-five years saving money in black banks and investing money in black businesses. How 'bout that?" chimed another member.

Chins—double, triple, and scalpel-tightened—lifted a little higher. Ada, the singer's daughter, had finally arrived: respectable in her own right, not despite of her father, or because of her husband.

As appetizers were served and some lettuce was doused with sweet and fatty dressings and some lettuce was eaten naked, the

Lunch Bunch settled into a raucous and significant chat about black green, about the niceties that served, and the niceties that prevented blacks from thriving. The ladies came to a few conclusions: A blues aesthetic of raw truth and lyricism was beautiful; blues economics of starve and steal were not. And blues health is plain illin'—and not in a good way.

Money and Food and Material Mess were the Achilles' heels of modern African American culture, according to the ladies of the Lunch Bunch. What, the ladies wanted to know, do we do about a culture, our culture, us, in which the phrase "She's a mess" is a term of endearment? It all came back to the stuff Ada was calling blutter. She shared the word with the group. Somebody said, "Suffocates me every day." Somebody else joked, "Blutter the dry drown of black folk."

They had brought it back to brass tacks. To the small things that hold the floor of our world down.

Now that Ada was doing a little something-something about blutter in her body, she realize she had long been wishing Preach would do a little something-something about blutter in their bankbooks. It seemed an easy thing to ask him for, until she realized he might be hiding some woman in the economic record mess. Blutter obliterated, she might see something she wasn't ready to see. Yet.

Ada let her mind drift back to the conversation at the table. The ladies were talking about the same thing she was thinking about.

"The politics of beauty lash black women harder, the politics of economics lash black men harder."

"Our women make green bank, and our men make white women."

"Lord, have mercy today."

By the time it was over, half the women were drinking the governor's water, tap water. When the waiter brought the bill, two thirds of everybody present vowed next time their bill would be the lowest.

In the midst of juggling twenty-eight separate checks, the waiter with the inky black eyelashes leaned over to Ada and said, "I'm going on your diet."

Ada gave him a great big tip. She tipped on the amount she would have eaten in her old days. It's one thing to be thrifty, and another to be mean.

24

MANAGE PORTION SIZES

IT WAS THE day to embrace Gargantua, lunch at the Cheesecake Factory followed by dinner at Maggiano's, the day after
Lunch Bunch. Gluttony was walking with the devil, and all Ada
could try to do was grab one by the tail and beat the other.

Ada hated what she called "Our Holidays," the season that
stretched from Thanksgiving through Valentine's Day that
seemed to be full of nothing but overeating.

She took the first snatch at gluttony's tail by walking to
Queenie's instead of driving.

It took Ada a lot longer than the twelve to fifteen minutes
the twins had separately assured her was all it was going to take.
And the hill up Blair, which didn't look like a hill in her car,
felt like a mountain in her pink-and-black Nikes and a thick
enough sweatshirt to keep her from freezing.

The only good thing about the walk was, she crossed paths
with the redheaded boy who rode the crazy bike. As he zipped by
Ada, he shouted, "We're getting it!" This remark pleased Ada.

Most acquaintances who passed didn't recognize athletic
Ada—naked of makeup, hair tied back in an improvised do-

rag, hands out front pumping to burn more calories—as Ada. She waved at a few folk she knew, passing in cars, who didn't wave back. She enjoyed being this flavor of incognegro.

What she didn't enjoy was being two blocks from the house and needing a toilet. Bad. The coffee and the exercise hit at just the same time. To hold it, she had to walk with the peculiar wriggling gait she saw daily on the playground, when she told kids to "hold it" and wait their turn for the toilet. It was a gait she knew to be completely undignified.

She had forgotten how hard "holding it" could be. Something about the absurdity of a fifty-year-old woman being in a five-year-old situation tickled Ada. If laughing hadn't been likely to cause her to soil herself, she would have laughed.

Shuffling down the street, squeezing little muscles for all they were worth, she gave herself some harsh reprimands. Accept the realities of the body. Let children pee when they need to. And finally, don't be embarrassed to desecrate your mother-in-law's perfect powder room!

Ada, who had called Queenie to tell her to have the front door open, rushed in without stopping to kiss or be kissed by Queenie.

Queenie was standing at the stove when Ada got out of the bathroom.

"Now, come give me some sugar, baby."

Queenie met her halfway cross the room, walking with three hundred pounds of grace that made Michael Jackson's moonwalk look like a stutterstep. Queenie pulled her daughter-in-law close in, like she was trying to smell her.

"You not abusing laxatives, are you?"

"No!"

"The way you just rushed into the bathroom—"

"No. How do you know about laxative abuse, anyway?"

"I saw it on *Oprah*."

"*Oprah*'s off the air."

"I didn't say I saw it yesterday." Ada settled in a seat beside Queenie. Queenie had some playing cards on the table in front of her. "You want to play a quick hand of bid whist?"

"A quick one."

Queenie shuffled and talked and dealt and talked.

"You know, Preach doesn't like skinny legs. On girls or chickens."

"Everything isn't about Preach."

"Don't tell him that."

"You should have told him."

Queenie waved her arms to create a swirl that included four or five dozen pictures of Lucius—baby, toddler, boy, and young man—crisscrossing the American South, standing at, on, or beneath various tourist attractions from the arch in St. Louis to the Everglades in Florida.

"We moved so much. Every two, three years, sometimes eighteen months. Preach got too good at making people like him right off the bat. And he was good-looking, and smart girls just told him what they thought he wanted to hear. Then you showed up, talking about what you wanted to talk about, and he started paying attention to somebody beside himself who wasn't standing over him with a strap."

"You make him sound selfish."

"He was till he met you. Then he decided you was his gift

from God, and he loved God real good. And he decided he needed to be the kind of man you would want to marry."

"When I married Preach, I thought we might get to move, that the church might move us, but that didn't work out."

"You wanted to marry a military man."

Ada tapped the brag book lying on the fake butler's table that sat beside the sofa on Ada's end. "I've been on my fair share of tours of the Holy Land."

"Yeah, but you had to put up with all the church ladies to see it."

"Preach does have his devoted ladies, but that doesn't bother me none."

"It would bother me."

"Shoot. My high school girlfriends used to have crushes on my daddy. He'd get up on that stage and start singing, and they be unbuttoning their blouses when they came to our house for dinner and putting on lipstick. My mama always said a man another woman can steal from you ain't your man no way."

The last card fell. Ada won. Pondering the everyday miracle and everyday misery of marriage, Ada walked back home.

An hour later Ada was at KidPlay, seated at her desk writing a subsitute teacher schedule and worried about lunch. Once a year, with board members acting as substitute teachers, all the KidPlay teachers treated themselves to lunch to celebrate recertification. At first there was a big debate about where to go. Then there was a place that pleased everybody. This year that place did not please Ada. She stopped and doodled a note to herself on a Post-it: "Embrace Gargantua without being gargantuan." Ada was headed toward perilous temptation: the Cheesecake Factory.

The ladies carpooled from KidPlay to the mall. In her head Ada heard the *Jaws* theme music. As she walked across the parking lot toward the Cheesecake Factory, the restaurant looked like a Disneyland version of the Taj Mahal, or perhaps something from a dream of the Arabian Nights—if the Arabian Nights moved to a suburban southern shopping center. Ada sensed danger.

The menu was exhaustive, pages upon pages, a food wish book of sorts, a cruel dictionary, or encyclopedia, not of flavor, but of food wishes. One of the older teachers said it reminded her of the old Sears, Roebuck catalog.

Ada got it. The old Sears, Roebuck catalog was a way to get shoes and gravel and underpants and washers, but it was also a way to learn how to live a middle-class life, a tip sheet of desire. This little spiral-bound book, the Cheesecake Factory menu, was, by Ada's lights, a cheat sheet of desire.

And it was a few other things as well—a food orgy, a diet disaster, and a kind of printed-language MSG. All the words and all the pictures dulled the palate before the food came out. When the food came out, everything tasted brighter—because the palate had been dulled.

That's what Ada noticed most, settling into her seat: everywhere, sensory overload. The colors were bright. The sounds were loud. The upholstery was slick. Sensory overload. Except smell. So few smells for so much food.

But paging through the book/menu, Ada had to acknowledge that there was something for everyone on offer. The seduction had begun. Against her will, the abundance pleased her; she became glad they had come.

She told herself it was a black thing. She told herself black folk, after all the starving they've done, deserve to be fat. She told herself it reminded her of Diddy Wah Diddy. She told herself it was good to remember Diddy Wah Diddy. *Whatever.*

There was American and Chinese and Mexican and Tex-Mex and Polynesian and things that were hard to describe, like the bikini martini, and there was Greek and southern. There was French and Japanese, and there was Thai, and that was just appetizers. Moving to main courses, there were burgers and calamari and even English fish and chips. There was old-school Chicken Marsala, and Chicken Piccata, and there was Ahi Tartare. And there was Jambalaya Pasta—the Cheesecake Factory's most popular pasta, and a dish that would perplex most Cajuns and all Romans. But maybe they would understand the Jamaican Black Pepper Shrimp or recognize the Mahi-Mahi Mediterranean, except Mahi-Mahi are not found in the Mediterranean. They are found in Hawaii and in the Caribbean Sea and off the Atlantic coast of Florida, and sometimes in Southeast Asia. Her head was spinning. There were even dishes alleged to be for managing weight: an Asian dish, a Mexican dish, and what was a kind of French dish if you consider pear and endive French. And she didn't know if a Cuban sandwich should be considered Cuban or Floridian, but she knew it should be considered. And then there were all the cheesecakes, including two low-carbohydrate versions.

She was salivating in anticipation of ordering the jambalaya when a family entered the restaurant, parents and a son, not one of them less than two hundred pounds. Her blood was in the water, and the shark was circling. Ada asked for grilled salmon and asparagus and asked that they both be cooked with as little oil as possible and no sugar. She told them to hold the potatoes. In her head she saw herself shooting the big white shark with her bigger black shark gun. When the plate of salmon came, she held her hand over the top of it, figured out how much would fit in the palm of her hand, and started cutting away at the rest, which she passed on her bread plate as tastes, leaving just a piece about the size of a deck of cards on her plate to eat. That was the depth charge. Blew the crazy hunger shark right out of the water. The *Jaws* music stopped playing in her head. She was victorious.

The asparagus were good, hot and crispy and a little salty. She savored that. And she savored being beneath light fixtures that reminded her of what she thought the roofs of Saint Petersburg, Russia, or some casbah in Morocco might look like, gorgeous bulbs of color, or what they had looked like in a Turner Classic movie or two, and a Bollywood extravaganza or three. Looking at the lights made the asparagus taste as good as the jambalaya she had wanted to eat.

In thanks for the extravagant surroundings and not wanting to be thought cheap she ordered Fiji artesian water and eventually a double espresso.

Most of the other teachers and all the aides ordered Caramel Royal Macchiatos, and she did her best to remember, from earlier visits, what she was missing.

When it came to dessert time, she ordered the original cheesecake but only ate one naked forkful. The 770–calorie, God-knows-how-many-carbs dessert was suddenly a shape-shifting low-carb boon. And by not adding hot fudge when it was passed around the table, she saved three hundred calories. By only eating a bite, she saved six hundred calories—and so it was that in the land of excess Ada found success.

Portion control and indulgence in dollar-expensive but calorie-free drinks (artesian water and espresso) allowed Ada to focus on what she was really paying for—an elaborate fantasy of abundance in an over-the-top exotic setting—and stop focusing on the so-so food. She had never enjoyed the Cheesecake Factory more.

She enjoyed it so much that for a moment it flashed through her head that she should found a string of restaurants called Diddy Wah Diddy, after the mythical land of food for black people, where the chicken run around cooked with a knife and fork in them. It would be an all-you-can-eat buffet, but everything would be healthy, and there would be amazing distractions that kept you from wanting to eat—too much. Diddy Wah Diddy—a place where we feed our health and our beauty.

She let herself be happy enough, knowing she had gotten out of the Cheesecake Factory under a thousand calories, with no carb damage. She was saving the carb damage for Maggiano's.

When the KidPlay birthday lunch and the annual Interdenominational Leadership dinner fell on the same day, it was easy to believe that God did not want Ada to get fit. The only way to keep her winning streak alive and get out of Maggiano's without gaining weight, she figured, was to study the calorie and carb counts before she got there. With the afternoon free, she locked her office door. It took a lot of poking around and Googling, but finally on Photobucket she found the Maggiano's nutrition info. Maybe God did love her.

The only thing remotely good for Ada's diet was the minestrone soup. Half an herb-roasted chicken was 1890 calories and 108 carbs. She wished she ate steak. She didn't, even if filet mignon was 800 calories and 13 carbs. Ada liked cows.

Looking for the lowest-carb chicken dish, she settled on Chicken Marsala at 970 calories, 25 carbs, and 1190 milligrams of sodium. If she focused on the Pellegrino water and the wine and just ate a bit of her chicken and a bite or two of the greener vegetables, she would be part of the feast but not part of the fat.

Ada was back to thinking about starting a restaurant chain. There was a carnival atmosphere to both of these restaurants that appealed. Something about eating at the Cheesecake Factory and Maggiano's on the same day was provocative. They appealed as a place to arrive hungry and be filled; they appealed as a place where hunger was historical.

But the commonness of hunger collects us too. Ada wasn't certain she would banish hunger completely, if she could. Much as she preferred the welcome of feasts, she understood there was radical union in hunger.

Squatting on the toilet in Maggiano's, peeing off a bit of the wine and the coffee, Ada understood a few new things about the shitty realities of abundance. That a purpose of largeness is to make us understand what it is to be small. That a purpose of the body is to be a clock, ever reminding us not just that time passes but that time runs out, just like shit. And sitting on the toilet, she knew this too, as she knew we deal so differently with our children's diapers and our spouses' diapers and our parents' diapers. Our children tell us we will die; our lovers promise a taste of infinity before we do.

Realizing she would not know this if she had not tasted infinity on Preach's tongue, once, some time ago, and that she did not know if she would ever taste it again, Ada let tears run down her face.

Back at the table, the bill arrived. It was larger than anyone expected, besotted as they had been by all the mundane abundance. Preach, who owed less than many, was the first to say, "Let's split it equally." Ada had to smile. Some of Preach's generosity was pure, "Lets keep everybody happy," not "Let's have everybody love me." Some of it was even, "Let's not forget what it is to be hungry and poor and the honor to be found in carrying each other." Generosity was something she liked about her husband, and it was something she hated; and generosity was something she liked and hated about herself. Like it or hate it, it was going to be with them awhile. They, Preach and Ada, would usually do their part to make that moment the bill came, that moment Preach had taught her had a name, *la quart d'heure de Rabelais*, the quarter hour of Rabelais, less chilling.

Having danced and intending to dance again, Ada was scraping together pennies and pounds for the piper.

25

EAT EVERY THREE HOURS

JARIUS'S GRANDMOTHER LORETHA was about to spend the weekend in jail, paying off a DUI. Loretha had been ashamed to ask for help till the last minute of the eleven o'clock Wednesday-night service, but she had sidled up to Ada during the last hymn and spilled the beans.

Loretha's breathalyzer had been over the maximum allowed, but not by much. She had been to a party with her friends after a long week of work, cleaning rooms at the Opryland hotel. It was Friday, one of the friends was getting married the next Saturday, and they took her out, put a fake tiara on her head and a fake veil, and started drinking sweet drinks that turned out to be stronger than the ladies thought they were. At the end of the evening, the bride-to-be, watching her weight, was the least drunk of everybody, so she volunteered to drive. And they got pulled over. Loretha switched places with the bride-to-be, who had had a DUI before. And so she had to serve forty-eight hours. At fifteen, Dorian was too young to stay with her baby by herself overnight. Besides, Dorian wanted to go to the church-sponsored lock-in.

Ada was in, and Dorian would be locked in—it was all settled before they got to the last verse of "I'm So Glad Jesus Lifted Me."

Standing before Ada in black leggings, flip-flops, and one of Preach's old shirts, Loretha barely looked the twenty-nine years that she was. Baby Jarius on her hip looked to be her son.

Ada felt sorry for Loretha. She didn't usually let herself feel sorry for Preach's congregants or KidPlay parents and grandparents. Usually she focused on the person and the problem at hand and the future. Usually she refused to think about their past, but this moment she did, and she felt sorry, almost "tore down," for Loretha.

Loretha had worked for Opryland since she was sixteen, since a year after Dorian, her only child, was born. Loretha had always kept a job and an apartment, and she didn't do drugs. Dorian liked watching cooking shows. Loretha had begun imagining Dorian as a famous chef. She had imagined Dorian getting to be eighteen and getting into the culinary arts training program at the hotel. Then Dorian got pregnant and wanted to drop out of junior high school. Loretha stopped imagining. She circled back to caring for a baby on a dime. She circled into drinking. She circled into fear that she would not have a life, and her daughter would not have a life.

As she stood on Ada's porch with Jarius on her hip, there was fear for Dorian in Loretha's eyes.

For baby Jarius, Loretha had hope. Baby Jarius was a boy. An impossibly long infant with beautiful hands. He was going to be a basketball star. Loretha knew this for sure. She kissed Jarius's fingers. Kissed her grandson's long baby legs, kissed his baby feet.

"He gonna buy me a house. He gonna go straight to the NBA. 'Fore he turn twenty years old he gonna be a millionaire. His daddy gonna wish he been good to this baby. That other grandmamma gonna wish she bought him some diapers. He gonna buy me a house and send his mama to cooking school, and he gonna get the Preach something for the church."

Ada reached out to take Jarius from Loretha. The boy didn't cry; he knew Ada too well. A moment later Preach was standing with them on the doorstep. A moment after that, Preach walked Loretha to his car, a shiny but conservative and powerful Chrysler 300. They all hoped Preach taking Loretha would mean better treatment at the jail.

The car that had scared Ada when purchased might be a part of Loretha's good luck. It *is* a rare ill wind that blows no one good.

Walking back into the house with Jarius in her arms, Ada realized he was soaked. She improvised a changing table on the floor with towels, then realized, too late, that she didn't quite have the right size diapers, or at least not the ones big enough to easily wrangle Jarius into and get the sticky tabs stuck tight. Jarius giggled and wriggled. As Ada tried to secure the right side of his diaper, the left side popped open and off. Before she she could duck and cover, Jarius was peeing straight up and into her face. Ada laughed so hard Baby Jarius started laughing too.

"I think you going to be a preacher like Preach. You already baptizing me. Preach used to baptize the puppies in his neighborhood with Kool-Aid."

Diaper secure, Ada wanted to kiss Jarius on the head but was worried about "potty mouth." She was just wondering what she should do with Jarius while she cleaned up when she heard him exploding a giant poop.

Holding Jarius straight out in front of her, Ada mounted the steps to her bedroom with its big shower. Jarius was too big and in too high spirits to change a messy number-two diaper without an extra set of hands. She, and other volunteers at Kidplay, had learned that the hard way.

The shower made up for the extra set of hands. Diaper off. Wipes wiped and flushed. He fussed through all of that, but when Ada turned on the shower and poured bubble bath on his feet and let the bubbles rise around his toes, Jarius was mesmerized. He plopped down in the suds. They made soap sculptures. He put suds on her nose. She little-piggied his toes. Then she rinsed him off again and plopped him in the playpen she had set up in her bedroom with three of his favorite books. Jarius alternated howling for her attention and turning the pages of *The Little Caterpillar* while Ada washed her face and got on some dry clothes. It wasn't until she started singing "Rise and shine and give God your glory, glory," that Jarius started laughing again. Clearly at Ada.

"You don't think I can sing. I can sing, now."

Baby Jarius screamed louder, even though Ada wasn't singing.

"It's not my singing. You hungry!"

Baby Jarius liked to eat every three hours, on the hour. Let his meal be late, and he would howl loud enough to wake the dead. But if you fed him right on time, he was pretty perfect.

Ada had to poke at his mouth to get him to take the bottle, but after she poked two or three times gently, he latched on and sucked vigorously.

Watching his contentment with his simple feast of milk and suck and repeat, Ada wondered if she wouldn't enjoy, at least for a little while, being on a liquid diet.

Wanting to be a happy baby herself and wanting to get past the plateau she was on, Ada decided to go online and order a month's supply of Medifast and think of it as adult baby formula.

Rocking Jarius to sleep, a latex nipple in his mouth, a cotton blanket across his back, it came to Ada's mind that she might even drink some of it, her adult milkshake, out of a baby bottle. The idea made her laugh, and the dreaming baby burped in her arms. She smiled, kissed him on the head, and tucked him into a huge Moses cradle she had placed at the bottom of her front hall stairs.

What she could do for herself at this moment was walk. So she did it. Up and down her house stairs, while the baby slept. For the first time in months, she was not walking to Matt Mason.

Knowing that she and Preach were a part of Jarius's best chance made it hard to step toward Matt Mason, hard to step toward any man but Preach, but not impossible. She had come too far to stop walking, so she kept stepping. For the moment, Ada was walking to Ada.

26

SAVOR *HOT* AND *COLD*, THE POWER OF HERBAL TEAS AND FLAVORED ICE CUBES

A DA STEPPED ON the scale: six pounds down! Medifast was the bomb. The diet bomb. Instrument of rapid change. Except she was bored.

Boredom was a treacherous territory. She jumped on the treadmill at the Dayani and started walking, not exactly to herself but past boredom. The first song she played shouted, "If you're going through hell, keep on walking, you might get out before the devil even knows you're there."

The devil got her thinking about fire and ice. Lines she had memorized in the seventh grade popped to the top of her mind. As she punched the numbers up to 2.7, then up to 3, then up to 3.2, then down to 3 and 2.7 and 2.5 and 2.4, before making her way up to 3.2 again, she amused herself by constructing a little parody of the long-lost Frost... *Some say my skinny life begins with fire, some say with ice, from what I've tasted of desire, I hold with those that favor fire ... for reconstruction, ice is also nice and will suffice.*

Fire and ice. She needed more of both in her life without adding calories. What would it take to get back into Lucius's arms? Getting beyond wanting a baby bottle might be a start.

Still, she was rocking the Medifast, at least for a few days longer. And on the treadmill she figured out that she would make herself a feast of fire and ice by making a tea drawer for herself—that would be the fire, the boiling water—and then by making herself wonderful ice cubes.

One of her Link sisters had given her a gift of some tea from Mariage Frères, and someone had given her some Fauchon. She had been saving these treats for a special occasion. There was one called something like Evening in Paris, and one called something like Afternoon in France, or was it the other way around? She was breaking out that fancy tea. When she went to look for the tea, it was gone. Snagged by the daughters, no doubt. She called Naomi: "You were just saving it!" She couldn't be mad. Naomi was right—and there was tea to be had, walking distance from her house. Ada never treated herself to it, but she had seen it on the shelves, and dismissed it as a foolish luxury. She set out on a tea safari in her neighborhood.

She walked north from her house, the seven funky up-and-down blocks that dropped her into the commercial district closest to home.

Her first stop was Davis Cookware. She sniffed a variety of black tea sacks, eventually settling on some lapsang souchong that was scooped into a ziplock. She went into Fido, the local coffee shop, and picked up some special pretty, flowery teas in sachets. Then she crossed back across the street and bopped into the French bakery, Provence, where she picked up some local fair-trade tea from Partners Tea Company. On her way home she stopped at Harris Teeter to get her oldie-goldie favorites from her college days, Twinings Earl Gray and Irish Breakfast.

Home again, she organized a tea drawer. She loved looking at the combination of shiny gold tins and paper pyramids and just plain boxes and plastic bags marked with black marker. Loved it so much she couldn't bring herself to use any. She'd put her nose in there and smell. For three days she savored just opening up the drawer and sniffing and looking at the teas. *I am Bird's daughter.*

On the fourth day she took out six cups and made herself six different cups of tea. She sugared none. She milked none. She sipped from one cup, then another. She sipped in the order that seemed to mean something to her, like she was picking out notes of a melody, one note at a time. Three sips of Cinnamon Apple Spice followed by a small sip of Lemon Zinger followed by a long sip of Soir de Paris filled her with all the solace of a fireplace and all the promise of sparklers. Then she sipped a bit of chamomile and a bit of the spiced chai and a bit of the Safari Rooibos, and it was like she was sliding up a musical scale, into a hit of clean serene. *I am Temple's daughter, too.*

Sip by sip she finished a third of three of the cups and half of three. It was a calorie-free feast that she would not soon forget. A feast just for herself, and it was good for her, an innocent first. A young-old woman's first innocent first. *I'm me.*

She didn't make six cups again, but daily she would make herself a cup or two or three, sometimes as an hour's entertainment, sometimes as an antidote to boredom, sometimes as reassurance. The cups became places to hide as her body dissolved. One day she looked into the cup and saw a fragment of her body floating in the cup; then the light shifted, and the reflection vanished.

Watching herself reflected, then vanished, she started thinking of the ice she had thought she would make but hadn't got to yet.

In her childhood her mother's mother, MaDear, had frequently frozen fruit into the ice cubes she made: maraschino cherries, slices of fresh peaches, pears from cans, it all depended on what MaDear had on hand. Ada loved the way her grandmother's ice looked in jelly jar glasses that frosted over.

Thinking of these ice cubes, Ada decided to make ice cubes out of her tea. When her ice was frozen, Ada made herself a tall glass of water filled with the new cubes and slices of fresh cucumber and mint leaves and slices of lemon. This was dessert, this was delicious, this was change, and it was frozen. The next week she went back into the kitchen to whip up another batch of ice cubes, this time orange peel and rosemary. The very next morning she served herself orange and rosemary ice cubes topped with Fiji water splashed with a drop of rose essence in the water. She served this with a little bread plate of herbs: a sprig of tarragon, a few chives, a bit of mint. She nibbled and sipped for a delighted quarter hour.

She was celebrating getting to 168.

27

DON'T INITIATE CHANGE
YOU CAN'T STICK WITH FOR
FIVE YEARS

SHE WAS SICK of Medifast. It wasn't that it tasted bad. It tasted fine enough for the good it did. But all the deprivation, despite the little treats of ice cubes and tea, was setting her up to gorge, and she knew it.

Before she knew it, she had snuck off to Burger-Up, her favorite neighborhood restaurant, and eaten an order and a half of crispy-on-the-outside, tender-on-the-inside sweet potato fries and a chocolate brownie made with local Tennessee chocolate—along with a most excellent chicken sandwich with a more-than-tummy-yumming sauce. Dinner was water and boiled egg whites.

She had a new rule: Don't do anything you can't do for a lifetime. It takes too long to get used to new stuff, and she didn't want to make the effort to get used to anything that was going to help for just a little while. She was saving her remaining powder for the last big long bang.

Nobody half a century old was meant to be drinking milkshakes three times a day and trying not to move too much or do too much exercise because you might pass out because you were taking in too few calories.

On the other hand, she had to admit that during her four weeks on Medifast she had lost sixteen pounds, and a sixteen-pound weight loss in a single month was hard to come by, mid-diet. She said one last "Praise the Lord for Medifast." Then chanted aloud the way forward: "Eight hours sleep every night. Eight glasses of water every day. Walk for thirty minutes every day. Eat protein and salad. Drink only red wine and tequila. When in doubt, eat chicken and broccoli for dinner. Snack on unlimited amounts of sliced cucumbers. Eat something every three hours from eight to ten, then nothing from ten to eight." Even better, Willie Angel had told her when she called to check in and get a blood pressure medicine refill: Don't eat from eight to eight. Simple rules. Every day, every day, healthing everafter.

Visiting Preach once a week in his office was another simple habit Ada wanted to get back to. Not visiting Preach was a thing she couldn't keep up. Wanting more than a wifely peck on the cheek, she headed to church.

The preacher was surprised by his wife's visit. He was sitting at his desk contemplating stealing from Peter to pay Paul when his wife walked in. On the desk were three ice-cube trays.

"Watching ice melt?"

"Trying to decide which of these credit card companies is most likely to cut me some slack."

"Credit card companies?"

"I've got credit cards frozen into the ice."

"Gimme some scissors."

"You don't need to hack 'em out; hot water works fine."

"I need to cut them up!"

"Ada . . ."

"You've loaned another one of your congregants our money—without asking me. Again?"

"The bail money for Jarius's grandma."

"And what's this you about to thaw a card out for?"

"Jesper Phillips."

"Jesper Phillips?"

"Blood thinner. The insurance company will only pay for Coumadin, but there's an injectable that's better. Just till I sort it out with them."

"How much are we spending in meds every month that we don't have?"

"I haven't added up the numbers. I don't want to know. If I know, I won't be able to get up tomorrow and do what I got to do."

"And if we don't know, I can't get up in the morning and do what I got to do, make the ends meet."

"We always manage."

"Managing is managing me into a stroke. Not living in a house we own. Not knowing where I will be living when I get old if your mama doesn't die and leave us her house—because my daddy is leaving his to our daughters—because I might give it to the church. And I'm the fool who loves you so much, I might give it to the church. Yep, we managing me into a stroke!"

"I'm gonna buy you a house, Ada."

"How many years you promise that?"

"Too many."

"If you lucky, I'll probably just drop dead in ten more years and you won't have to worry about retirement, just go move in half the year with Naomi and half the year with Ruth."

"I'm gonna buy you a house."

"Don't say it. It's a lie."

"It's a promise. If I have to smother my mama, I'm getting you a house."

"You could stand up to the vestry."

"If I knew how to do that, you already have a house."

"You should probably use the MasterCard—Temple paid a little something on it last month."

"You know about my little accounts?"

"Yes. And there's something else I know."

"What, baby?"

"I'm going to get my body together, and you gonna get our bankbook together! I'm not leaving any of this blutter for our girls to drown in! Blutter is a river too deep to dredge—no telling how many is lost in it never to be found. Our future son-in-laws, maybe. I'm over blutter! All of it! Everywhere."

"Just don't be over me."

"You're not blutter, you butter."

"I like that."

"I want you to like it."

Preach kissed Ada on the lips. Hard. She opened her mouth. He squeezed her hands, then dropped them like he had something important to say.

"Every which way you ever looked, or could look, did look, do look, or will look, I love to look at you."

"Listening to talk like that is how I got hooked up with a blutter-loving man with credit cards frozen into ice blocks and body blutter hanging off me. I ain't listening, and I'm late for work. And late for your mama's, and before the day's out I'm gonna be late for my mama too, then come home to a home I don't own! All listening to you."

Ada put her hands over her ears and marched out of the office. She was thinking, If I don't get that fine man back into my bed, I sure as shit need to find a way to get him out of my head! Then she thought a little something worse: He put the words on me, but he didn't put the moves.

Sometimes the rule she liked best was her very first rule: Change it up. Crossing "Change it up" with "Walk every thirty minutes," she decided to get off the Dayani Center treadmill and start walking the path around Radnor Lake in addition to walking the neighborhood.

Unfortunately she decided to try the outdoor walk close to dusk, and the mosquitoes thought she was a banquet just for them.

Three days later she was in the hospital with West Nile virus.

Ada wondered if it wasn't a sign from God that she shouldn't be exercising. Preach said it was a sign from God she was supposed to be wearing mosquito repellent.

Mason called from Greenwood. He was staying at the Alluvian Hotel. Ada, just out of the hospital, full over her West Nile and emboldened by brushes with her mortality, allowed herself to enjoy the call, as recompense for recent suffering—and by telling herself, silently: I will talk. I will not cheat.

She would not cheat. But she might move on. On the phone with Mason, she let herself know this.

For a long time she had been less than content with the hiatus she and Preach had stumbled into, less than sanguine that he had become more her preacher than her man, that she no longer called him by his first name, that she would not be pleased if her daughters at their half century had what she had.

As Ada listened to Mason tell her all about Club Ebony, about the folks that remembered her father and her mother, as she heard him saying that he had kept the record collection she had left at the apartment all those years ago, that he was wanting to either give them back to her or give them to the B. B. King Museum, she didn't know how she would bring herself to hang up the phone.

It almost made her cry to hear Mason say that he might give the records to the museum, because it was like he was saying, Neither of us knew how valuable what we had was when we had it. And it was like he was saying, I figured it out first, and I can give it back to you, or I can give it away if you still haven't figured it out.

She tried to imagine herself starting a KidPlay in Los Angeles. She suspected funding would be easier to find out there, that some of the great big stars might help out. Perhaps Mason would get her invited, in person, to the NAACP Image Awards she had watched on television, and maybe she would meet Queen Latifah and Latifah would fund her and work with her and she would create a black *Sesame Street* and it would be aired on BET.

She already knew what he didn't know, or didn't care about: that Mason's friends in Los Angeles would find it easier for her to be smaller, that black Hollywood might even want her to be tinier, if she was spending time in the undressed West, in La-La Land.

She didn't think Mason would want her to be smaller. She wasn't even sure he would care that it made her life harder if she wasn't. She hoped it was what it was unlikely to be—that he was attracted to her exactly as she was, not that he too was besotted with the iconography of bigness.

Ada was hungry for a romantic adventure. Some days it seemed she was really close to finding a new man at home inside her old man. Some days it seemed like her own bed was the last place in the world she would find her next passionate kiss. She kept zigging and zagging between getting tickled by the possibility of an affair and being horrified she could even imagine one.

Still, she wouldn't cheat . . . unless she had proof Preach was cheating. If she had proof Preach was cheating, Ada would step out with what Memphis Minnie would have called her back burner boy. For the very first time in her life Ada hoped Preach was cheating.

Zigzagging again, clearing away blutter each step of the way.

28

FIND AND CREATE DNA-BASED GO-TO MEALS

THE THOUGHT DIDN'T stick at the front of her mind. What came to the front of her mind was: home cooking. If you don't want the home cooking, maybe it's what you're cooking at home.

Medifast and baby food had her brain a little fuzzy, but not so fuzzy that she didn't recognize that one of the reasons baby food and its adult equivalent had been so attractive was that feeding herself was too much work on top of too much work. Ada decided she needed a go-to frozen meal that worked with her DNA. She needed a go-to specialty of the house that was E-A-S-Y.

She had never served herself or her family a commercially made frozen dinner—but she was about to start. And she would have a signature dish she was proud to serve every day of the week, instead of priding herself on never repeating the same meal in a single week and usually not in the same month. She was going high and going low—she was getting out of the fattening middle.

After scouring the grocery aisles, the Weight Watchers site, and a bunch of food review message boards, she decided to try Kashi Southwest Style Chicken. It had 15 grams of protein, less salt than a lot of the Kashi meals, and it was supposed to taste good.

It came in a little plastic black container with cling wrap on top. To Ada's eyes it looked half cool, half pathetic. She vented it by slicing into the plastic film, then microwaved it for about four minutes, stirred, then microwaved it for four more minutes. After that, Ada served it to herself in a bowl. She took a bite.

Cheap. Fast. Healthy. Pretty tasty. Good to look at. She wished she had discovered Kashi when it first came out. The daughters laughed hard at her when she called to tell them she had discovered and succumbed to store-bought ready-made entrées. The twins already knew all about them.

Daughter Naomi allowed how she preferred Lean Cuisine. Ruth preferred a fat-free minestrone soup as her go-to fast food.

When she told them she was creating a specialty of the house, they both said, at the same moment, "Roast chicken with lemon and garlic." The very first dish both of the girls had learned to cook agreed with everybody's DNA. There was a God. And she probably had given Ada the recipe in her sleep.

You take a whole chicken, rinse it off, and pat it dry. You lay the chicken on its back, breast up . You slip a knife between the chicken skin and the breast meat, being careful not to tear the skin. Into that space you place sprigs of rosemary and cloves of garlic sliced in half. Inside the cavity of the chicken Ada put a whole onion studded with clove. She rubbed the chicken skin down with olive oil, then she put slices of onion atop the olive oil and slices of lemon atop the onion, course-ground a bit of pepper over the whole, then roasted the bird for about an hour at 375.

One chicken, two onions, a lemon, a few cloves of garlic, rosemary, a grating of pepper, a bit of olive oil. A dish you can get into the oven in fifteen minutes.

Her go-to side dish was what the family called Link green salad: sliced cucumbers, fresh basil, and green beans, with a few tiny dried peas thrown in as garnish instead of croutons to give the thing some crunch. The salad didn't need to be dressed; instead she just salted and peppered it and tossed it with olive oil over which she dashed a tiny amount of white wine vinegar.

Dessert would be fresh strawberries and Jack Daniel's for the no-fat folks; goat cheese and dark chocolate shavings for the no-carb folks; and a bit of goat cheese with a few plain strawberries for the balanced-carb-and-fat folks.

Keeping all these plates spinning was getting easier by the day, particularly when she had some basics like chicken and green salad to fall back on that worked for everybody.

Everybody. She didn't have everybody to cook for very often anymore. It made her sad. But the truth was the truth. She didn't. And she didn't have time to be slicing cucumbers and snapping and blanching green beans or spending the money for dried peas if the girls were not coming home. She grimaced.

It might be a little boring, but the go-to dinner was going to be roast chicken with plain broccoli roasted and just drizzled with olive oil, or spinach the cleanest way possible: rinsed, thrown in a pan with a tight-fitting lid, covered, set on low to cook until completely soft, then sprinkled with nutmeg.

And if she was too busy to do that, there was always peanut butter on a spoon and a plain baked sweet potato roasted in the oven.

29

USE CONSULTANTS: TRAINERS, MASSEUSES, NUTRITIONISTS, AND PRIESTS

ADA WAS FIFTY-FIVE pounds down. Ada was fifty-five pounds down. Ada was fifty-three pounds down. The number on the scale had finally changed. She had gained two pounds.

She was doing what she had been doing, and one thing more each week—and it had stopped working. Ada was verklempt.

When her body wasn't doing what she wanted it to do—shrink into a small, dark, and lovely queen—it was hard for her to have faith in her body.

Standing in the shower, letting the hot water pour down onto her, Ada tried to count her body blessings. She was glad that she even had something she wanted her body to do, shrink, so that was blessing one. She was glad she had a word—"shrink"—that made sense to her. She had felt swollen, inflamed, too stretched. She was glad to be past swollen, inflamed, and stretched.

Still, shrinking was a diminishment. She grimaced at the present difficulty: how to be big enough, grand enough, to be willing to be small.

She was at fifty-five pounds down, she was at fifty-five pounds down, she was at fifty-three pounds down; she had put on a brake.

She was a new kind of scared. She had reached the pinnacles she had reached large. Faithful wife of twenty-five years. Grown children well raised. College graduates. The kind of women the baker lets touch the bread.

It was hard to let go of the pounds that remained. They were an anchor to her good life. They were protective padding for the battle of life. They were an old, old beauty ornament.

Because she treasured the beautiful brown largeness of black women, it felt a little like she was robbing herself. Or it felt like she was denouncing herself.

She believed the truth of a radically different black beauty aesthetic. It complimented our kink and our curl, our big butts and flat round noses and the shape of our beautiful heads. It celebrated all the volumes, all the proportions, all the bronze difference. In the swirl of change, she feared losing all that. She feared breaking with black beauty.

It seemed that 165 pounds was almost too small for five-foot-two Ada.

And so all change had stopped. Every ounce of her knew—and in this moment she was thrilled there were so many ounces of her—every ounce of her knew she could not afford to lose her faith in black beauty, or her faith in her right and ability to change and still be a black beauty. She was the mother of beautiful brown twins.

She wouldn't move back, and she couldn't move forward. She was the kind of stuck that can only be resolved by faith and prayer and a willingness to throw out the pattern book and blaze a new silhouette.

It was time to call in the consultants. She would find somebody who still believed. First stop was Jenny Craig. She bought a week's worth of food and got a spiel on "goal attainment" from an hourly wage worker and true believer. She paid eight dollars for a drop-in yoga class on Twelfth Avenue and got a quiet talk on how drinking just a bit more water and taking yoga lessons would change her life and change her body. She went down to some funny house near the Baptist Hospital and had her tarot cards read in relation to the question "Will I be successful on my health hunt?" And she thanked God, her Judeo-Christian God, that the cards said yes. Then she went down to see a very old friend, someone she knew before she dropped out of divinity school, the Reverend Becca Stevens.

Ada called Becca the sexy brilliant priest. She was blonde, married to a handsome songwriter, a Phi Beta Kappa math major, and the mother of three boys. She was a radical progressive, always working from a hyperearnest heart, and a crazy house not far from Ada's.

Their paths crossed not often, but always with sparks.

Becca did not let her down. An hour after she called, they were sitting on Becca's upstairs balcony with bread and wine before them.

Becca gave Ada communion. She said, "Take this bread, it is my body, take it and eat, do this in remembrance of me." She said that, and she said the rest of the words.

But because there were only the two of them at the table, after they had taken the bread and the wine, Becca held Ada's hands and looked directly into her eyes. Ada looked directly and deeply back into Becca's eyes.

"What does it mean, God puts Jesus in our mouths and in our bellies to know he is in the world in our lives? What can it mean but your body is beautiful? Do this in remembrance of me. We remember with our mouths and bellies. We build with our mouths and bellies. I have faith in your body. It is a gift from God. See yourself and serve yourself with the truth of what I have put in your belly. Be any kind of black you want to be. Show me how to be any kind of blonde I want to be."

Becca's words scared Ada. She would not be as she had been. Becca wiped the tear from Ada's face with the fringe of her blonde hair.

"Jesus wept too," said Becca.

Eventually, Becca waved Ada off from the balcony. Just before Ada slammed her car door, Becca hollered, "Massage your own feet."

"What?" Ada hollered back.

"Reflexology. Google it," Becca hollered.

"Massage my own feet," Ada said, finally getting it.

On borrowed faith and consultants' wings Ada floated down four more pounds in a single boxed-food-, prayer-, and yoga-filled week.

Ada was 163 pounds.

30

MASSAGE YOUR OWN FEET

MASSAGE YOUR OWN FEET.

At first she just did it. Sitting on her bed, she grabbed one of those ugly tired things and started making little circles with her fingers. That was good. But what was really good was when she pressed down hard beneath the pad below her big toe. Pressing with her fingernail just below that bone, she felt something release—like a snap of tension, then a wave of electric calm. She had hit a pressure point.

The old zing took her back to her teenage days when Temple and Bird made friends with some hippies who lived on the Farm, the commune a few hours outside of Nashville. Back at the Farm, folk had rubbed her feet, and she had liked it; then she had forgotten about it, after Bird had said she thought it was "nasty."

Bird was referring to hygiene. This time Ada was worried whatever she was doing could be a different kind of "nasty," worried that reflexology sounded cultish, and wasn't something a good Christian preacher's wife should get involved in. A quick Wikipedia search assured her that reflexology was solidly in the world of traditional or alternative medicine, not a New Age religion.

The first time she did it, she did it dry. It amazed her how much benefit she got just from rhythmically squeezing each little toe. *This little piggy went to nirvana.* Walking her first two fingers around the perimeter of the sole of her foot. It only got better when she added lotions and oils.

She had had some of this same feeling when she had gone for a pedicure gifted to her by her daughters. Except pedicures gave her the heebie-jeebies. She didn't like being approached with sharp instruments held by strangers.

Reflexology was noninvasive. And it was storied. Some say it is practiced on four continents. Some say the Cherokee practice a form of it. Ada found that on Google. She liked the idea.

Looking for some more information on the Cherokee form of reflexology, which she couldn't find, Ada found instead a story called the Cherokee Legend.

A grandfather was teaching his grandson about life. He said, "A fight is going on inside of me." The grandson looked afraid when his grandfather said this, but the grandfather kept speaking. He said, "The fight is a vicious fight between two wolves. One is an evil wolf. He is everything bad: anger, envy, sorrow, regret, greed, arrogance, self-pity, resentment, false pride, superiority, and ego. The other wolf is good. He is joy, peace, love, serenity, humility, kindness, benevolence, empathy, creativity, generosity, compassion, and faith. The same fight going on in me is going on in you."

Now the boy looked even more afraid.

"Which one will win?" asked the grandson.

"The one you feed," replied the grandfather.

Rubbing her own feet was a way to feed the good wolf. When Preach came to bed that night, she tried to introduce him to the practice. He made a face.

"Don't be going Wiccan-woman on me now. You are the preacher's wife."

Ada paid Preach no never-mind. She called Delila, off playing at a club in New Orleans. Delila didn't pick up. Ada left her a text.

Next morning she called Willie Angel. Caught her on her cell phone as she was out of the office for a week, probably on vacation. But Ada wanted to know, and the office said she was taking patient calls.

Willie Angel wasn't too hot on reflexology for weight loss. "Reflexology? If that does anything, it's just a placebo effect."

"Shoot!" Ada said, and kept rubbing and pressing her feet, looking for the deep zings and finding them. Much as she loved Willie Angel, Ada ignored her. She made a new rule: Massage your own feet at least once a week.

Even if it was a placebo effect, Ada would welcome any good effect.

DRINK CAUTIOUSLY: NO JUICE, NO SOFT DRINKS, NO FOOD COLORING, NO CORN SYRUP, NO FAKE SUGAR; EXAMINE ALCOHOL AND CAFFEINE INTAKE

PREACH HAD A surprise for Ada. He invited her over to the inner sanctum of his office to show it to her. She took a seat. He asked her to close her eyes and hold out her hands. When her eyes were closed and her palms were outstretched, he placed a file and a ledger in her hands.

He had the taxes ready for the accountant. He had bought a shredder and two boxes of file folders. He had taken an online Quicken class. And best of all, he had one quarter—January, February, and March—of perfect records of income and expense. Those records were printed out and pasted into the ledger he had put in Ada's hands. The tax return was in the folder. The backup documents were scanned and on a Zip drive.

Ada was so excited she stood up and kissed Preach twice, very solemnly, on the lips.

"You're not the only one who can obliterate a little blutter."

"Lucius Howard, blutter obliterator."

"Have Quicken, will conquer."

Ada kissed Preach again. She was stunned by the miracle of records that worked. He was high on pride; she was high on relief. Only the sound of the morning "guys" coming for their coffee had kept her from stepping toward him to explore these emotions carnally.

Ada sped by Queenie's on the way to KidPlay. Queenie had a surprise for Ada as well.

"I got some hard-boiled eggs in there. And I picked up some celery Friday."

"Thank you, Queenie."

"Don't thank me. Less cooking means more time to play cards and some money to spend on clothes."

"And I just may take you shopping."

"Now that we not eating so much and cooking so much, I got some extra time."

"Imagine that."

Ada hugged Queenie and was out the door, rushing to Kid-Play. Keshawn's mama was waiting for her.

"I found an old Popsicle cart, the kind you pedal. And I remember I've got an auntie lives in the country, she got a greenhouse. Tomatoes and greens all year round, and cucumbers. She gonna give me the vegetables, and I'm going to sell 'em, and we gonna split what we get. I was thinking I could sell them here when school gets out."

"KidPlay would be honored."

"Strictly cash and carry."

"Strictly cash and carry and receipts."

"No food tax on farm food."

"Who told you that?"

"Miz Inez."

"Then it's probably right, but see lawyer Angel."

"I'm a food island. I call my truck Keshawn's Island. He's my firstborn. Every truck I get, I'm gonna name for one of my babies."

Ada, who never cried at school, let tears fill her eyes. Keshawn's Island tickled her sweet potato orange.

Ada had been putting off something. She read and reread her body journal, but she hadn't paid that much attention to her food diary since it told her to eat sitting down. Seeing Preach's ledgers prodded her to review her own. Even if her diary was going to give her another hard rule.

Rereading her food diary, one thing became perfectly clear. She needed to drink more cautiously.

Too much salty bubbly water, too many chai tea treats, and too much red wine. At the beginning it had only been a glass a day, then eventually two, and now it was too often three and occasionally even half a bottle.

Reading the food journal, Ada decided she would drink very cautiously: no bubbles; no juice; no soft drinks; no food coloring; no corn syrup; no fake sugar; no more than two glasses of wine most days, and never more than three—and as much coffee as she could drink and still go to sleep at night. The food journal made one bend in the road obvious; her road to health and beauty included more caffeine and less alcohol.

After all the highs of the day, less alcohol was hardly a hardship.

32

BATHE TO CALM OR BATHE TO EXCITE: RECIPES FOR BATHS

WEDDING SEASON WOULD be there before she knew it. Thirty-two weeks into her healthing campaign, nothing Ada had worn in recent wedding seasons, except her beads, bangles, and shoes, fit. And the shoes barely fit. Ada stood naked before her bathroom mirror. The image reflected appeared alien. As she gazed at this picture of her new self, she was overwhelmed by a sense of loss.

Her body didn't look like it had looked when she was young, plump and brown, with a tidy triangle of jet-black love fur; it didn't even look as it had before the diet, immense, imposing, and just extraordinary in that Hawaiian princess, earth mama, sugar mama, blues empress way she had been proud to be.

This day she looked wriggly and wrinkling, like empty bags. This was not the new she wanted. This was an inferior old.

According to the Internet, hot baths and cocoa butter would help. Building muscle would help. And she was glad that she loved a man who cared more about the firmness of her opinions than the firmness of her abdominal wall.

Her ass was still fine and firm and high. Some things simply do not change. When they are the right things, this is very good.

Baths as a sanity preserver were another of the things that had not changed. A thing she had come this day, this hour, to lean hard into.

She missed cooking. Or more specifically, as she still cooked, she missed concocting without limits, and passing her concoctions along.

And she missed dessert, the sweet and froufrou end of a meal that said night had come and night was sweet. She missed giant slices of tall and quivering lemon meringue pie, and she missed wet-with-chocolate, almost pudding-like brownies made with East Nashville chocolate.

She would find a way to eat these things in community, on occasion, but she needed a bow to tie on the end of her evening.

Contemplating her wishes: She wanted to play with recipes—freely. She wanted dessert. It came to Ada, like a strike of lightning, that she could create a dessert that she got into, instead of a dessert that got into her. If she could not have Preach or pie, she could create bath recipes—her own bath recipes.

The first bath she created was nostalgic. She called it "Over and Out." Its ingredients:

1 boom box
1 *Purple Rain* CD
1 bundle of fresh rosemary

1 copy of *Cane* by Jean Toomer
I cup forget-me-not flower tea
A square of dark chocolate

The second bath she created was "Get Up and Go":

1 boom box
1 Al Green CD
1 fresh lemon
1 bunch cinnamon basil
1 copy of *Yes I Can: The Story of Sammy Davis Jr.*
1 piece crystallized ginger
1 cup ginger tea

The third bath she created was called "Dove":

1 boom box
1 Bach's *Art of Fugue* CD
Crabtree and Evelyn rose bath and shower gel
Dried rose petals
1 volume Emily Dickinson poetry

The fourth bath she created, she called "Home Truths":

1 boom box
1 CD *Aretha Franklin's Greatest Hits*
1 copy *Their Eyes Were Watching God*
1 tall metal "glass" of homemade Lipton iced tea
1 carton Epsom salts

The fifth bath she created, she called "Smoke":

1 boom box
1 Jimi Hendrix CD
Sage to purify the air
1 cup lapsang souchong Tea
1 oz smoked salmon, cut into little pieces
3 cinnamon sticks to throw into the bathwater
A candle
A cloth to cover the eyes
Very hot water

After five days of hot baths—feeding her nose, feeding her ears, and feeding her skin—Ada realized she had found the best way to feed her Joy wolf. She had only lost 1.7 pounds that week—but it was a particularly tranquil 1.7 pounds. She had been on a five-day spa adventure, and it hadn't even cost her fifty dollars.

And she was feeling pretty firm.

33

INVENT DNA-BASED CARE PACKAGES THAT WORK FOR YOU AND YOURS

K NOWING THAT HER father, Temple, was planning a special treat for her, and feeling guilty for all the brownies and caramel cakes that she had sent to Washington, D.C., when the twins had been enrolled at Georgetown University, Ada packed up the ingredients to all the baths (except the boom boxes, which she ordered on Amazon) and sent one box to each daughter.

The girls would raise their eyebrows at the boom boxes. Ada didn't mind. IPods get ruined in the bathtub. The girls had killed three with water—all different ways. And boom boxes were cheap. Less than fifteen dollars. *Let them raise their eyebrows.*

Thinking about her daughters kept Ada motivated. And it didn't encourage selfishness, like always thinking about her own health, or nastiness, like thinking about Matt Mason. She thought about her daughters.

A box to Mississippi, a box to New Hampshire . . . it had surprised Ada when the girls had decided they wanted to land in very different parts of the country after graduation. It didn't surprise her when they announced they would pursue the same profession.

Naomi had wanted to taste a bit more of the Northeast, wanted a closer glimpse of northeastern boarding-school glamour. The only students she had envied at Georgetown had had that particular polish on them. Naomi coveted that shine.

For Ruth, the icy gloss of the boarding-school kids never intrigued. She wanted the deep and sunny South, the place where her grandpa's music was born. She wanted to be what her mother was, some kid's very good chance.

New Hampshire and Mississippi were the ends of Ada's earth. One daughter was in a place that was very international, with kids from every state and from every continent. The other was in a county many people living in had never been out of.

Each of her girls was getting worn down in a different way. Naomi had no privacy. She lived on campus. She got up and had breakfast with her students and ate her other meals with them as well. In the late afternoon she did sports with them before teaching her last class in the dark in the winter and returning to eat with them. Again.

Ruth had hard days but came home to a sweet apartment, a lovely place on a lovely street, and she was always home before dark.

Thinking of her girls struggling, Ada wanted to feed them. And she wanted to feed them right. In addition to the bath care package, she would send food—but not the same food, and not the old food.

To Naomi, who was a serious fat restrictor, she sent a great big box of apples straight from Washington State. To Ruth, down in the Delta, who needed balanced carbs and fats, she sent peanut butter. Ada ground the peanuts herself at the local Wild Oats.

One got Johnny Appleseed. One got George Washington Carver. Both got a little bit of their mama's love in the thought. And a bath box.

Temple had his boat back in the water. He wanted to take Ada on the first spin of the year around the lake. Walking down the pier, Ada put her foot through a rotten wooden plank. Ada and Temple both laughed.

It was a good laugh. It was good they could laugh, good they could know the problem was the plank, the pier, the rot, the weather. The problem wasn't Ada was too big. A year before, they wouldn't have laughed. This day she pulled her foot out of the hole and kept stepping, leaving her daddy to be embarrassed by his slipshod maintenance of the property.

"Your gals will inherit all this."

"You're sure? Not me?"

"You might give it to the church."

"I might give it to the church."

He stepped from the pier to the boat deck first. After he got his footing, he offered her a hand and she was aboard. They didn't talk as he got the engine started and the anchor up. They tied on life preservers. Temple stood at the wheel and steered them out of the cove. Ada lay on her back, looking up at the sky with the water below her. Soon the house had vanished.

"When I bought the house, I thought every day would be like this. Turned out your mother didn't like wide-open spaces."

"She liked them better when I was little."

"I'm sorry."

"For what?"

"You ain't enough to get her over Mag and Glo and Evie."

"Don't be sorry for that."

"I'm sorry for that."

"Thank you."

"You whittled down pretty."

"I couldn't get rid of the clutter in the house, so I got rid of my blutter."

"Blutter?"

"Black clutter."

"Get the blutter out of the place before you let your little gals see it."

"I'm not ashamed to let them see it now."

"I am."

"I love blutter."

"I know. And you gave it up. You a good mama."

"I learned from a good mama."

"Thank you for saying that."

Temple kissed Ada on the top of the head. She stood on tiptoes and kissed his cheek. They zoomed around the lake until the sun began to fall from the sky. It was a good grown-daddy-grown-daughter day.

Temple had arrived at a place he could tell Ada he was sorry. It had taken him almost too long to get there, but Ada had the patience that allowed him to be just on time.

Love, Ada thought out on the lake that first spring after-noon, is largely a matter of paying attention and good timing. Like her daddy had said long ago, when a dangerous storm was whipping up the lake and it was hard to get to the pier with the waves pushing the boat away, "It's an easy jump if you know when to do it."

That afternoon Temple tapped the rhythm on Ada's shoul-der, and he sang it out loud, "My gal love to jump, my gal love to jump, my gal jump, NOW." And Ada jumped, right on time, to the safety of the pier.

She had been a fortunate girl. It is easy to coordinate time with a loud-singing man.

They were anchored and shivering and he was playing a har-monica when the first star of the night showed itself. It winked, and Ada did what Ada had long done when she saw the first star of the night on the lake—made a wish.

She wished it wouldn't always be her father who made time for her girls on the lake, and that instead her mother would make space for them in the house. She wished she would keep on keeping on letting go of her own clutter, the pounds she had hoarded, to compensate for losing her mother, to shield herself from Preach's withdrawal, and to simply enlarge the external space she possessed as the internal space she possessed became smaller and smaller. She wished she wouldn't always have to compensate, shield, and enlarge to find something about her-self she loved.

All the pounds she had held on to had not been hoarding. Some had been out of pure love of a black beauty aesthetic that reveled in bigness. And some of it was the reality that fat makes a mighty fine veil. She hoped she would find a way of retaining a measure of privacy even with the shed pounds. She prayed the loss of her big curves didn't mean the loss of a certain kind of seclusion.

Ada had treasured the seclusion fat afforded. And Ada had enjoyed using her body as a hard-to-read symbol. Ada was ready to be done with all that. Her body was not a metaphor or an aide-memoire. It was her body.

Out on the lake with her daddy, Ada was beyond everything that went into making her brown father's eyes green, without being beyond his green eyes.

"Do you still carry two harmonicas in your pocket?"

"Always when I'm going on a walk with you."

They walked up the pier, trading riffs. When she went back into the house to say good-bye to her mother, Bird was in the shower, having just woken up from her long night's day.

Temple walked his daughter to the car. When she was behind the wheel, he leaned in for a last hug and a question.

"How you and Lucius doin'?"

"I don't know."

"You better find out."

If Temple was worried, there was reason to worry. Ada was scared.

34

DON'T STAY OFF THE WAGON WHEN YOU FALL OFF THE WAGON— AND YOU WILL FALL OFF THE WAGON

D RIVING BACK TO Nashville, Ada had a sullen mantra. *Get on the treadmill, get on the treadmill.* But she didn't. She preferred to think about sailing on the lake and to not think about Preach. For three days Ada didn't step near the Dayani treadmill, the path around Radnor, or the blocks around her house. Distracted by a strep running through KidPlay, Preach's mama having a fall, and Dorian getting diagnosed with HPV and ADHD in the same seventy-two-hour period, Ada was fall-ing into old habits: stay up late working, get up early and con-tinue working, work through lunch, then grab whatever was floating around KidPlay for lunch, never stop to drink a single glass of water.

To top it off, both of her girls were up to their eyeballs in trouble. Naomi in boy trouble in New Hampshire; Ruth with no boy trouble in the Delta. That was part of the trouble of the treadmill. She needed to think and listen, and she did that better sitting down in a chair close to the phone that still had a cord.

There was a part of her imagination that was very literal.

Talking to her girls at home in a chair or on her bed, connected by a cord, she felt more connected.

Walking fast on the treadmill, or walking Radnor Lake, or walking the neighborhood, walking and talking on the cell phone, Ada talked more, interrupted more, heard less. Preferring to be a good mother to being a skinny woman and angry at herself for turning that into an either/or proposition, again, she stopped getting on the treadmill.

She had eaten breakfast. That was a step in the right direction, if not a step on the treadmill. She had eaten breakfast in the car, as she was headed to the nursery school.

Preach had put a cup of yogurt with almonds and spices in her hand. She didn't know he could do that. Cook anything that wasn't barbecue or a fish fry. The surprise excited her. She had stood up on her tiptoes and kissed Preach. That surprise had excited him.

He had put his arms around her and had kissed her again in response. With his arms wrapped round her, he felt there was distinctly less of her. He felt it, and she felt him feel it. She felt: and still too much. He felt: and when I close my eyes, I miss the curves that don't pillow me—like something dear snatched away.

He said to himself, I must get inside her snatch to snatch it back. This startled him. That he would say in his head "snatch," that he would give her sweet woman parts a name other than the gentle and black "jellyroll" or their private "Eden," startled and thrilled him.

He hadn't known the thrill was gone until it started to come back. Until he told himself what he felt: How hard it is to let her go out the door to help and teach those babies, when I would like to sit down in the nearest kitchen chair, take off her panties, and have her jump on top of me. As he handed her a paper cup of yogurt and got an open-mouth kiss in return, he hoped she could read his mind. Until he was startled by the smallness of her into acknowledging what he had seen in other minutes in other places—times she was headed out the door to walk around the block, on the treadmill—not just that she was losing weight but that he might be losing her. Not for certain, but might be.

Her body had changed. The body she had now, he had never seen fully naked in the daytime. And he had never been inside it. He wanted that privilege, to get inside the soft abundance, and he wanted it more now that she put the soft abundance on the inside, where only he could get to it, than he had wanted it when it hung on the outside like globs of fatty love for the kids and every comer to grab.

He wished it wasn't that way, but it was. He looked at her now and wanted her in old ways. I want to get inside Eden. Eden was his name for her most precious lady part. Eden.

He wanted to say so many things that seemed too late to say, so he simply noticed she had not gotten down to make her breakfast, noticed she had not been to the Dayani Center in three days, so he made breakfast for her and put it in her hand. She had kissed him. He prayed that the body she was working toward, he would be invited into. He prayed he would be able to enter it.

She felt that prayer. He was her husband by more than law. Silently she said amen with him.

Then she prayed for herself. "Please God let me know why I am doing what I am doing. Am I walking back to my old body, or walking toward a new body, or stepping toward a future love I have not met, or stepping toward my husband, or am I doing all those things at once?"

One more thing that needed to be done that she didn't have time or money to do—see a therapist to sort this part out. The only way she could think to afford that was to steal a guitar from her father. Except she wanted him to give her one. She didn't want to steal a guitar from her father.

She did the next best thing. She would drink eight glasses of water today and sleep eight hours and walk on the treadmill for thirty minutes. She would act like a sane person until she was one. She would act like someone who loved her body and was settled enough in her marriage to get her sexy back and still act sensible.

One day at a time.

35

GET THERAPY

Not long enough after their close encounter with West Nile, Preach was out golfing with his friends when somebody got struck by lightning on the same course.

Ada started to think exercising was dangerous. Refusing to count Mason as a "bad thing," she wanted to know when the next bad thing would happen.

"Bad things come in threes," Ada said.

Preach contradicted her.

"In the Christian tradition, good things come in threes. Jesus. Mary. Joseph. Father. Son. Holy Ghost."

"Something's comin'."

It wasn't lightning that struck. It was a parked car wielded by a sixteen-year-old girl.

Ada had continued to encounter the redheaded boy on the strange bike on her walks through the neighborhood. After months of his calling out to her, "I'm getting mine, you getting yours," Ada had hollered back a question.

"Exercise?"

"Our pretty-pretty back."

Ada had nodded her assent. The boy was fitter than he had been at the beginning, when he seemed a huge bronze bear on a bike too frail for his weight. Now the bike seemed too big. She hoped he saw she was fitter too.

The week after Preach was on the golf course that got zapped by lightning, Ada was looking at the boy, noticing that he had metamorphosed into a handsome young man, when she saw him lift his cap. Ada called out, "Looking good," just as she noticed a blonde girl sitting in a Prius. She could have been the encouraging biker's skinny sister. The girl opened her car door, a car door that the young biker didn't anticipate. How it was the girl in the Prius didn't see the formerly fat redheaded boy on the tiny and tall bike, Ada couldn't imagine. Later she was told that the girl was texting as she parked. But that seemed an inadequate explanation. Ada would have thought the girl should have been able to feel, not just see, the passing extravagance.

There was no small warning for any of them. Ada was walking, the boy was pedaling, the girl was texting, then the door opened and the boy was still pedaling, and Ada stopped walking.

She saw the once chubby redheaded cyclist fly through the air, smiling. It appeared he was certain he would land, that he was enjoying the sail over the handlebars into the air. Then he landed in just the wrong way, on his shoulder, then on his head—and matter from his head that Ada prayed was just blood stained the street, in a flashing, head-bouncing second. The girl who had opened the car door was screaming as Ada spoke with a quiet and steady voice to the 911 operator. She wanted help to arrive as soon as possible. She knelt beside the boy. He said, "I'm fucked." Then he laughed, squeezed Ada's hand, and died with a smile on his face.

And so the young man—the obituary would say he was a busboy, but he was in Nashville writing songs—was dead before his first song had been recorded.

Later Preach said, "Bad things don't come in threes; these bad things came in three."

That night in bed Preach held Ada as she cried. She wanted him to make love to her but couldn't find the strength to kiss his neck and let him know. He wanted to make love to her but wasn't sure he should even try, that it wouldn't be all wrong.

Ada went to the funeral. As a preacher's wife she had been to many funerals of people she didn't know. This one was different. She sat off to the side, and she cried hard for this boy who had been a fellow traveler. She prayed he knew he was beautiful, but she didn't think he knew. She prayed he knew his encouragement had meant much to her. She hoped her hollers back had meant something to him.

Healthing was dangerous. Ada had suspected this; now she knew it for a fact. Three very strange things had happened that wouldn't have happened if the family hadn't been exercising more. She didn't want to stop, but she was stopped, by the Prius car door. She didn't walk in the immediate days after the funeral. Every day she ate an ice cream cone with hot fudge and nuts because she was going to die and she didn't know when. Young people don't believe death is coming. Old people beckon it near. Middle age gets scared.

On day four Inez Whitfield, summoned by Preach, came for a visit. The women sat in the living room. Ada brought them both a bowl of vanilla ice cream topped with warm homemade fudge.

"You haven't just fallen off the wagon, you've gotten yourself run over by the wheels."

"Run over by the wheels."

"What you gonna do about it?"

"What should I do?"

"Get back on."

"I don't know how."

Her friend handed her the name and phone number of a psychiatrist. He specialized in issues related to death and dying. He was in semiretirement, but he agreed to see Ada, for Inez and Preach's sake.

They figured out what was bothering her in a single session. The boy had had no tomorrows. He would have been better off enjoying getting fat or even getting fatter.

The shrink only had one question for her. "Do you expect to live for a thousand more tomorrows?"

"A thousand tomorrows?"

"Three years."

"Yes."

"Well, then."

The day after the visit to the psychiatrist's office, Ada got back on the treadmill at the Dayani Center. She ate her yogurt for breakfast, a Kashi meal for lunch, and chicken and broccoli for dinner.

That night she wrote a new rule—Get therapy—in her body journal, then she rewrote a previous rule for new emphasis: When you fall off the wagon—and you will fall off the wagon—get back on.

Even if a mule kicks you off. Even if that mule is God.

36

CREATE YOUR OWN SPA DAY

THE FIRST SWALLOWS of the long June that would be wedding season were the invitations. The first one to arrive carried a stamp Ada hadn't noticed before—a tiny man carrying a great big heart.

By the time all the invitations had arrived and wedding season had actually begun, engraved, e-mailed, handwritten, xeroxed, and calligraphed invitations were all waiting to be hung up on a special board Ada made each year with ribbon and cloth. This year, as in earlier years, the day Ada hung the board was the day she considered wedding season officially begun.

The first decade of her marriage, she had loved this time in the church year. Every wedding she attended was a chance to renew her vows. In comparison to the young brides, she felt wise—she was proud to be a young matron. She liked the display of everyone knowing that she was having virtuous sex, the kind that produced the laughing babies who attended the wedding with her, or who toddled down the aisles as flower girls, then as junior bridesmaids; living proof of her beauty and her and her husband's passion.

Over the years, all that had changed. She and the girls got to be too old to be in the bridal party. Then the girls were off at college, now off at work, and she had to attend weddings sitting alone in the pew. Preach was still at the center of each wedding event. Preach was still in the wedding party. Ada was not.

She had accepted that. Then the girls started to be asked to be bridesmaids, and Ada was alone in the pews. Or they were just away at work. Either way, this was a new hard. And a new old.

Weddings were so much about the babies that would come. They made she-who-had-no-babies-to-come feel painfully irrelevant. She tried to think of weddings more politically, as strategic alliances. She tried to think of weddings more psychologically, as frames for growth. She couldn't. She knew what marriage was for—consecrating sex play and making babies.

With her husband maybe out hound-dogging and her daughters all grown up and no prospect of grandchildren on the horizon, Ada would almost rather be anywhere than at a wedding.

She had to do something about that. Diligence has its limits, and she had arrived at one. Diligence wouldn't get her through wedding season with a smile on her face.

Using wedding season as an excuse to go on a beauty hunt just might. Ada was going on a beauty hunt. The First Lady was supposed to look good at weddings. In recent years Ada looked like a cold mess. Wedding season was the perfect excuse. She needed a lift. She needed encouragement. She needed a break. She needed a time out. A Sabbath. Vaycay. She needed a spa day.

And she needed one cheap. She fantasized about checking into a day spa at Escape, where she had had her nails done, but even a half day in a day spa was something like four hundred dollars, and she didn't want to blow the last of her spoon money in one place. Besides, she wanted more than four or five hours of spa. She wanted about twenty. And she wanted it soon. To-morrow. *My baby loves to jump! My baby loves to jump. My baby loves to jump, now!*

She pounded through an hour on the treadmill at Dayani brainstorming. Eight of the twenty-four hours would be spent sleeping. To prepare, tonight after dinner, she would do a deep clean of her bedroom, dust everything from baseboards to the highly carved mirror, which she would dust using Q-tip swabs. She would change the sheets. She would pick out a book of poetry to be her day's meditation, probably something by Lucille Clifton or the poets the twins had given her, Pablo Neruda and Yehuda Amichai. Clifton, Neruda, Amichai. These were the poets she would use to romance her body. She wanted an affair with herself. She wished that she had kept the vibrator Delila had given her as a fortieth-birthday present. No worries, she would make a little bouquet of flowers that had a scent, and she would place it by her bath and by her bed. She would buy her-self a new squishy pillow. She would lay herself down.

She was walking faster and easier, well into a second hour. Planning a day of body self-indulgence got her adrenaline go-ing. She wanted a theme. She quickly narrowed the choices to Native American and roses, then chose roses. Roses were old and fresh. And roses were weddingy. Roses it was.

But roses meant she had to go to the mall on her way to the gym.

Upon waking up on spa day, she would take a shower, and she

would spa-a-fy the shower by choosing a rose soap at Crabtree and Evelyn. Or, if she was really indulgent, she might even buy herself something from L'Occitane en Provence, a fancy body shop in the mall that had to this day intimidated Ada. So far the spa shopping list was rose soap, squishy pillow, lotion. She added pumice stone, dental floss, and emery boards.

Then she called in sick. For the first time ever. Asked one of the board members to fill in for her for the day. She didn't even think she was lying. She thought—I am sick. I need this mental health day if I am to make it through these weddings. I need to air out my brain.

She went to the mall. She cleaned her room. She cooked the meals she would eat the next day. She warned Preach to get out of her way. She went to bed exhausted.

Intending to spend most of the day walking and as much of it in sight of water as possible, Ada began her spa day morning at Shelby Bottoms, marching along the Cumberland River. Around lunchtime she would walk around Radnor Lake. In the afternoon she would walk out at Cheekwood through the gardens that overlooked their pond.

The day went as planned. Between the second and the third walk Ada headed into the bathroom for an old-school Epsom salt bath. Up to her ears in hot water, she covered her eyes with a warm wet washrag and blasted Billie Holiday from her little boom box and counted her favorite body memories.

Mind spa. The current moment was a favorite body memory. That was good. Very good. She sunk deeper back, wanting to remember her first favorite body memory, one before sex, one before babies, a true girl memory. She counted backward from one hundred. She took ten-second inhales and ten-second exhales. She came to: the *vroom-vroom* feeling she had when she first went fast on her first tricycle; then the first time she noticed the sun hanging like a red ball in the sky; pressing in the tips of her nipples when her chest was still perfectly flat; the sway of a swing seat beneath her feet as she pumped hard; the scent of honeysuckle and cigarette smoke mingling with perfume, going out to her first summer-night high school party; the day Preach put the baby in her, in a tent in the rain, and she knew before morning it was two, not one baby, that was coming to that tent, to that rain; that touch of his hand on her face. The girl memories dissolved into the woman memories.

In the hot water Ada welcomed it all. She came from a culture of warm water and song. She couldn't prove it, but she knew it. Like she knew that drinking herbal tea while she soaked made her more able to retain what she needed and shed what she didn't. Finished soaking, she rubbed her arms with a pumice stone and her legs with a loofah. It felt good to shed a skin. So good she almost took too much off. Looking down at her red elbows, she wondered if there would be a scab.

She had been in the bath for an hour. It was time for her late lunch. She ate the gazpacho and chilled shrimp she had prepared the night before. She ate it listening to Miles Davis, trying not to think of anything at all. To help her with that she counted to one thousand.

For her afternoon walk she took herself to Cheekwood Botanical Gardens. She dawdled through the Japanese garden and the rose garden, and around the swan lawn, then out to the gazebo, where she had read books to the girls when they were young. She had spent a lot of time in these tame gardens. And just for the moment, tame was what she needed.

She came home, cut open a lemon, stuck one elbow in one half and one elbow in the other to bleach away the rough brown points on her. It didn't sting, so she figured she hadn't pumiced too much off. She showered again. This time, when she showered, she shaved.

Then she soaked in the bathtub again. This time, as she soaked, she read *Coming Through Slaughter* from beginning to end.

An Episcopal priest friend of Preach's had suggested the novel to her years before. She had avoided it because she had found the priest, Virgil, an infuriatingly vanilla brown man. Reading the book, she realized she didn't know Virgil as well as she thought she did. She liked the book.

Out of the bath, she brushed and flossed her teeth. She lotioned her legs and breasts and hands. She took all the polish off her nails and gave them a quick emery boarding.

It was time to take herself to the pool. She didn't swim laps. She floated. She cherished her remaining lush fat buoyancy.

Much to her surprise, a day that had been about giving herself escape had become a day to become recommitted.

"Let the weddings begin," she said before submerging herself beneath the Dayani Center's chlorinated waters.

37

GET BETTER HAIR

ADA'S HAIR LOOKED hinky the morning after her spa day's dip-without-swim-cap. She headed straight to Big Sheba's Little House of Beauty, calling from her cell phone en route. Sheba bounced a med student from her chair. Sheba's daughter attended KidPlay; Sheba attended Preach's church. She gave her First Lady preferential treatment. Ada settled into the salon chair with a smile and an announcement.

"I need new hair."

"You need to leave your hair alone."

"Because?"

"Because you got too much change going on. You going through the change, and you making a lot of change, and that's too much change. Something gonna get dropped. If everything ain't where it supposed to be and where you used to it being, things happen."

"What's not where it's supposed to be?"

"To start with, your titties."

"Where are my breasts supposed to be?"

"Somewhere up closer to yo' shoulders."

"You are lucky they're not dragging to my knees or out to next door."

"You fifty years old. Get 'em up high and squished in, so they look all round and pretty—"

"And that wouldn't be change?"

"Preach loves your crazy hair."

"I want new hair, and I'm getting me some new very hard-working underwear, and I'll be ready for wedding season."

"You get you some new hair to go with that underwear and you most likely to get yourself in trouble, or get Preach worried. He's gonna start asking questions."

"Questions like what?"

"Like who you doing all this for?"

"You don't even have to ask, don't pretend you need to ask, you know I'm doing it for Preach," Ada lied.

Opal Herbert, Sheba's most in-demand stylist, who had walked in halfway through the conversation, decided to open what everybody on Jefferson Street called "the mouth of the South."

"Lord, child, you got your eyes more open than I thought you did. Fight the good fight. There bad women on every corner looking for somebody's husband, and there's always a few who think they gonna get to heaven by kissing one of God's true angels. Jezebels in every congregation."

"What you talking about, Opal?" asked the med student, who Opal was staring right at as she spat "Jezebels." Sheba wasn't studying on the med student's guilt or innocence. She was worried about Ada.

"Opal ain't talking about nothing, at least nothing but her

paranoia. She think everybody after yo' husband because she want to drag her tired old half-yellow black ass after him. Everybody with sense know the preacher don't have eyes for anybody but his First Lady," said Sheba.

"It's a good thing I started going to church with the Episcopals," said Ada.

"I ain't so sure 'bout that. I say the cat's away, the mice will play. I say get your butt back home and into the front pew e-v-ry service, and not just Sunday," said Opal. Sheba was shaking her head in reluctant agreement.

"How can I pray, thinking about everything but God, thinking about who's looking at my husband, and who's voting for his raise, and what does he think about what I'm wearing, and what some Little Miss Jezebel is wearing. And I would not say a word of this past this beauty shop, but this is a sacred place for me, sacred as the sanctuary, with sisters more darling to me than my Altar Guild ladies. So let me be clear. I have one, and only one, thing on my mind now. I *need* you to hook up my hair and get me out the door with not one more worry than I came in with. Trust me. I hear one more piece of bad news, I'm going to snatch myself baldhead. I don't want to know nothing more bad."

"Let's get this head together."

"Give her something classy."

"China chop!"

"China chop?"

"Straight bangs across, straight sides."

"Cut it up just above her shoulders."

"That keep it fresh."

"My grandmother wore that hair back in the twenties."

"It's back."

"Put you a real pretty real diamond clip in it."

"I've got one of those."

"I know. I remember when your daddy bought it for your mother before you were born."

Big Sheba's Little House of Beauty returned to the usual hubbub of morning chaos. If Ada had been thinking about anything but her hair, she would have noticed what wasn't being said. It was written all over the faces of the silent. Sheba and Opal were both thinking the exact same thing. Ada's request for a new haircut was an open confession that she knew Preach was cheating. That she knew all about it. But they kept on smiling and kept on acting like all she wanted was Better Hair.

Whatever was coming, Better Hair would help. That hippie-curly mess she had all over her head was *tired*. Everyone in the shop knew it. Everyone in the shop agreed on that. What they differed on was what was coming.

Whatever it was, Ada would greet it with her chin up and a China chop.

38

FAKE IT TILL YOU MAKE IT: FINE FOUNDATIONS AND WIDE SMILES

DELILA LEE WAS back in town. If Delila Lee had not been Ada's oldest friend, and Delila Lee's mama had not delivered Ada in the back of a band bus, Delila Lee would probably have been way too wild for Preach's congregation to tolerate as the First Lady's bestie.

But Delila Lee had been there from the get-go, and she was the First Lady's bestie, so Delila Lee got into a lot of clubs: the Lunch Bunch because she was wickedly funny, and the Altar Guild because she had the deep purse to buy the expensive flowers for Christmas and Easter, to name her favorites. Because she would never on God's green earth get into any Links chapter in America, there was no chance in hell for Delila Lee to take over. And she was fun. Eventually the congregation didn't just accept Delila Lee as Ada's bestie, it embraced her—whenever she was around, which wasn't often.

Delila Lee liked to run up and down the road. Ada's best friend was usually gone, particularly these last two years. Ada remembered how that seemed to come to be: There had been a few parties where Delila got too drunk, then she put herself in treatment, then she hit the road, playing more and more out-of-town dates.

Ada hated that.

Strangely enough, Delila Lee (she had christened herself Delila early, as soon as she knew she would be wanting and needing a stage name) was a year younger than Ada, but she looked ten years older, only foxy.

Delila had bumped around clubs in New Orleans, and Memphis, and Austin before landing in Nashville with two obscure CDs to her credit and a convertible that she claimed Isaac Hayes had given her. Delila Lee's Isaac Hayes was a white "farmer," an old blue-blood aristocrat, pink and skinny, who once had been in cotton and now grew corn. Cottonball white, with a black interior, Delila's car was the one thing she possessed she would not sell or rent.

Delila never slept with men for money or serviced men for money, but she would shack up with an adoring patron of the arts who enjoyed a private blues concert once or twice a month.

Her lovers were all white, and she was always convinced they loved her voice—if they didn't love her. Delila Lee didn't love anybody but Ada.

Her very last lover had been a very old man whose name was not Isaac Hayes. He had tried to get her to go with him to AA meetings, but she never did. One fall day he went out dove hunting and got tangled up with a fence, his rifle, and his head. In his will he left a house to Delila Lee, who he described as his housekeeper. He also left her a little income of $40,000 a year, and health insurance to be paid from an ongoing trust account for as long as Ms. Lee was alive, with the wish that she get sober, and the promise she would be taken care of dry or wet. The adult children complained that they didn't have a housekeeper. Their mother told them to shut up.

The wife of record insisted on meeting Delila to give her the deed to the house and the once-a-year check for $40,000. On every such occasion, she said the same thing: "Better you than me." Delila Lee just said, "My pleasure."

Ada shook her head, thinking about Delila Lee. Strange things were always happening to her. Strange good things and strange bad. It came from Delila Lee always chasing after the juice in any moment. When they were children, Delila had confessed to Ada, "The one thing I'm true scared of is being bored." She had been talking about having to go spend a summer with her father's grandmother in Chicago in a perfectly clean house where all she had to do all day was sit on a proper couch reading books. "I may drown myself in her perfectly clean toilet."

After a flurry of missed calls and text messages, they met at the Pancake Pantry in Hillsboro Village. Delila liked it because it was around the corner from a noon meeting she liked at the church in the village.

Ada told Delila Lee about Matt Mason. Delila Lee near peed her pants. Ada told Delila Lee not to get too excited, she probably wasn't going to do it. Then she added, not as a tease but as the truth, "But I just might!" Then Ada changed the subject.

Something bigger was bothering her. One of the weddings this wedding season was an interracial wedding. The girl was marrying a boy from Belle Meade, in a two-minister ceremony. The other minister's wife was skinny and blonde and looked like she could have been a pageant girl in an earlier life. The grandmothers on both sides, black and white, looked great. Ada had to represent. Ada didn't want to let the side down. She could pull off her own brand of power black frump—she'd been pulling it off for years—but she didn't think it translated to the white world.

"And I do not want to embarrass the church."

"Honey, you looking good, better than you've looked in years."

"My old clothes are too big, and my titties are trying to hang down to my knees."

"Fake it till you make it."

"Fake it till you make it?"

"A big smile works more wonders than a face lift. Put a great big smile on your face, and people will start smiling at you, and then you be happy for real. The fake turns real."

"Fake it till you make it?"

"And let those biddies wonder what you got to smile about."

"Is there a fake-it-till-you-make-it body remedy?"

"Sho 'nuff."

"What?"

"Rebecka Vaughan."

"Who's that?"

"It's an old-fashioned foundation shop. Go in there and get you a modern girdle, and a body suit, and some Spanx, and a brassiere that gets the boobs high and separated and sucks in the waist. And buy you some black tights with a panty girdle built in to put on top of that girdle, and you can be two sizes smaller by dinner tonight.

"Fake it till you make it."

"Why?"

"Honey, it's women who don't know nothing about men think it's the clothes you wear that makes them want you. Any man over fourteen years old or who ever been to one whorehouse knows, it's not how you look in clothes, it's how they feel when the clothes come off and the light go out, and the only way to know anything about that is looking at a woman's smile and her underwear. She can be big as three houses but got her on a pretty purple silk panties and bra, and he's probably in for a good time; and she can be skinny as a rabbit, if she's got on some skanky frayed panties that don't look like nothing and no bra, all that skinny bitch is probably gonna do is give him disease. And if she's wearing grandma panties and some big ole mummy-bag slings, you know she ain't about to give up anything with anything except you be her grandbaby looking for love and a sugar tit."

"I wear this one-piece black stretching thing with underwire that's like a swimsuit. It's like I'm always covered."

"It's like you a modern nun. You can't even pull 'em down to pee, let alone have sex. Have mercy, that's just a frigidity protector. What does it have, four hooks and eyes right at your twat? Get you some pants to pull down. Get you a bra. Get you a short little slip if you just need to be covered. Your mama was a stone fox. You should know some of this. What is wrong with you, heifer?"

"Missing me some you."

"You got me . . . I get my two-year chip this week. And I'm staying in town for a while. I'm going to take some of my money and make me a new album. I'm gonna sing some of that Memphis Minnie shit nobody even knows about anymore. And you gonna sing backup."

"You get you another show in Nashville, and me and the girls be right up on the stage with you."

"Your girls ain't getting anywhere near my stage. They too young and too pretty."

Ada looked at Delila, looked at her hard, like she was accessing new possibilities. Delila smiled back and said, "I love your China chop. You keep rocking that, babygirl."

"I will. Just for you," Ada said, then she kissed Delila on the cheek.

Delila was skinny and brown with big huge eyes and long hair that was almost all gray. There was a lot of Indian in her African, Ada guessed.

Ada wondered where Delila's mother was. Somewhere out west, she had heard. Married some Indian man who had some casino money. He was her seventh and, she said, final husband. Delila's daddy had died when she was just three or four. Ada's mama always said that Delila had more or less raised herself.

Just seeing Delila be so bold and so wonderful after being orphaned took some of the pressure off Ada about her being a good mother and about her worrying about her babies' mothers. Delila had turned out great with hardly any mother at all.

But that wasn't the best part of Delila for Ada. The best part was, Delila got happy just looking at Ada. It was good to still have that power—except she wanted to be looking across a pillow at someone and feeling it.

Not this day. Today she was keeping a move on. Today she

was getting her nontrifling ass to Rebecka Vaughan and seeing if she couldn't find a trifle that might fit.

She was putting a big smile on her face, and she was buying herself some new underwear. She was going to undress like a woman, not like some ancient baby.

Underwire or no underwire, she was over the stretchy black middle-aged-woman onesie they called a lingerie bodysuit. It wasn't a shape maker, it was a no-one-will-feel-your-shape maker.

For three years she had pulled the between-the-legs part over to pee and had had to shit only before it was put on. She had made a lot of accommodations to wear what was a fundamentally inconvenient garment, a garment that only made sense if you wanted to see as little of your private parts, as seldom as possible.

That night Ada threw every one of the strange pieces of underwear away.

In their place she folded black cotton panties and bras that looked like the woman who wore them liked sex, and herself, and style, and the environment. Ada prayed they looked just a little like she should be wearing them.

39

UPDATE BEAUTY RITUALS
AND TOOLS

L EAVING THE PANCAKE Pantry, Ada had called Naomi in New Hampshire. It was easy to catch her; she had a cell phone and could use it between classes. Ruth in Mississippi never got breaks. They could only talk at six fifteen in the morning and after four in the afternoon. The last few days, she wasn't even reaching her then.

Ada was calling Naomi to find out if she knew why. She didn't, except she thought Ruth was starting to explore the Blues Trail. Ada got on with her other business. She was thinking about updating her makeup in time for the big luncheon and in time for her upcoming birthday.

"Mama, you do an allover face. Nobody does that anymore. Do lips *or* eyes."

"Lips or eyes?"

"Either do bright lips and barely anything around your eyes, just maybe eyebrow pencil in your eyebrow, not even mascara— or go the other way and do nude lips, or near nude neutral lips, and go wild on your eyes: liner, mascara, shadow, or two shadows."

"Lips or eyes. What about base?"

"Go back to Sephora. They have every base in the world. Don't just take the first salesperson. Find someone good at matching colors, our skin colors, and see what they come up with. I'm betting Smashbox or maybe Stila, but Stila's probably too young."

"I want Chanel."

"Maybe Chanel, if you try one of those new Perfection Lumière shades. Do a virtual makeover. They have a thing to do it at Essence dot com and there's one at Seventeen. They're free. I like the Seventeen one. It will let you see if you prefer lips or eyes . . . you'll have to upload a picture of yourself, but after that it'll let you try on different shades, and different colors, even different hairstyles, and you're in the privacy of your own room . . . I think you would like it big time."

"You know your mama."

"I know my mama."

"How's your diet going?"

"Going. I wish I had the same type you have, or that Ruth and I had the same type. I'm not loving being in Daddy's type, and Daddy can eat three times as much as I can—and it feels too boy to be Daddy's type."

"You are not too boy."

"I can't get a date here. I shouldn't have taken this job."

"You should get into Boston more."

"I should."

"But—"

"You know your daughter."

"So the but is—"

243

"Now that I'm making all this change, I don't want to meet anyone new until I finish making the change. I don't have a lot of first impressions left in me."

"You have thousands. You are twenty-three, not eighty-three."

"Have you read that most black woman graduating from college this year will never get married?"

"That won't be you."

"How do you know that?"

"Because if we have to rope in some one-eyed old man who has somewhere deep in his history great genes, I going to rope you into marrying him and him into marrying you, at least long enough for you to get some great babies."

"Before I did that, I'd just do it with one of my gay friends."

"Families start a lot of different ways."

"But—"

"But I'm hoping for true love, a big ring, a big wedding, and a big family you raise with the person with whom you made the babies. All that, I want for you."

"And what do you want for my sister?"

"I'll discuss that with your sister."

"I want us to marry two brothers, not twins but brothers. I want the older one."

"Sweetie, that's strange."

"What's up for you the rest of the day, aside from your thirty minutes on the treadmill?"

"Updating my beauty rituals."

"I haven't had any long enough that they need updating."

"I was once that young. But when I was that young I didn't have beauty rituals."

"Because you were a blippie?"

"A blippie?"

"A black hippie."

"I was bit of a blippie, back in the day. The hippies were just a little bit ahead of me, but Nashville is a little bit behind in the world, so I guess I was a blippie. I guess that's why my beauty roll never got started right. Instead of wanting to be like my mama, who was glamorous, I wanted to be like those women out on the Farm, except that was the place for straight brown hair and skinny thighs and no-butted beauties."

"Sounds like Exeter now. How did you let me come out of the South? I never knew I wasn't beautiful till I came to New Hampshire."

"You had to find out sometime."

"That I wasn't beautiful?"

"That everyone doesn't know it."

A bell rang. Naomi had to get to class. She wasn't ready to get off the phone. She was uncharacteristically willing to be late.

"I miss seeing myself in your eyes. I remember sitting in your lap touching your breast and seeing myself reflected in your eyes and knowing I was the luckiest girl in the world and one day I would be a mama and my daughter would sit on my lap and know she was the luckiest girl too. What if that doesn't happen for me?"

"It will, darling."

Ada was walking toward that truth, wherever the walk took her.

40

SHOP FOR YOUR FUTURE SELF

EVERY YEAR IN January, Bird and Temple would choose the days they would celebrate family birthdays and Christmas and Thanksgiving and Easter. Once the dates were picked, they were sacred and didn't get changed. Originally the dates were picked according to Temple's band's schedule.

The day had come they had chosen to celebrate Ada's birthday out at the lake.

The party started in the living room. For the occasion, Bird had arranged the sofa in a rectangle. And she placed a birthday cake she had made by molding store-bought ice cream into a Bundt pan on a plate atop a guitar case right in front of the couch. Next to it was a giant bowl of pasta puttanesca. So Ada didn't have to do the cleaning up, Temple had bought paper plates and plastic forks.

Every year Ada's birthday celebration conversation started off the same way.

"Ada Howard, all y'all a lot of work, but you the little bit of fluff we picked up from the summer fields."

"That's what you said, and that's when that crazy bass player said, 'Let's call her Cotton,' and it stuck for a hot minute."

"Half a hot minute."

"Then it changed up to Honey."

"I had to buzz around a pretty flower to get you."

"You buzzed around a lot of pretty flowers to get Honey. Had to make her mama hot jealous. Not easy to get that woman to uncross her legs," said Maceo.

"That's right. I had to buzz around a lot of pretty flowers to get you," said her daddy.

Her mama was busy sipping and eating and thinking about something, trying to remember something, then forgetting that she was trying to remember. Maybe it was that little tiny strokes kept her mind jumping the track, but for the time being, she skidded back onto the track almost as fast as she skidded off. Bird squeezed Ada's hand. It was a birthday. She was making a special effort.

"You my velvet-chain baby."

Ada didn't know if that was a skid on, or off, the track. "What's that, Mama?"

If the mother had wanted to answer, she would have had to shout down the daddy.

"Your mama tried to name you Velvet," said her daddy, like it explained something.

Her mother laughed, spewing soup. She patted her brown face with a starched and scorched white cotton napkin. She was wearing a holiday bright red kimono.

"Your daddy was a hard dog to keep under the porch—till I 'tached him to it with a velvet chain. You my velvet chain."

"Porchlight babies, we used to call 'em, they lead a man home," said Maceo, who was tapping the browned top of a square of macaroni and cheese tentatively, with his fork, like he wanted it to be a snare drum.

"When did we start eating macaroni and cheese?" asked Temple.

"The sixties," said a new tenant, one of three brothers who called themselves the Chesterfields. This emboldened the two other new tenants, his brothers, to join in the conversation, but first Maceo joined in.

"I don't remember macaroni and cheese way back. I don't 'member it before Pyrex casseroles. And I don't know when the white folks up North got 'em, but white folks down South didn't get Pyrex and CorningWare till after the war, and we didn't get it till the sixties. Macaroni and cheese came in just about the same time as Jimi Hendrix. Caught on fast when it came. I like the way it looked cut out in a square, all brown and orange on top," said Maceo.

"About the time everybody said, Say cheese, when they stopped to take your photograph. Remember those old instant photographs you had to rub with a wax crayon stick?"

"Kitchens don't look the way they used to. Bedrooms look just the same."

"That's something to think about."

"I'm still thinking about Velvet. I forgot we called Honey that for a hot minute. There was that new TV show and the girl looked just like Elizabeth Taylor, and I always thought Elizabeth Taylor looked just a little colored, and her name in that movie was Velvet Brown. Velvet Brown could be colored."

"Maceo, you is sho'nuff crazy."

"Not so crazy. I was the one who said we giving this child entirely too many names."

"There was no compromising, so we just added on."

"She wanted to name you Velvet so she could laugh at me and know you tied me down. I named you Honey, 'cause I buzzed around a lot of bees to get you."

"And then you didn't buzz no more."

"I got snipped."

"Like a puppy."

"I was the first man I ever knew to do it."

"First one of us."

Ada wondered if by "one of us," her father meant musician or black person. Or black musician. She assumed he probably meant all of the above—her father was a happily hyphenated man. Years of playing music, smoking reefer, talking to his dead daughters in his head, and texting his living grandchildren with his guitar-speeded fingers had sweetened him.

"Thank you, baby," said her mother.

"Thank you, baby," said her father.

She couldn't tell if they were thanking her for all the food and caretaking or for being the velvet chain. Lately she had fed her parents and their boarders collard greens and black-eyed-pea soup with sweet potato broth and lots of fresh thyme. And she had left them a few sweet potato pies made with just sweet potato and egg whites, to give it some protein. She smiled to see that her parents were shrinking a bit too.

"You looking good, girl," said her mother.

"Real good, child," said her father.

"Don't get too skinny," said Maceo. "Whatever men say they want, or think they want, they like a little meat on the bone. I never let myself get too skinny."

It was a funny family. Her mother treated her more like a sibling than a child, her father treated her like an adoring fan. But she loved them.

Sitting in the house her daughters would one day inherit, a house that looked like a junk shop and smelled like one too, dusty and musty, Ada shook her head against the blutter. Black clutter, a particular kind of too much and unsorted, the kind Ada hated and loved. She took another sip of the sweet and bubbly wine her daddy was pouring and savored the contradiction. For the very first time.

Usually, on her birthday, they tried to do something to let her know, without telling, how sweet she was. *You are the sugar in the plum.* This year they almost told her out loud that she was their treasure. Then they didn't.

But Ada knew from the time Temple let her suck on his knuckle and she had let herself be quieted, from the very first weeks of her life, that he had allowed her more. Her sisters had had sugar tits made of handkerchiefs dipped in sugar water. Ada had her father's knuckle. She was the first flower of their middle age. She was a passion flower.

The first three daughters were noisy babies who did not let him sleep in the night when they did not sleep through the night.

Ada was different. She sucked on his knuckle, lying in her little crib, then she slept through the night. After this baby was born, the mother liked sex more than before. After this baby was born, everything was better.

The sisters pulled together to share in her care; they started visiting home again. He still went out on the road, but now the road was all singing and no kissing. His songs got better.

Everything Temple had to give anybody who was not his woman or one of his four girls or his band brother, he gave on the stage.

Some girl laid up for him in the men's room of a club one night. Standing crouched in the shit stall, and when he came in she pounced, and he told her, "You got my best already. I don't want to see the disappointment in your eyes." He never slept with another one of the girls who follow the boys in the band again.

He owed Ada something more than what he had given. And it was her birthday. He didn't like birthday presents. It had been too many years of not being able to afford to get good ones that did that to him. But he didn't have to be that way. He had an old guitar he had picked up in a pawnshop in 1952. A guitar he had bought for twenty-five dollars, and it might bring Ada twenty-five thousand.

Looking at Ada with her China chop, in her sweatpants and pearls, with her Burberry coat, the preacher's wife and the R&B singer's daughter, he knew a big part of why she was tired and broke was she lived in so many worlds, too many worlds. She lived in the music world of honor among thieves and the church world of thieves forgiven by Jesus. She worked and she mama'd and she wifed and she daughter-in-lawed and she preacher's-wifed, and she, somewhere he knew, tried to be, and wanted to be, Lucius's lover. Ada was Bird's daughter. Temple was proud of his girl for juggling it all for so long.

"So it came down to Rose, or Honey, or Cotton, after we threw out Velvet, and we couldn't pick, and our last name was Smith, and so we just called you Honey Rose Cotton on top of the Jacqueline and Vicksburg and praised Jesus our last name was Smith, then we came to our senses and put Ada at the front of it."

"And we filled out the papers at the hospital before we had a chance to sober up, so there it was, turned into Uncle Sam. Ada Rose Honey Cotton Jacqueline Vicksburg Smith. Thank God you married a Howard and dropped the rest of that mess."

"Ada Howard is a good name," said Temple.

"If you like stripped-down," said Ada.

"It was Lord Byron's daughter's name," said Bird.

"And Bricktop's," said Temple.

I will not underestimate my mother. Every year Ada had a birthday present for herself, something she would improve or change about herself, a secret improvement. Until this moment she had not known what this year's would be. Now she did. *I will not underestimate my mother.*

And she would focus on Preach. She would find out if he was cheating, and she would start calling him by his name, Lucius. And she needed to be doing some work she truly *wanted* to be doing *now*, which was writing *Home Training* or getting a degree in nutrition and a degree in counseling and teaching others how to do what she was doing for herself. It was time to change more of everything up!

Ada was going to buy herself something gorgeous to wear, something her mother might have worn if she had been the preacher's wife. *I will not underestimate my mother.* She would dress as the woman she wanted to be.

Her father was tucking a bundle into the backseat of the car. A blanket wrapped around an old guitar.

"I don't play guitar, Daddy."

"Take it to Corner Music. Or down to Gruhn's. They'll know. You don't take less than ten thousand dollars for it. Cash. You might get near to twenty-five thousand."

"What is it, Daddy?"

"It was a lot of things. What it is . . . is a break for my baby."

"How fancy, Daddy?"

"Ain't fancy at all. It's a poor boy's guitar, dozens of 'em floatin' round near like it. It's a tool, an ax, it's nothing. But that one belonged to somebody who knew how to do something with it had never been done. Genius touched that box. Corner or Gruhn's will know."

"It's your Indianola guitar. I can't take that."

"Be my music walking, girl."

Before she pulled off, she put down her window to blow her father a kiss.

"Go straight to the shop with that. Don't get it stole. This is Nashville. Keep it in that ratty blanket. Too many folk 'round here will know what it is."

She went straight from Corner Music and bought herself a $49, size-10 stretchy black dress from Target.

41

TAKE *ONE* BITE OF ANYTHING AND NEVER MORE THAN *TWO* BITES OF ANYTHING DECADENT

THE TWINS FLEW in for Ada's actual birthday. With the help of their daddy, they pulled off a surprise fish fry in Sevier Park.

Before rushing out to pick up Ruth and Naomi at the airport, Preach brought Ada a birthday breakfast in bed: a bowl of ripe plums.

The gesture made Ada cry. In the bowl were four purple, perfectly imperfect, dark spheres. Ada reached for a plum with brown fingers. Her fingers touched the smooth, poreless, tightly encasing skin. She held the plum close to her nose. There was no scent and only the slightest sound when her teeth pierced the fruit, releasing the burst of flavor. First the dark and shiny smooth, almost slick, surface, then an acid layer, sharp but not bitter, then the sweet flesh, yielding, wet, dense. The flavors were ripe purple and acid green, then the acid green faded off, leaving only the sweet.

Ada closed her eyes, and the plum melted onto her tongue. A taste of self-recognition. *I am the sugar in the plum.* The sweetness that lightens and abides.

The things you taste become a part of you. *I have tasted you.* Ada took a woman's pleasure in relishing her most intimate sense. She took a black woman's pleasure in relishing the least assaulted sense. The swallow after a black beauty tastes is a precious swallow.

She ate a second plum. She drank her milkless coffee. She awoke. She was grateful to Preach for his bruiseless gift that spoke a language they had almost forgotten. How many carbs were there in a plum? In a banana? In an apple? In a little sip of honey for her tea? In a tablespoon of mascarpone? Thank God there were none in a kiss. And the kisses of Preach's dark mouth were sweet. She had to have them. That night she would tell him so. *Happy Birthday.* Happy 150 pounds.

Ada reveled in an afternoon to bite with abandon into a fried fish sandwich dripping with hot sauce and mayonnaise smothered with melty yellow cheese all jammed between two square pillows of Wonder Bread. Ada loved a "hot fish sammich." She loved the smell of sizzling oil, the salt and pepper and cornmeal goodness of the crunchy skin of whiting or catfish or red snapper.

Wandering, in white cotton pants and white cotton shirt, along the bank of the little stream that wiggled through the park, watching many of their church friends and their KidPlay friends hula-hoop, and jump double-dutch, and chase, and hand-clap and dance to the music that was blaring from the hot fish truck speakers, Ada felt deeply easy.

She felt light enough to make her way into the jump-rope lines. When it was her turn, the old rhythm found her and she was wheeling her feet, right, left, right, left, and she was inching them into a turn, right, left, right left, and she was getting short of breath and she knew the ropes would be falling on her shoulders soon—but not yet. Right, left, right left. Mamas from her school were handling the ropes, and they knew how to turn. She was jumping for all she was worth until she missed the beat and the rope got caught around her ankle and she was lying in the grass laughing and the twins were screaming, "Mama, are you crazy?" and the kids were screaming, "Look at Ms. Preach" and Queenie was hollering at the top of her lungs, "Lord, help me Jesus today! Lord, help me Jesus today!" and Preach was whispering on his knees beside her, "Ada, are you all right?" And he seemed to be talking about her good sense leaving her as much as he was talking about her knees and her face.

She didn't remember the last time she'd laughed so hard. She didn't remember the last time she had grass stains on her knees and on her butt and on her side. The ropes got going again, and this time Inez jumped in. She jumped in and jumped six or seven times, then jumped out. Her suit stayed pretty. Then she put an arm around Ada and said, "I wouldn't have done that if you hadn't." When it was Becca and Ada's turn to turn, Delila jumped into the ropes.

Eventually, it was time to eat. Seated at a picnic table, Ada brought the sandwich to her mouth and she took one great big bite. She closed her eyes and chewed. If there hadn't been so many children everywhere about, she would have said right out loud, "A spicy hot fried fish sandwich made right is as good as sex." Only it wasn't. She put the sandwich down.

She had forgotten about the zing. Her zing wasn't in the

sandwich. Her zing was jumping in the ropes. Her zing was dancing. She got up, and she and Preach showed the young kids the Stroll, and showed the old folks they still could stroll. Somebody started handing out icy paletas. Ada got a hibiscus-flower one. It was purple and it made her lips look pretty, but it wasn't a plum. There was no acid to set off the sweet.

Bunny came up to her, rolling a hula hoop. Bunny wanted to try hooping with Ms. Preach. Bunny stood right close to Ada and let Ada's hips do most of the work. As the plastic hoop spun round them, Ada realized Bunny was at least ten pounds lighter than she had been at the beginning of the year. Bunny was no longer in a pudge predicament. Ada was prouder than proud.

When they had hooped till Ada was panting, Bunny dropped to a blanket and grabbed her supper, grilled halibut wrapped in lettuce. Ruth and Naomi had figured that recipe translation out. With hot sauce, of course. New hot fish sandwiches. When Bunny started delicately nibbling on hers, making sure not to get any sauce on her T-shirt, Keshawn called her Miss Priss. Bunny shook a strong fist at him, and Keshawn ran off, laughing.

Ada grabbed her new hot fish sandwich and settled onto a blanket with the girls to eat it all with big bites. When the sauce dribbled onto her lips, she licked it back. She told her girls the recipe was the best birthday present they could have given her. Then she told them, "There's not a thing in the world you can't eat one bite of. And never eat more than two bites of anything decadent. But it's nice to eat something you can let loose on!"

She looked around the park, searching for the man she loved. Lucius. He saw her looking for him. Soon he made his way across the park to Ada. It was that kind of good day. When

Lucius settled in beside her with the abandon that belongs to true feast days, with a plastic plate with two fish sammiches on it, Ada kissed him.

"It time for the big dog to eat," said Lucius.

Ada put up a prayer that he was talking about more than fish-fry food. She knew that compared to the other ladies, she looked a little old-fashioned. All in white, she could be a nurse or an attendant in one of the fainting Baptist churches. She hoped she looked real good to Preach.

Healthing became Ada. The way her feet didn't hurt, the way her shoulders didn't hurt, the way her back didn't hurt. She felt these absences as pleasures.

The presence of her girls, seeing her look better than they had seen her in years, was a greater pleasure still.

When most of the guests had left and the trash had been tied up into big black garbage bags and someone had ridden Queenie around the corner for her early bedtime, the family and some of the closest friends gathered on picnic benches and opened presents and drank coffee from thermoses as the first stars came out.

Most of the presents were accessories. Maceo had planned it.

"Your mama used to say all a woman needs to get through life is a good name, a big smile, and the proper props: a great scarf, a fabulous pair of shoes, an alligator purse, some glamorous sunglasses (my gift), and ladylike gloves. Since all your other sizes are changing, we decided to get you the good props," said Maceo proudly.

Ada took the scarf and tied it around her neck. She threw the purse over her shoulder and put the sunglasses on like a headband; she slipped out of the shoes she had been wearing and into the shoes she had been given.

She no longer looked like a nurse or a church attendant.

Looking at herself in the Tahoe's side mirror, walking back to the car in the parking lot, Ada realized for the very first time that looking good could add to feeling good. She let out the last good-time holler of the evening, "In the immortal words of James Brown, 'I feel good.'"

The little dog had to eat, too. That night. With the little bowl of plums sitting on their chest of drawers, Ada invited Preach to her body. He declined the invitation.

Next morning, as soon as the twins hit the front door in a taxi to the airport, Ada called the divorce lawyer.

42

UNI UP: GET YOURSELF A UNIFORM FOR DAY AND FOR NIGHT

JOEL ANGEL, ESQUIRE, couldn't see Ada till noon. Aside from being a member of the vestry and having the office closest to the Manse, Joel Angel, Esquire, was the lawyer who had drafted up their wills and handled the small matters to do with Preach's father's estate.

He was surprised by Ada's call, and relished this moment of power. More so than in vestry meetings, it felt as if the future of the church was in his hands. He had no intention of letting either party walk out wanting a divorce or in search of a lawyer who might actually help his pastor and his First Lady move toward the dissolution of the marriage. He had let Ada make the appointment and notified her that he would be notifying Preach, as he was the family's lawyer. He said that if they decided to move forward, he could help them each find counsel that would work in tandem for the benefit of all involved. But Joel Angel would not let push get to shove. Thinking that a noon appointment would give Ada time to cool off and Preach time to prepare to grovel, without leaving either to brood too long, he set the time.

Noon worked perfect for Ada. It was time enough to get on the treadmill and try to hold on to what was left of her mind before heading to KidPlay.

There was a hole in Ada's biker shorts. She noticed it just as she was about to wriggle into them and head out to the Dayani Center.

The day before, on the treadmill before leaving for the park and her party, she had told herself, and told herself, nothing was irritating her. She had told herself she was imagining things.

But she hadn't been. If there was a hole in her bike shorts, and there was, some of the pudge of her thigh would have barged out of the hole, forming a round, brown bubble. Every step she had taken, the seam of the other leg of the biker shorts had grated against the naked pudge, chafing and chapping her skin.

She spread her legs—she sought and found evidence, the slightly red circle, then thanked God for unbroken skin.

She took another look at the hole. This time she looked because the hole was a funny little triumph. She poked her finger through the hole, oddly delighted.

She had walked far enough to fray fabric. She had worn something out that wasn't herself. It was her anti–John Henry moment. She had *almost* hurt herself—she *had* worn the pants out.

She grabbed another pair of biker shorts to walk in, and her iPod, and headed for Dayani. On foot. Victorious. When she got there, she hopped on the treadmill and cranked up "Spike Driver Blues." It wasn't the only John Henry song on her iPod, but it was her favorite. Ada thought a lot about the hammer that killed John Henry. She loved the way Big Joe declared he wouldn't let John Henry's hammer kill him. Ada wasn't going to let it kill her either. No, sir. She sang along way too loud and didn't care who looked. Another victory.

Then she was humming along to another John Henry song she loved, "Nine Pound Hammer." How could she roll when her wheels had come off? She couldn't except she put them back on. Listening to "Nine Pound Hammer" she was ready to do just that.

Ada had a strange relation to tools. Until this day she had thought them dangerous, like John Henry's hammer, or unnecessary, like fancy cooking equipment. She didn't believe a craftsman was only as good as his tools. She couldn't. She was Temple's daughter.

Healthing had taught her different. Having the right tools, and taking care of her tools, helped get the job done. Tools facilitate and buffer. And just at that moment, wearing out a tool, instead of wearing out her skin, was a big triumph. She could, and did, throw the shorts away and start again. And she prayed she would walk enough to wear out another pair.

As she pondered tools on her treadmill, she asked herself what else she needed in her tool kit. Quickly her thoughts went to clothes—to the stuff that went under the props that she had been given. She needed some new everyday clothes. She was tired of walking around in sweatpants and a raincoat.

She was especially tired of it if she was about to get a divorce.

An acronym and a slogan occurred to her at once: Keep it simple, sexy. She liked calling herself sexy where some would call themselves stupid. And she knew that part of keeping it simple was to have a uniform for day and for night.

Many people had black. She didn't want that. Except Preach liked black, and it was cheap and simple and sexy, and her proper props would set it off right. Besides, she knew it: Divorce was a kind of death. If she was getting divorced, her go-to uniforms might as well look like mourning. Black would be her go-to color.

She would buy some size-10 black dresses, stretchy and knitty and good quality, and she would fit them. She would get two good day dresses and a good night dress. The dresses would be a uniform. The uniform was a cushion and a signal, a tool. It said, I have figured out how to look good now. She liked it. And she could afford it.

She had sold an Oscar Schmidt Stella Jumbo twelve-string guitar with a peculiar provenance. Which also meant she had enough money to pay the divorce lawyer.

Joel Angel stood in front of his great big desk with arms outstretched. Ada and Preach sat frosty in Angel's beautiful large chairs. Angel had asked who wanted to start. He had expected it would be Ada, as it was Ada who had called, wanting to file for divorce. No one was saying anything. No one had said anything for too long.

"Well, Ada, what grounds were you thinking of?"

"I think it's called . . ." Ada couldn't finish her sentence.

Preach was clearing his throat. "You need to leave the room." He was staring at Joel Angel.

"This is my office."

"And we need it. Right now."

Joel Angel looked at Ada. She nodded assent.

"I'm safe with him. I don't know if he's safe in here with me and that heavy-looking paperweight I see on your desk, but he can take his chances."

Joel Angel nodded his head in very grudging assent.

"Fifteen minutes," said Joel Angel.

Angel left the room, curious about who would be standing when he got back.

When they were alone again, Preach placed his chair right across from Ada's and took a seat. Their knees touched. He took her hands in his. She took hers out of his. She put them back. Much as she didn't want to, she still trusted him.

"What is it?" asked Ada.

"The money, you being my congregant, not just my wife, the people calling all day and all night, everyone looking to me to be a big wheel because the church is grown, the getting fifty, the high-blood-pressure medicine, I . . . I . . . ."

"Slept with someone else."

"No."

"Started gambling?"

"No."

"What?"

"Can't perform. The big dog's too tired to stand up and eat."

"Winky's on the blink?"

"Ada."

"Handle your stuff! There's medicine for that."

"I can't go into the pharmacy and get those pills and have every Negro in north Nashville know!"

"Rob a drugstore. Get some samples."

"I've been seeing a head doctor, pro bono, trying to get everything in order . . . I'm too young for this."

"We are at our half century. Get the little pill."

"I want to take you on a anniversary trip, but I was waiting till I had this situation under control."

"You let me worry I wasn't pretty enough, and you were cheating, because you too proud to handle your stuff? I'm not sure I believe you that stupid. Some men need Viagra because they trying to do too many women . . . I saw that on *Big Love*."

"That's TV. That ain't you and me."

"Sometimes TV is just like real life."

"I love you, Ada."

"How often do you *want* to love on me, lately?"

"Every day, baby."

"It's hard for me to believe the big dog isn't barking. Somewhere. I need a few days to think on all of this. *If* we gonna have a reunion, we both have some getting ready to do. You got to get that pill. I may need to beat you half to death once, first. Or put you in some time-out for messing with me over nothing, over mythic-Mandingo-male drama. I don't want a mythic big wink. I want your big wink, or maybe I will want it, in a week. I don't know if I believe you."

"Come over here and let me half show you."

"Naw."

Preach gave Ada his best pout. Ada gave him a smile. He sidled on over and kissed her on the lips. She opened her mouth. His tongue distracted and his fingers slid up her thigh and into her panties. In a few minutes she was sighing like a happy old married woman.

They walked out, past Joel Angel, Esquire, thanking him profusely for he didn't know what. Ada looked so satisfied, Joel Angel, Esquire, wondered if his preacher and his First Lady had resolved their differences on his sofa.

43

FRONT-LOAD: EAT BEFORE
YOU GO TO PARTIES;
DRINK WATER BEFORE MEALS

WITH WEDDING SEASON in full swing, Ada felt like an engaged virgin, lusting and uncertain. She and Preach had picked a day and a place to revisit their vows and their bodies. Privately. At the beach on an anniversary trip. Willie and Joel Angel had been all too happy to loan their house at Seaside. Ada was excited and anxious. The exciting part was, she and Preach were a bit like strangers to each other now. And the anxious part was, she and Preach were a bit like strangers to each other now. Had all his little flirtations been a way to mask ED? Or, had Winky been on the blink because he felt guilty for cheating?

She was counting on ignorance being bliss. So far it was a motley bliss—but bliss nonetheless. Ada had never in her life been as excited about wedding season as she was this one that would end with their—Big Bang.

With full-on sexing on the horizon, it was time to put the finishing touches on her sizing and her primping.

She was trying to knock off and down fifteen pounds that were hugging her tighter than a punch-drunk boxer in the twelfth round hugs the about-to-be-champ. She took that as a sign she was about to win.

And she also took it as sign to work just a little bit harder. She had gone to nine weddings in four weeks and gained three pounds. Approaching the tenth, she decided to reinvent her definition of both the good wedding guest and appropriate wedding behavior.

She would imbibe every noncaloric detail, not only the scent and sight of the flowers but also the soft of the petals and the poke and scratch of green fronds and leaves. She would lift the goblet for the wine, feel the heft and see the sparkle, but she would have it filled with water. She would not only smile at the bow on the back of the chair and the bows in the little cousins' hair, she would touch their smooth shine.

And she would carry and share the kit she took to every wedding over which her husband was presiding: needles and thread and tiny safety pins, an extra set of wedding bands, an antinausea patch, extra pairs of pantyhose in at least three different shades, an extra two hundred dollars, three sizes of tampons and thin pads and thick pads, a package of condoms, a few travel-size bottles of mouthwash, and a package of chewing gum.

And Ada would dance every dance she was asked to dance, with little boys, with old men, with whomever it was that needed being taken off the bridal party's hands.

And she would admire the colors and the folds of the linens and the sparkle of the table-toppers, as she took a napkin to her mouth, or as the cloth brushed her knee. She would even sip a tiny bit of champagne when the appropriate moment came.

As for the food, she would eat whatever lettuce was available, undressed, and exactly four other small bites of whatever it was least distracting or wasteful to have four bites of.

And she would not be hungry. She would not be hungry because she would eat at home before she went to the wedding. Halfway through wedding season, she had figured it out.

The thing to do was arrive with a full tummy. Like the thing to do at the start of a meal or twenty minutes before a meal was to drink a glass of water or maybe eat half a grapefruit: front-load. Before a wedding, she did a big front-load, then allowed the sight and scents and feel and talk and sway of the reception to delight every sense but the tongue.

This was easy to do when the meal was a buffet and the food so-so. It was harder when the food was good.

It was hardest if the dinner was seated and the food was amazing. And there was a lot of that. Black folk love a delicious wedding. When the food was amazing, she would remind herself that this was not the last great dinner she would sit down to. And amazing as the meal was, it was not as amazing as the bride, or the love in the room.

Before she went out that night, she ate a special frozen Kashi meal, Chicken Florentine, because it reminded her a bit of Romeo and Juliet and a little of hotel wedding banquet food. She planned to feast at the wedding reception on the sights and sounds and touch and love in the room.

Until she got to the museum where the tenth reception of her wedding season was being held, and read the seating chart, she didn't know how very fine a feast it could be.

Matt Mason was on the seating chart. Matt Mason had come to the wedding. He was a distant cousin of the groom's. He had RSVP'd at the last moment.

When the mother of the bride told her all that, Ada hoped the problem would be magically solved by the fact she had lost another twenty-something pounds, and he was a fatty-chaser.

It wasn't. He saw her across the aisle and the pews at the wedding before she had seen him, and he thought, She is the best of both worlds. When he smiled at her across the tables at the reception, it was a smile of unveiled invitation.

Seeing Mason, she knew that if things hadn't played out *exactly* as they had, if Preach hadn't been *afflicted*, if Winky wasn't on the blink, she would have wanted her one dalliance. She would have felt some kind of human right to be free in the place she was sexual. It was disturbing to discover that the sexual reawakening of midlife was as hungry and reckless, was as itchy, as the sexual awakening of adolescence, when the itch must be scratched. She had gone fully latent, fully underground, like a flower bulb in winter. Preach, she sensed, had stayed at a slow burn, his fire never fully extinguished. And he had not come to her for anything this last year, or slightly more. Was it two? Had he gone elsewhere for something? That niggling question did not stand alone. It braided into two other hot topics. What does it mean when the mother is the least sexually experienced person in her family? And, Is it easier to forgive a cheater if you've cheated yourself? Taken together, these three questions had Ada bothered by Mason's presence.

If she knew for sure Preach had cheated, Ada might have lured Mason into a coat closet and made love to him.

But she didn't know, so she took him out onto the dance floor. She thought it the safest place in the room. She was wrong. Matt Mason started singing one of her father's original songs, a song her daddy had sung to her over and over in her babyhood, into her ear, while the band played a long instrumental in the middle of "My Cherie Amour."

Then the band played "The Way You Do the Things You Do," and they didn't talk at all. They danced, and he danced different than Preach. It wasn't better, it wasn't worse, it was different and somehow interesting, particularly because his dancing different caused her to dance different. Delila, dancing with Joel Angel on the other side of the dance floor, smiled at Ada's new "get down" moves. Ada held tighter to Mason. She thought: This man is a bomb I can use to blow up my life—or blow me out of it.

He was talking about a lecture he was giving at the B. B. King Museum in Mississippi. He was joking about getting B.B. to play at one of the girls' weddings. He was teasing her about running away with him to Los Angeles.

These were missteps. She didn't want any old man but Preach at her daughters' weddings. She thought of all the parties her father had played for so many years, all the times he had sung covers instead of originals, and she knew her daddy's blood, sweat, and tears were in the Southland. She would not leave the South. Preach had known that about her before she had known it about herself. Matt Mason was saying there were worlds of good she could do in South Central L.A. And worlds of good she could do with a black educational television show. He said all of this like he was talking as her friend, as a consultant, but he also seemed to say it in a way that was meant to imply she could be more to him. She couldn't be.

"I'm a Dixie girl."

"That's what I love about you."

"I'd wither far from home."

"It could work."

"No."

"Did you ever read about Garrison Keillor and how he left his wife and married his high school sweetheart and took the wife's name out of all his books?"

"Do you mean the Lake Wobegon man?"

"Yeah."

"You comparing me to the *Prairie Home Companion* guy?"

"I'm saying it happens."

"I'm saying, if you see a clock going backward, it's broke."

"That's your daddy talking."

"Naw."

"What is it?"

"That's the Deep South talking."

"That's Preach's wife talking."

"Yes, it is."

"What's he got?"

"You see me. We be we."

"That's silly."

"It isn't."

"What is it?"

"A language I don't have time to teach you."

"Preach is a lucky man."

"You'll get lucky."

The band laid into "Baby Love," and they were back at Hampton, doing the Bop in a dorm room on a Sunday afternoon. They were as close as they were ever going to come to sex, and so far away from it. He left the reception early. Early to bed, he hit the highway first light.

She woke up Sunday morning two pounds lighter than she had been the Sunday before.

In the excitement of her upcoming reunion, these two pounds seemed a paltry thing. And the text from Mason, saying he had met Ruth and some of her friends while touring the Dockery Plantation, seemed absolutely inconsequential.

44

DRAW A MAP OF YOUR BODY

MONDAY MORNING ADA was back at KidPlay, subbing with the five-year-olds, showing them a globe and an atlas of the world. She was pointing out Nashville and North America and the Atlantic and Africa. Somewhere between their questions, and the beginning of their drawing outline maps of Africa, Ada knew she wanted to draw a map of her body.

During her lunch break she closed her office door, took out a sheet of paper, snatched up a few crayons, grabbed a pocket mirror from her purse, and started to draw. She had no skill, but she wasn't trying for something artistic. She achieved the shape of a pear with big watermelon breasts.

Then she started adding details. She began with the toes and went all the way up to her original curly head. On her map she did not wear a China chop. She drew some of the stretch marks. She nodded to the fact that no bones had been broken. She drew on the belly button.

The belly button seemed important. And blighted. When she had had her own daughters, so efficiently, two girls, one pregnancy, her belly had become marbled with the light marks.

It had broken her heart. Later, after the girls had been born, she had gotten back most of the flatness of her belly.

Thinking of that, she drew a cesarean scar on the map, and she put a date. She drew her hymen and put the date it got broken through. She drew the skin tags on her neck and put a date. She drew the lines in her forehead and her knees, and the scar on her knee. In the margins she wrote the details that seemed important. The day her ears were pierced, the year her wisdom teeth were removed. She drew the inner body parts that she could remember and thought important: her heart and kidneys and ovaries and bladder and uterus; and because all of this was somehow related to being under Preach and taking him into her body through the slit between her legs, she drew that.

It was a work in progress. And it was a new rule: Draw a map of your body. If she was leaving something, or some part of herself, behind, she wanted to know what it was.

So she drew a map of Lucius Howard. It was a silhouette of a man with a giant question mark inside it.

45

UPDATE YOUR GOALS

S HE TOLD PREACH she was running down the road to see
Ruth. It was the first outright lie she had ever told him. She
had four names on a list, and none crossed out. Beside the names
were four addresses. Ada was on a truth hunt. It was an overnight trip.

Naptime had done it. She had been sitting in the playground
with baby Jarius on her lap, chanting a Paul Laurence Dunbar
poem, "Little Brown Baby," when two girls sitting nearby
started playing an old tickle game, the one where you pinch and
squeeze and grab after you finger-walk and blow air: "We're going on a treasure hunt, X marks the spot, three big dots and a
question mark! A pinch, a squeeze, a tropical breeze, blood
running down your back got you!"

It was time. The little brown angels were telling her so. She
had gone on her first honeymoon innocent. She needed to go
on her second honeymoon wise. Armed with celery sticks and
turkey jerky, 149 pounds of Ada hit the road.

★   ★   ★

"Are you sleeping with my husband?"

"It took you long enough to ask," the girl said flatly. As if she was almost bored. She was a pretty girl, the color of coffee with a splash of cream. She wore her hair in a little halo of braids. She was wearing a backless dress that made it obvious she wasn't wearing a bra. Her unharnessed breasts were small and round, perfect apples. Her legs were hard biker's legs, and she had a yoga ass. There was one tattoo visible on her ankle and another on the inside of a forearm. On the arm that wasn't tattooed was a silver chain with a heart from Tiffany. It had been a sixteenth-birthday present from Ada and Preach. At the time it seemed the perfect gift; at least, it was the standard present they gave goddaughters on the sixteenth birthday. The heart dangling from the chain on this girl's wrist terrified Ada. She didn't want that heart to be her husband's heart. And if it was her husband's heart, the idea that she had pinned the medal on the child made her want to vomit.

The girl—her name was Thea, and she was twenty-two now—saw the wave of nausea cross Ada's face. Thea didn't know what she was seeing. She let it be what she wanted it to be, her mother's remorse that she had let her stepfather fuck her every day for a week after the year she turned sixteen. Then Thea had stopped it. Blackmailed him. Moved across the country with the money.

"Am I fucking the preacher?" The girl asked her question with the smile she smiled to mask confusion, a smile that looked dumb and smug and pretty. A smile that vexed other girls because it was a smile boys wanted to put themselves inside.

Ada slapped the girl. Slapped the smile right off her. Ada's hand flew up before she could stop it. Her hand was on the girl's face. All at once she felt the hot, hard contact of her flesh against the child's soft skin. She had done something she hadn't meant to do. Her hand just flew up before she could stop it. She just touched the girl before she knew what she was doing. And she wondered if this was exactly how it had been for her husband. His penis got hard before he could stop it. The child said something vulgar and unexpected, and before he knew it, he was touching her face. Ada didn't mean to do it, she just did it. Maybe it had been that way for Preach too.

The absurdity of the entire situation got Ada laughing. Much to her surprise, the girl, Thea, started laughing as well. The slap had brought her to her senses.

"You a mess," the girl told the woman. It was a case of the pot calling the kettle black, but Ada didn't think it wise to point that out. She had slapped a young woman she had known from infancy because she might have been Preach's lover. Only she couldn't believe that. Standing in front of the girl, even with the nasty words said, even with all the girl had implied, it was impossible to believe Preach would steal an inch of innocence.

On the other hand, touching this girl might not be a matter of stealing innocence but rather a matter of swimming in sin. The girl's eyes were older than Ada's own. Her eyes were like the old folks say, older than salt, old as pepper.

"I go to work in an hour. I'm not inviting you into my house. Meet me around the corner at Starbucks."

It was a long twenty minutes. Eventually Thea showed up. Eventually Ada and Thea were seated at a small round table sucking down tall chais.

Ada felt like she had felt sitting in the doctor's office waiting for mammogram results, waiting to find out if her life had turned to shit while she wasn't looking.

"I tried."

"You tried?"

"There were two summers I saw Preach a lot. The first was the summer we got rid of my stepmonster-rapist, and the second was my first summer after college. I had tried to kill myself that first year away. I told him, and he kept me under him the rest of the summer. I ran the paint table at vacation Bible school. He was good to me. He even got me a shelter puppy. I named him Chaos. He was a little dustball. He slept with me in the bed. I carried him to camp in my purse. One day Preach said, looking at me painting Chaos's toenails, "I would like to be Chaos," and it got me to thinking. When we were alone in the art room, later that day, he turned to do something. When he turned back, I was standing there naked except for my sandals and my bracelets and my jewelry. I had pulled the dress up over my head and dropped it on the floor. I didn't wear panties. I still don't wear a bra. So I was just like Eve. He just stared at me. I knew I was good to look at, so that didn't surprise me. I thought he would stare for a moment, then he would come jump on me. I even knew how I wanted to do it. But he didn't move, and I thought he needed some encouragement, so I asked him a question. I asked, 'You ever seen one all grown up and bald? You ever see one pierced?'

"'Lord, child.'

"'I'm nineteen, I'm not a child.'

"'Our second date, my Ada made a box out of playing cards that blew smoke rings.'

279

" 'Bar trick.'

" 'I was impressed.'

" 'When was the last time you slept with your wife?'

" 'I'm not going to answer that question.'

" 'Why?'

" 'It's the wrong question.'

" 'What's the right question?'

" 'When's the last time I wanted to?'

" 'When's the last time you wanted to?'

" 'Right now.'

" 'You looking at me, looking like this, and you want that fat woman?'

" 'That fine fat woman got something make a man crawl over glass and fire to get to again after he get to it once. A whole lot of that is a good thing. And she bought the shoes you're standing in. Put your dress back on.'

" 'You're not getting any.'

" 'I can wait.'

" 'It's that good when you get it?'

" 'It's that good when I get it.' "

Thea shivered as she came to the end of her tale. It was a shiver of relief. It felt good to confess, so she plowed forward.

"I kept a crush on Preach. I've got a boyfriend, but I've kept a crush on Preach. He didn't take it, but the way he pushed it away, I felt special for just being a woman. Wouldn't mind having what it takes to make a man feel the way Preach feel about you."

"Why did you act like you were sleeping with him?"

"I don't know."

And she didn't. She only knew she was sorry. And she was. Ada refused to judge Thea for the betrayal. The child, and she was a child, had been through too much. She was thinking she would go strangle that stepfather, except he was already dead, and if she ever saw that mother again—well, she hoped she didn't.

Ada walked out of the Starbucks door thinking about the magic box she had made of cards a very long time before. And she was thinking that girl's whatnot was not the first one Preach had seen grown and bald. Ada had waxed for a first and near only time, back when waxing was very, very new, back before she got pregnant and dropped out of graduate school. She wanted to prove to Preach divinity school students could be very wholesome and very sexy. She remembered he laughed and told her it looked "too young to fuck." She had slapped him and bitten him for saying "fuck," and then they had made love. So long ago.

The second address was on West End Avenue. On the way Ada pulled into a drugstore where she bought, then guzzled, sixteen ounces of water. Portia, the other preacher's wife, scared Ada. Somewhere between a size 6 and a size 8, she was small but not too small. At five foot eight, she was tall but not too tall. In every way she was what the old folks called one of God's best days of work. Portia was an intimidatingly perfect woman.

And she was the woman Ada had wanted to poison.

Where Ada's house was always clean, fairly neat, and antiquey, Portia's house was immaculately clean, perfectly neat, and modern. Her aesthetic was stark and glossy. Her children, five boys, were tall and lean and usually gone. They did however, show up for all the appropriate holidays: Thanksgiving, and Christmas, and Easter, and birthdays, bringing presents and pictures and clippings of accomplishments. Each was married, and each had a single boy. When the grandsons got together, it was like Portia was a young mother again, except her husband was gone. Everybody thought she would go to pieces when her husband died, but she didn't. After a while it was hard not to notice that widowhood seemed to become the woman.

Portia, once the queen of the frozen chosen, had periods of thaw. Unfortunately, the sun that seemed to be melting her was Ada's very own Preach.

At the beginning, it was just leaving both of them baskets of vegetables on their back porch. That became baskets of the preserves that he loved and the pie that he loved. Eventually a dinner, once a week, appeared as well. When Ada settled deep into her diet and said something about the pies and fried chicken that Portia dropped off being too tempting, Portia used that as an excuse to stop bringing "the family" dinner on Tuesday. She started bringing the preacher lunch on Thursday. And strangest of all, at least to Ada, was when she started baking the communion bread.

Ada hated that. She hated not having thought of it first. She hated not having done it for Preach herself. Portia made Ada feel all kinds of ways inadequate.

Once when she had been invited to Portia's house for a Link meeting, Ada did something awful. She peeked into some of Portia's drawers. Perfect rows of perfectly folded silk cappuccino-colored panties, and perfectly matching C-cup brassieres, one cup spooning the other, filled the top drawer of her lingerie chest. In the next drawer were lace nightgown sets, all in a champagne or light coffee color. Folded in one of the nightgowns was a handkerchief monogrammed with Preach's initials. She prayed Portia was a thief.

Ada looked at the pristine bed with monogrammed linens, and she wondered what sex had been like in it for Portia when her husband was alive. Ada could only imagine it had been efficient. As far as she knew, neither of them liked mess of any kind. But they had had five children, so surely they had had sex. Ada shuddered as she walked out of the room.

Standing on Portia's doorstep, uninvited, ringing the bell, listing to Portia's bell echo through Portia's house, watching her open the door, surprised, Ada was wondering if Preach had ever rolled in Portia's monogrammed linens.

Portia opened the door. Even with a blue bandanna tied round her head, wearing jeans and a denim shirt, Portia looked every inch a frozen mochaccino husband stealer.

"May I come in?"

"Of course."

Portia led Ada through the front hall back to the kitchen—a room Ada had never sat down in, had barely passed through. The kitchen could have been a surgery. Everything was bright and white. There was even a little bowl of eggs on the counter. A Swiffer mop leaning against the refrigerator and a box of Swiffer pads out by the sink, together with the jeans outfit, told Ada Portia had just finished cleaning house. Portia moved the

mop and pads and washed her hands before opening the refrigerator and pulling out two green bottles of Perrier. She offered
one to Ada, and they both took a seat at her kitchen table.

"Are you in love with my husband?"

"A little."

"Is my husband in love with you?"

"Not even a little."

"Have you had sex?"

"No."

"Thank God."

"Thank your husband."

"Did you try?"

"Just after Justin died."

"What happened?"

"I asked him to comfort me. And when I was in his arms, I
asked him if, when he died, he would want you to be comforted
as intimately as possible."

"What did he say?"

"He said he would want you to have anything you needed."

"And then?"

"I said I needed him. And he said, 'Anything Ada might
want, I got to save for Ada.' I told him Justin only wanted me
starched and pressed and dry, still and quiet. I said, God would
understand. And he said it had nothing to do with God or vows
or propriety, just love. He loved you and he couldn't do anything about it. He said he wanted to be my brother.

"I told him it gave me hope to know a man could love a
woman like that.

"He said, once he woke up and there was a feather on you, a

pillow had broke, and he thought for a second he had died and gone to heaven and you were an angel he had made love with. He saw a feather on you and thought you were an angel."

Ada remembered the time the pillow had broken. She had seen the feathers too; she had thought, for a moment, almost the very same thing.

"He'd be too messy and stinky and loud for you," said Ada.

"If I had a man thought I was an angel loving him in heaven, I would set up house in a tent above a pigsty."

Portia rose. She was finished. Ada took in the full measure of her beauty. Ada had thought Preach might be curious to slip between perfectly ironed sheets, or far more sadly, between her perfectly proportioned and thin tapered thighs. She had been mistaken.

Everything about Portia's body was too neat for Preach. When the children had been young and they had all gone to the one or two black homes with swimming pools on Sunday afternoons in the summer, Ada would be in a muumuu and Portia would be in a bikini. You could count her ribs. She remembered telling Portia years before, "You have an amazing body."

Portia had replied, "I have a boy's body, and we grafted some big breasts onto it a thousand years ago. It photographs well."

That summer day, long past, almost forgotten, Ada knew the other preacher's wife was profoundly lonely. She was telling Ada what she should have been telling a best friend. And she told me because I idealized her, she thought. Me, not Preach.

Ada pointed her car toward Sylvan Park. When she arrived at her destination, she reached into her glove box and pulled out a jar of sugar-free peanut butter and a plastic spoon. It was snack time. She didn't want it to be C.J. C.J. was her friend.

C.J. was the fifty-something blonde woman who the kids at Preach's church affectionately dubbed Granola Girl. She had first showed up at Full Love Gospel Tabernacle when she was thirty-two, with two small kids and husband.

Ada had been surprised by the family the first time they showed up at a Sunday service. At the time, they lived just a few doors down from the church. Over doughnuts and coffee in the fellowship hall after the first service, it came out that Granola Girl had lived for a decade on the Farm, the hippie commune where Ada had spent a few weekends growing up. They knew some of the same people; friends had sent them. The slumming hippies were welcomed with open arms.

It was one of the things that was eccentrically endearing about Nashville: It is ringed by utopian communities. The Farm and Rugby, the best known, were polar opposites. The Farm was a haven for a multicultural group of hippies. Rugby was founded by the second sons of British lords.

Granola Girl had roots in both communities. She had grown up going to Rugby on weekends, traveling from a tiny house in Belle Meade, Nashville's most posh neighborhood. One Wednesday night, in the seventies, Granola Girl had gone to a show at the Exit/In where she had met a steel guitar player who called himself Twang, renamed herself Star, and played in a psychedelic country band called Spur.

When she turned eighteen, Twang and Star lit off, not for the territories, like Huckleberry Finn, but for the Farm.

Twang, who didn't like farm work but liked bars and sorority girls more than he had let on, did not last long. Star, who took to midwifery and other people's baby-tending, settled in for a long stay.

Eventually, a decade of babies and bickering and working every day left Star played out.

She asked her parents if she could move back home. First thing when she hit town, she ran straight to Ivan, the hairstylist her friends from growing up said was the miracle worker who could transform her brownish hippie frizz to Belle Meade blonde.

Ivan worked his magic. Granola Girl took possession of the house, repossession of her life, and started calling herself C.J.

She enrolled in TSU, very, very quietly, because the historically black university gave scholarships to white kids. She got a nursing degree and a husband, who wanted to be in a band, but was a lawyer in a Music Row law firm. She had a boy and then a girl. Eventually she started getting bored. Then she started volunteering with the Baptists, after meeting Preach at his church.

For a decade, C.J. had led a neonatal prep class out of the Full Love Gospel Tabernacle basement. She had helped many, many babies come into the world healthy; she had helped many mamas deliver unafraid.

Granola Girl was days away from her fiftieth birthday when she opened the door for Ada. She was excited to see Ada on her doorstep. The church usually gave her a birthday present, and Ada usually delivered it. Granola Girl showed Ada into her living room, a mixture of Indian rugs, family antiques, flea-market pieces that had been smartly refinished, and DIY extravaganzas, thinking she knew the purpose of the visit.

Ada nestled onto a sofa bed made of wooden packing pallets and blankets. Granola Girl settled into a painted director's chair across from her. An easel obscured Ada's view of Granola Girl. The oil-in-progress on the easel depicted the library in Rugby.

On a table near the easel was a pot of tea, two cups, and local honey. Ada had called to announce she was on her way. Granola Girl poured Ada a cup. Ada squeezed in a bit of honey, then took a sip.

"I hope you like sassafras."

"I thought it was illegal now?"

Granola Girl shrugged. "The law is not in this room."

"Happy birthday." Ada pulled a small suede bag from her purse. She handed it to Granola Girl, who opened the package. It was a pouch full of beautiful one-of-a-kind beads.

"Nice. Very, very nice. I can use some of these in my half-century necklace."

Granola Girl got out of her chair and walked over to a desk on which there were many, many tiny drawers. Opening one, she took out an intricate piece and fastened it about her neck. It almost looked Egyptian. Granola Girl sat back down in the chair and began fingering the beads as she talked. She was rubbing what appeared to be a black pearl.

"It's a reckoning. A reckoning for my birthday. The numbers of babies delivered. This"—she now pointed to the black pearl—"was the first black baby I delivered. Years lived. Concerts attended. Men kissed. Lovers had—"

"Lovers—you cheat?"

"I don't do everything. I do what wives don't like to do and hippie chicks . . ."

"And that would be?"

"BJs."

"Blow jobs?"

"Exactly."

"God!"

"They can be very reviving. BJs are not really cheating."

"You are using Clinton/Lewinsky logic?"

"I didn't do it in the wife's house, or with anyone working under me."

"Did you ever offer one to my husband?"

"In my thirty-something youth, and maybe once in my forties."

"What did he say?"

"He said he was already completely taken care of in that regard."

"Thank God!"

"Then I tried to blow it off by saying BJs weren't really sex, and he interrupted me and told me that when you, I will never forget his phrase, 'addressed him with your mouth most quietly,' it was 'most decidedly sex.' He said it was entering into the center of the universe."

"My baby said that?"

"Your man said that. Last year I asked him what he had meant when he said it. It wasn't a come-on. I wanted to know. He told me. He said, when he entered into your body in the regular way, it was like entering into your soul. But when you took him in your mouth, he felt like he was entering into the center of the universe."

"My baby said that?"

"Why do you think he wanted a shower in the office during the renovation?"

"I haven't been able to figure that one out."

"He thought he was coming home too funky for you to want him."

"Funky how?"

"Funky playing basketball with the young bronze gods that run through that church basement. All the hospital germs. The plain smell of death."

"Do you think he cheats on me?"

"He'd betray God before he betrayed you."

"Good people cheat. I'm looking at one."

"If he said it once, he said it a dozen times. 'God's got everybody. Ada got me.'"

"And he got me."

"You ever don't want him, pass him along."

Some say the distance from Nashville to Sewanee is two hours and one hundred years. Crossing Monteagle Pass, Ada was thinking about distances and dangerous angles. Once she was inside the town limits of Sewanee, all she could think about was cozy.

And taking a walk. As strange a day as it was, Ada was walking her thirty minutes before she knocked on her last door of the day. Once inside the Sewanee gates, first easy place to park, she did. Taking note of the time on her phone, she walked seventeen minutes straight ahead, then thirteen minutes back. Then she did ten more minutes. Her last stop might be her hardest.

Ada and Virgil sat across from each other in front of the fire in a room Virgil called his parlor. The room was tailored and plaid, in every way moderate. If a Brooks Brothers suit could be a house, it would be Virgil's sensible cottage.

When she came up to Monteagle or to Sewanee, she preferred to stay in Clifftops, with its modern and extravagant mansions, rather than in the Assembly, with the picture-perfect cottages, where Virgil lived. She had felt too loud, too black, and too bluesy for the Assembly.

Virgil fit right in. Part of it was the collar. The simple black Episcopal pants and shirt and jacket didn't hurt either. But Virgil didn't need the collar to achieve black Anglo-Saxon Protestant respectability. He was trim. Quiet. Reserved. Fastidious. Classic. Right now he was playing Bach's *Art of Fugue*, and he was pouring Ada a second glass of a fine malbec to go with the Stilton cheese he had already served. She was sitting on Virgil's plaid couch, clutching a cashmere pillow, charmed and worried.

She had walked into the pages of the southern preppie handbook—the entry that read "black Episcopal." On his walls were all the books they read, books she had seen on the shelves of certain of her Link sisters' homes as well: Shakespeare and C. S. Lewis and Evelyn Waugh and *Black Ice* and the collected speeches of Wallace Thurman and Martin Luther King and more Shakespeare and always a King James Bible from childhood.

"Which room does Preach stay in when he stays with you?"

"The library—it has a pull-out couch."

"You have three guest bedrooms, and he sleeps in the library?"

"He likes sleeping with the books. He likes the fireplace. He likes being on his own floor and having his own bathroom. I like having him in a room I love."

"That sounds stranger than you meant it to sound, or did you mean it to sound strange?"

"It sounds stranger than I meant. I always put a stack of books by the bed for him. I like to prepare for guests."

"He told me that."

"He told you."

"He tells me everything."

"Does that sound stranger than you meant it to sound, or did you mean it to sound strange?"

"Do you pick from what you've been reading, at random, or for who's coming?"

"For who's coming."

"What did you pick for me?"

"*Waiting to Exhale.*"

"You funny."

"I thought you would enjoy a Terry McMillan heart-lift."

"Does Preach sleep well in this house?"

"I hope so. We stay up fairly late figuring out how to fix the world and the church and how to best confess to God our sins so that we might be forgiven. But he's down in the kitchen fresh in the morning, so yes."

"Your fishing trips are fishing trips?"

"Our fishing trips are fishing trips. I did put the *New Yorker* with *Brokeback Mountain* by the bed. It's probably still up there somewhere."

"Did he read it?"

"He never said. He never said if he read *Gentleman Jigger* either. Or *Other Voices, Other Rooms*. The only book he ever really talked about was *A River Runs Through It*. I told him I was in love with Emily Lloyd. He didn't see the attraction. I liked that."

"Episcopal priests can marry."

"Not a man. Not and be black and stay happy on this happy mountain."

"That's sad."

"And it would have to be a white man. There are few black men up on this mountain, except for Lucius, when he comes to visit."

"That's sad, too."

"I spend a lot of time alone in this house, reading."

"Have you and my husband ever been lovers?"

"If I say yes, will you run out of the house screaming into the night?"

"Probably."

"Then I would like to be able to say yes and see that."

"Are you saying yes?"

"No."

"No?"

"I invited him once. But he turned me down."

"In this house?"

"No. Out on the Domain. I had just caught a fish. It seemed the moment. It was 1997. The twins were about ten. He pretended he didn't know what I was saying to him. Last year I tried again. He seemed a bit lost. I was thinking he might be missing me, missing us, missing what we never got to be. He was missing you. We were sitting in this very room. There was a fire, and he said, 'You know, once, she wrote the entire Song of Songs all over my body.'"

"He shouldn't have told that."

"He told it."

Virgil closed his eyes. He was back in the room with her Preach, his Lucius.

" 'No, she didn't,' I said.

" 'Yes, she did,' he said.

" 'That might make me want a woman,' I said.

" 'You've never been with a woman?' he asked.

" 'I didn't say I never been with one. I said, I never wanted one.' That's what I told him. Then I said, 'What I never been with is a man.'

" 'Go find your true love,' he said.

" 'Even if it's a man?' I asked.

" 'Even if it's a man,' he said.

"Then he said, 'I would trade anything for two days of me and Ada when we good. When we good, I can do what I'm s'posed to do because God didn't make me wait for heaven to taste heaven. Sometimes I get a preview.'

" 'What kind of theology is that?' I asked.

" 'Baptist Sunday School 101,' he said.

" 'I thought that a soul was sufficient to know God,' I said.

" 'Nope. True love is a preview of heaven, and you do what you got to, to get it.'

" 'No wonder your pews are full.' "

Virgil opened his eyes. He was back with Ada.

"He said I was a preview of heaven?"

"A foretaste."

"Wow."

"Did you really write the whole Song of Songs over him in lipstick?"

"Just the best verses."

"I might just have to walk down and off this mountain one day—if I could find me a you."

She kissed him on the lips, as a gift from Preach.

When she went to sleep that night, she found the McMillan beside her bed. She read for a good long hour, then put down the book and searched for a pen and paper. She had a new rule: Update your goals.

An affair with Matt Mason was no longer on her list. Finding out if Preach was cheating was no longer on her list. She turned out the light.

In the dark, Ada exhaled, too.

46

CREATE YOUR OWN SPA WEEK

H ER HUSBAND WAS faithful. Lucius loved her. And she loved him. She got into her shower and made herself quake, remembering. It had almost been a year since they'd made love. His birthday. She had finally remembered their last time.

She had brought him breakfast in bed, and he had put the tray on the floor and pulled her into the bed. She was wearing a white cotton gown. Her teeth were brushed, but his were not, so they had not kissed. He had not taken off her gown. He had simply pulled her on top of him. They fit together so well and so quickly, it was over before it began. Or she thought it might have been, except it wasn't. He was just beginning. He unbuttoned the top of her nightgown. With one hand he found a breast. With the other he was drawing a pattern of flowers on her knee, a pattern that was trailing toward the top of her inner thigh. Then the phone rang, and he embraced her, not intending to answer it, and then it stopped ringing after two rings and then it started back again, and he picked it up, because that was how the old black folks signaled trouble—two rings, a hang-up, and a callback. Someone had died.

She had rolled back in the bed, sticky, wet, and abandoned. He left to go do God's work, and she cried.

That had been a day of rapid decline. In the middle of life the body changes quickly. Decline is never slow. Decline is always too fast. But that day had been faster than all others.

On this new day, as the water pounded down on her almost firm-feeling body, Ada cried again. They had found themselves lost in a dry and bitter desert. She no longer knew the most intimate truths about his body, about how quick her kiss could turn him ready for her, or even what "ready" for her was these days. She feared needing a bit of help from a jelly in a tube; she feared that as a final ignominy that would be too hard to face. Maybe that shame was why she had not let him approach her. But he loved her. He had stayed within garden walls, he had not strayed. She could face whatever she had to face. Just as, years before, she had fumbled with a diaphragm before he had been snipped, a little bit of lube was no more barrier than a little bit of spermicide and a rubber dome. And that was no barrier at all—she had the twins to prove it.

This dry time had at first been a bitter chasm in the fabric of love that threatened to unravel the marriage. Now the dry time was not a chasm, it was a hiatus. She could smell sex near.

But first she wanted a time to prepare. This would be no poke and sample. It would be pure claim, pure surrender, pure fusion without confusion, aided by science.

She would accept his invitation, and she would double down.

She would take two weeks off work—one week to prepare and one week to be with him. She would make a spa for herself.

She had arrived at the place where she could make a feast of her body for her husband. She would be his garden and his feast. He would be her garden and her feast.

She would emerge from her cocoon. She would get into his bed, and he would get into her body. And they would have high and low help from the pharmacy. He would get his prescription. She would slough off—exfoliate the layers of dead skin, polish her hair and her toes, remove every stray hair and polish every hair that should be there. She would reread the *Kama Sutra* and do Kegel exercises. She would get a full-out expert mani-pedi. She would go to yoga classes. She would get massaged on a dry table and in water. She would know the body she was giving away—and she would know it as beautiful. She would be a good gift and await an excellent gift of him.

If he would join her, if he would leave the church, the only mistress she was prepared to tolerate, behind for a week, they would leave the desert. Or discover they would not leave it again—or at least not together.

A week of him after a week of spa. Ada turned off the shower and grabbed a towel. She dried her hair, then wrapped the towel around her. It went all the way round. And it wasn't a beach towel. Another triumph.

She would listen to all of their favorite love songs. She would not look at old pictures. She wanted to be with this man now, this new man. She put a funny song on her iPod: "If you're thinking you want a stranger, there's one coming home."

She was prepared to disconnect with everything that wasn't Lucius and wasn't her body. The world would be there when they got back.

But first she had to let it fall away.

The problem was the lake. She had thought the problem would be town: KidPlay and the church. KidPlay and the church were okay.

Inez had volunteered to cover for Ada at KidPlay for both weeks. More important, Loretha, Bunny's mama, and Keshawn's mama had promised to talk to the other mamas about keeping "drama" to minimum during Ada's absence. On Preach's end, turned out the deacons were delighted to fill in at the church. But what about the lake?

The lake was a different story. Her parents couldn't manage a week without her, and there wasn't a person Ada or Lucius knew that they would allow in the house that could do the work of tending them and theirs. And if she sent a stranger, Bird would just tell them to leave.

Delila had an idea. Ada executed it. Ada hired a team of Mexican ladies to fill in for her out on the lake while she was gone.

The ladies didn't speak English, and her mother didn't speak Spanish. Ada, who spoke a fair amount of Spanish, told the ladies to do what they thought they should do—and trusted Bird didn't have the Spanish to countermand her instructions. And there was also always the possibility Bird would sleep through the cleaners' visits.

That didn't happen. The first time that they went to the

lake, the time Ada went with them, to show them around the place and make the introductions that needed to be made, what happened was, the ladies saw stuff they needed, and Bird gave it to them.

"I didn't want it thrown away. Didn't say nothing about giving it to someone who needed it."

"Thank you, Mama."

"You welcome, Ada."

Bird pulled the big doorknob ring from her finger. She pressed it into her daughter's hand.

"This one's real. Sell it. Hire somebody to clean out here. Tote this stuff away."

"For real, Mama?"

"For real. Go get your man. You looking good, gal."

And she was. Even before spa week got started.

47

GET BETTER HAIR DOWN THERE

THAT NIGHT MACEO, muttering about Buddy Bolden, died. He left Bird and Temple all his old suits and shoes. Left his old instruments to the W. O. Smith Music School. Left Ada his gold watch.

Bird sang "Welcome Table" at the funeral. It was the first time she had sung out of her house in a decade. Her house was too cluttered for the repast, so they had it at Ada's. Bird walked all around that house, asking for Ada, who was standing right beside her. After her mama left, Ada said, "I guess my mother's got her very own kind of diabetic retinopathy."

The earth kept spinning, just like eighty-five-year-old Maceo would have wanted it to have done. Everybody at the wake said it: "Maceo would have wanted y'all to have a Big Time. Go on yo' trip, gal."

Six days later, spa week was almost over. It was Saturday night. Preach was putting the final touches on the next morning's sermon. His bag was already packed and waiting in the front hall.

Ada had one thing left to do. She locked the bathroom door. From the back of her tampon drawer she pulled out a box of very special hair dye. She was a grown woman and proud of it. She wasn't waxing her privates bald as a prepubescent child, a porn star, or a 2009-era grown-twenty-five-year-old.

While Lucius put the final touches on his sermon, she put the final touches on her twat.

Thank God for Amazon. She hadn't had to go in anywhere and buy her box of Betty. She was going to get better hair down there. No gray. But first she had to use Bikini Nair on the stragglers.

First she took care of the sparse but distinct "happy trail," the little hairs on her belly that led from her belly button to her private parts. Noting that none of those hairs were gray, she smiled at the perversity of aging bodies, squeezed on a little depilatory foam, set a timer, waited the suggested minutes, then wiped off the foam and the hair with a washcloth.

Lying on a beach towel spread across the bathroom tile, she repeated the process on her inner upper thighs, then stood at the mirror to inspect her work. It needed a bit of refinement. It was time for a little scissor work. Armed with a tiny pair from her new manicure kit, she trimmed her triangle, taking care to only touch the few that were clearly longer or straighter than the rest. She trimmed only the obstreperous.

She took a quick shower, washing her breasts with antibacterial soap. When she got out of the shower she took a tweezers to the five—three on one, two on the other—fine but dark hairs she believed distracted from the beauty of her breasts.

Her woman fur was halfway to looking great. She took a deep

breath. She wasn't doing Botox, she wasn't going under the scalpel. She was taking advantage of the fact he hadn't seen her down there in the clear light of day since the gray had sprouted.

Permanent dye. No washout color. You didn't want it coming off on his tongue. She ripped open the box and got started. Forty-five minutes later, she would be head-to-toe beautiful, and she would know it.

As she lay sprawled on her bathroom floor with her legs splayed, dark brown goo slathered between them, singing along to the Godfather of Soul, it was clear to God, and anyone else watching, for real and for sure: Ada loved her some Lucius.

She cranked up the James Brown. She laughed to think that an entire generation of rappers and rock stars had probably never seen a woman with any hair down there—and James Brown had probably seen his share of gray.

Whatever. Lucius Howard liked a cute black thatch, and that's exactly the snatch Ada Howard was going to have.

Again, now.

48

SEIZE THE PROPER PROPS:
SCARVES, SHOES, PURSES,
SUNGLASSES, AND RESPECT

SUNDAY IN THE South struts in, sun and chin up, color-fully loud church hats on, just after the low-down dark deliciousness of Saturday night creeps off.

The older Ada got, the more she liked the juxtaposition.

What she had originally loved best about belonging to an independent tabernacle instead of a "regular" Episcopal or Baptist or Methodist church was, she never knew what Preach was going to say or how the service would be shaped.

Over the years this had become less and less true. Living the week with Preach, she could usually predict the subject of his Sunday sermon. Preach rarely surprised Ada on Sunday at eleven.

It was Women's Day Sunday. This year Ada suspected Preach might talk about their daughters, Naomi and Ruth, or the young women of the church. Usually Women's Day is for talking about mothers and grandmothers and elder women icons like Harriet Tubman and Sojourner Truth and Fannie Lou Hamer. Previous years Preach had talked about Queenie, had talked about Ada, had even talked about Bird. But Preach had doodled the phrase *the power and the possibility and the promise* on his breakfast napkin, along with *gift* and *God's best gift*. That was the tip-off.

Ada knew God's best gift was babies, was children, so Ada knew what Preach was preaching about—daughters, young women.

Sidling into the front pew, pink church hat on her head, Ada felt good looking a little glamorous. In a twenty-year-old size-8 white brocade suit stretched tight across her butt with the help of Spanx, a girdle, God, and an itty-bit of seam-letting-out, Ada felt just a little like a bit of God's glory was giving her a Women's Day glow. If the back seam of the skirt didn't rip as she flopped down on her knees and prayed to prepare herself for the service, she would know God loved her.

She flopped. The skirt didn't rip. God loved her. She had been waiting a very long time for a clear sign. Now that she had it, she seized on it. She told God what she really wanted. It had been a long time coming, this telling. She wanted a little—sometime soon, please, if it wasn't asking too much—toe-curling Saturday night s-e-x, crazy, hot, married love, s-e-x that promised love without ending, adventure without fear, and gave good sense-rattling pleasure beyond knowing. She wanted her husband to have gone to the doctor, gotten the prescription, and gotten it filled.

Her prayer was interrupted by Bunny bringing her a corsage made out of orange Kleenex tissue flowers and a safety pin. Bunny beamed as Ada attached the flower to the lapel of her suit.

The church was full way before eleven o'clock. Mothers and grandmothers and beloved aunts and great-aunts and even sisters were surrounded by people who loved them. Three pews back, Bunny's mother was wearing five pink flowers pinned to the bosom of her dress. Eleven o'clock came. The choir sang. Preach was ensconced near the altar in the chair in which he always sat. As the church rolled into the first hymn, Preach nodded for the head usher's attention. After Preach whispered into his ear, and he gestured to his team, the ushers proceeded to pass the offering baskets during the hymn. It was a change from the usual. Some of the old heads and many of the young heads nodded their assent to Preach getting the money part out before he got to the worship.

Preach moved from his chair by the altar to the pulpit. He stood quietly in his pulpit, looking out at his congregation, for longer than anyone remembered him standing without saying a word. He seemed to be looking into the faces of the women. Drinking them in, nodding, smiling at the beauty. Then he stepped out of his pulpit, took off his robe with a flourish, and laid it on the altar, reminding Ada a little of a cross between James Brown and Father Divine. This time, when he looked out at the congregation, he looked straight at Ada. There was a look of surprise on her face as Preach walked back into his pulpit, displaying the plain gray suit beneath his preacher's robe.

"I have a confession to make. Due to the nature of this confession, it's a good thing my mama and my wife's mama don't come to church. It's Women's Day, and I didn't love my wife last night. It's Women's Day, but I am standing here to tell you I have been unfaithful and idolatrous. The church is Christ's bride. And I have been acting like she was mine. God will take care of his church. God gave me Ada—and I have been cheating on her with you. And like a girlfriend, you, my church, tell me what I want to hear: that I'm a good preacher, a fine man, always there when you want me. Ada tells me what I need to hear. And sometimes she tells me without words. With her exhaustion I have refused to see and with her self-renovation I have refused to fully understand, I'm standing at a crossroads, see and understand, or lose Ada. Be a man, or lose Ada. This is Women's Day. I'm here to talk about something we don't talk about on Sunday morning at eleven. Saturday night. When a good man loves a good woman, God smiles. When a good man loves a good woman, God smiles so broad and bright that the angel guarding the gate to Eden puts down his fiery sword. I've been too busy to get to Eden. What kind of man is too busy to make God smile? I got things to do. You men out there, you know. You busy, too. You may be a truck driver or a teacher, or a doctor or a janitor or an electrician or a lawyer. That's what you call yourself. When God looks down and thinks about the work he put you on earth to do, he doesn't see truck driving or school teaching or doctoring or janitoring or lawyering or preaching. He sees lover! How many of you been too busy to take your woman to Eden as often as she might like to go? Man invented the car. Man invented the house. God made woman. God made man. But instead of prizing what God made, we prize what we made. Money in the bank. A promotion. A raise.

A boat. A trip. Now we got to work, but we got to know why we working—to serve our families, not to make ourselves the big shot. We got to 'umble ourselves in our work. Me first. Ushers, I want you to pass the collection plate. Again. I put my robe over there. Y'all can tell me if you want me to put it back on by what's in the basket. I can't be Ada's man, Ada's good man, without an assistant. We need forty thousand dollars for that. And I don't know whether you will give it or not. But I know this. I ain't above begging to do right for Ada. I don't care if y'all hate me, fire me, say I have embarrassed the church, or ruined Women's Day. I want you to know, God doesn't give a man anything more precious than a good woman. When I first came to this church, I said I would never pass the collection plate more than once a service. We gonna pass it three times today, and I don't care if nobody puts even a penny in it the second and third time it come round, 'cause it's not about the money we collect today. It's about me breaking my word to you so I can keep my word to God. When I married Ada, I gave my word to God that I would stand by Ada, would be her helpmate. The money I have not asked you for has come out of the too many times I left my woman alone, trying to do the job of two men, leaving responsibilities at home, Saturday-night responsibilities, neglected. Leaving Eden unentered. Leaving God's best gift to man, after grace, ignored. If God struck me down now, I would not be surprised. The gifts of God are for the people of God. When we love on the right woman, the right way, we are treasuring what the good Lord gave us. We are giving thanks and praise for creation. And the best of that is women, starting with the mamas who bore us, and the good women they were when they lay down with our fathers, like Eve lay down with Adam. I will not be cheating on this woman no more. I have bought myself a second phone. My wife thought it was for nefarious reasons—that's how much I have neglected her, she almost lost the excellent sense God gave her—but this second phone"—here Preach reached into his breast pocket and pulled out a phone that he lifted high to show all the congregation—"is for emergencies, real and true emergencies. And y'all best not abuse it. Unless you want to start looking for a new minister. My regular cell phone is turning off at eight P.M. every day God sends. I'm not cheating on Ada no more. Usually on Women's Day I give my wife what my mother-in-law calls the 'proper props.' The things most of us give our wives on Women's Day: hats and scarves and expensive purses. This year I'm giving her the 'true props' of respect and real good wide-eyed time-taking loving. That's what the Reverend Franklin's daughter meant when she sang about getting her props when her man got home. When a woman takes care of herself, she doing what God wants her to do. Ada showed me that. Look at all the grace in your First Lady. That's the Lord at work. I been interfering with that. A year ago your First Lady looked exhausted, and I was helping exhaust her. Not anymore. Not again. Will the church say, Amen?"

The church said Amen. Eight thousand, seven hundred dollars was raised in a single morning. Nine women had to be carried out by ushers, and six babies were born nine months to the week later. One member of the vestry resigned.

In the front row, under her veil, Ada cried. She did not cry like a baby, as some said later, nor like a bride, as others said later. She cried like a woman whose man had reclaimed her, in front of God and her neighbors.

The flight to Jacksonville, Florida, from Nashville is not long, but it was long enough for Ada to whisper into Lucius's ear a thing she wanted to do with him. And it was long enough for her to tell him that she had been to see his special friends.

"What did you find out?"

"That you talk too much."

"Anything else?"

"That you love me."

He reached out his hand to her, and she took it. He closed his eyes and brought her hand to his lips, and he kissed it. She pulled her hand back, and his eyes opened.

"Did you get the vitamin V?"

"Absolutely."

"Hallelujah!"

She took his hand, but he squeezed it, then let it go. He had a question of his own.

"Was any part of you getting big about me?"

"About you?"

"You know I love great big women."

"Was I trying to get bigger so you would want me more?"

"Yeah?"

"Maybe just a little bit."

"Is any part of getting small not caring what I want?"

"No part."

"None?"

"It's just that I figured something out."

"What's that?"

"Some men are heterosexual, some men are homosexual, some men are asexual, some men are bisexual, you are Adasexual."

"Adasexual. I like that."

And they played in a borrowed Seaside cottage like they were naked babies playing in Eden.

That had been her good invitation: "Come play like a naked child with me." She had whispered that in his ear, and that is what they did.

In a little white-and-blue bedroom she took the chocolate whiff puffs she had found and purchased on the Internet and blew them into his mouth. And then she made him a little feast of herbs, sage, and rosemary, and thyme and basil. She waved the savory bundle under his nose, then dropped leaves one at a time on his tongue. He dipped apples in honey and dripped the honey on her belly and licked it off while she nibbled on the apple. They sat in chairs just opposite each other in fluffy terry-cloth towels, and each of them held the other's feet in their lap, and she would press in a place on his and he would press in a place on hers, sometimes a responsive place, sometimes a mirrored place. They talked for hours with their hands and feet.

Eventually, she got down on her knees and kissed him with her tongue. She learned the new sight and scent of him, the sameness and the difference, the compelling truth of long-lived love. And when she climbed onto his lap, and they looked each other in the eyes, and he pushed deeply into her, and her legs wrapped round him, allowing her to pull herself tighter and closer, in that same moment they were two babies swimming in the womb of God, and they were fierce warriors on the road to freedom, and they were flowers blooming in an autumn garden, and they were everything exciting two as one can be.

When she slipped off his lap and they slept together until he woke her and this time she was on her back and her ankles were on his shoulders, he was a sugarcane stalk, or so it seemed, crazy drunk on well-aged crazy love.

Well-aged love is hallucinogenic. She hadn't known it until she had come more times in an hour than she could count. Till they were sitting alone on the balcony of their house, looking out to the ocean just at dusk, and his fingers made their way around and around the smallest circles of her and into the frills and folds of her, until she was wrapped in his love and saying, again, "Here, I come."

It was prophesy, predicament, and truth. "Here, I come." The place that she was going to was the place that she was. The place they were going to was the place they were.

The place they had was the place that they wanted.

49

DON'T STOP SHORT
OF YOUR GOAL

T HEY DOZED AFTER they made love. When they awoke, they walked to the little grocery store and bought coffee and cookies. As they nibbled, sitting at an umbrella table just outside the store, he on the cookies, she on his fingers, they took turns asking themselves "What were you thinking then?" questions.

Playing Scrabble back at their house after their snack, they both agreed the house afforded "a watch-God view." They were not talking about the balcony's view of the water. They were talking about the way Ada and Lucius inhabited the space and how it put them eye to eye with God's greatest creation.

They played Scrabble, their own version. One made a word, and the other had to name a way the word had been important in their life, and all the words they made had to have something to do with love.

It was something Lucius had learned in a "How to Save Your Congregants' Marriage" workshop. The one making the word got the number of points on the word, the one making the association also got the same number of points. The game always ended in a tie and a bouquet of shared memories provoked by the words constructed. It was a game he had taught many husbands but had not taken the time to play with his wife. And now they did.

They had an early dinner served in the room and fell asleep reading *Cane* aloud to each other.

Ada awoke early as the sun was coming up, and she got out of bed naked and walked to the bathroom, still naked. She did her business, and was going back to the bed when she spied the scale underneath the sink. She stepped on the scale; she was sixty-nine pounds lighter than the day she started. It wasn't the hundred pounds she had thought she wanted to lose, but it was almost just right.

She was very near to journey's end. She would drink hot herbal teas and suck on special ice cubes and restrict carbs, and sleep eight hours; she would walk thirty minutes a day, the rest of her life.

She would separate herself from one last pound and declare victory. She would finish what she started. And part of it would be celebrating the reality—she still had a magic box, and he still had a key.

She brushed her teeth and found her way back into the bed. Lucius was sleeping beside her, snoring loudly. The noise amused her. Wanting to see the dawn with her beloved, she started to bite him softly.

He awoke and pulled her to him. Then rolled away. He hit the bathroom, then the shower. Seven minutes later he was back in the bed, whispering to her, "Finish what you started."

She did. And after, while he slept, she walked naked up the

stairs to the balcony, and she walked naked beneath the sky when the moon and the sun still hung.

She had never stood naked in the open air. She didn't know how she looked, but she knew how she felt—wonderful. Awake.

Finish what you start. Drunk on all the possibilities of morning, particularly the possibility of making love to Lucius again and soon, Ada wondered if it was possible that God had invented orgasm not just to encourage us to have babies but because God wanted to teach us to finish what you start—and get well rewarded.

She was finishing what she got started. Once he had chosen her. Now she was proof he had chosen well. Once she had chosen him. Now he was proof she had chosen well. *I am a wall, and my breasts like towers, then was I in his eyes as one that found favor.*

How much more to be the one who had kept favor, the one who had proved *Many waters cannot quench love, neither can floods drown it.*

The road to freedom passes through discipline and creativity. Embracing limits and boundaries as well as desire, Ada had whittled herself down to an essential big brown beauty.

She went and found her body journal. In the euphoria of reunion sex, Ada found it the sweetest rule of all.

Finish what you start.

50

CELEBRATE DAPPLED BEAUTY DAILY: THE POWER OF THE IMPERFECT AND GOOD-ENOUGH

WHEN LUCIUS AWOKE, he was scribbled over. Head-to-toe flowers and love notes. Ada had done it with her new lipstick.

He smiled at her. In this place, all the surprises were good.

"What is this?"

"A reason to take a shower together."

"Isn't that how we got the twins?"

"Another advantage of getting old."

"Can you love a dappled thing?"

"Dappled you, yes."

He soaped her up and down, reciting to her the words he didn't expect had ever been recited before in a shower. He found the dichotomy uplifting. He continued to recite as he soaped her up and rose to the challenge of middle-aged morning.

"Glory be to God for dappled things—For skies of couple-colour as a brinded cow; For rose-moles all in stipple upon trout that swim; Fresh-firecoal chestnut-falls; finches' wings; Land-scape plotted and pieced—fold, fallow, and plough; And all trades, their gear and tackle and trim. All things counter, original, spare, strange; What is fickle, freckled (who knows how?) With swift, slow; sweet, sour; adazzle, dim; He fathers-forth whose beauty is past change: Praise her."

Ada slipped to her knees and took Preach into her mouth. For a moment he could continue to recite, "How many loved your moments of glad grace or loved your beauty with love false or true, this man loved the pilgrim soul in you and loves the beauties of your changing face." Then she stopped him with her tongue.

Just after, lavish with the hot water a hotel affords, they bubble bathed.

"I was born to be a self-absorbed bastard. I loved you too much to watch you not have what you need."

Ada and Lucius were up to their shoulders in hot water and soapy bubbles. They didn't move. They didn't talk. They didn't do it. It was their first taste of old-folks' sex, and it wasn't half bad.

5 1

CULTIVATE NEW INTERESTS

ONE FLY IN the ointment of the honied-moon was a call
from the Delta. The girls had been told not to call. Ruth
ignored instructions and called to ask her mother if she, Ada,
had ever dated Matt Mason, because she, Ruth, wanted to date
him. It seemed Ruth had spent an afternoon at the B. B. King
Museum with Mason; this followed on the heels of three Dockery visits, a dinner at the Alluvian, and God-only-knows-what-
else with Mason.

"He's fifty years old."

"He's brilliant."

"He's like an uncle to you."

"I've never met him before in my life."

"We dated in college."

"You married Daddy. And you didn't *date* date, did you?"

"No."

"Then grown is grown."

"Grown is grown."

Ada said it, and she meant it. Then her daughter said something she immediately forgave her daughter for repeating, but would never forgive Mason for saying.

"He says I look more like you to him, than you look like you."

"You look like you, baby. And you prettier than I ever thought of being, but I take that as a compliment. A big compliment."

"I think I love him, Mama."

"The thing about love, baby, only time tells."

Time had told Ada Preach was Ada's man, and Ada was Preach's woman.

That night, before they went home to Nashville, Ada had two confessions to make. She picked her moment. They were on the balcony, counting shooting stars.

"I've got something to tell you about Matt."

"Matt who?"

"Matt Mason."

"What?"

"He went on a date with Ruth."

Preach looked shocked. He expected Ada to start crying, to fall apart, to be heading to the roof to jump off. Ada was smiling. Finally he got it.

"You never slept with Matt Mason?"

"Never. Not even close. Wasn't even interested."

"Why you tell me you did?"

"It was the only way I was going to get you to sleep with me before the wedding."

"Matt Mason's seeing our Ruth?"

"They're probably about the same emotional age."

"He couldn't do better, but she could do worse."

"I'm sure glad you didn't let me make him a godfather."

"I knew."

Ada was lucky. He wasn't saying, but she could see that Lucius couldn't imagine why any man would want to start all over with a young twenty-something. Ada couldn't imagine that any man wouldn't want either twin at the center of his life.

She was no longer worried about the girls getting married. Her confidence in her own romantic choices had inspired in Ada a confidence in her daughters'. They were far more likely to marry than she was to learn the solo her daddy taught Duane Allman, and she was learning the solo her Daddy taught Duane Allman. She was bringing beauty back to her house every way she knew how.

And she knew a whole lot of ways to beckon beauty. Ada thought about them all on their flight back home. And she thought about something she promised herself she would not think about after the plane landed. She thought about how she had tasted Delila on Preach's tongue, Delila, from the time just before she got sober. Ada had felt it in her body. There had been a fifth name. She would not let it be a devastation. She wasn't about to ever lose Delila, and she wasn't about to lose Preach. Whatever they had done—once, not twice, she had not tasted that level of betrayal—had scared Delila into sobriety and might have gotten Winky on the blink. They had all paid enough. It was time to live and forgive. She would gift to Preach the forgiveness he had given her for Matt Mason. She didn't need it. Then. Now. Or ever.

Bird and Temple stopped the service when they entered Preach's church. Ada turned her head to see what had caused the quiet.

She thought it was the hat: a giant plumed purple and velvet turban. It wasn't the hat. Bird and Temple entered on a solo. When Bird lifted her voice to accompany the soloist, the soloist stopped singing. Bird's voice eclipsed. Temple nudged Bird in the ribs with his elbow while nodding with a bandleader's emphatic chin for the soloist on stage to continue. When she did, Bird and Temple quietly took a seat on the front pew beside their daughter. Bird eased in gracefully, like she always sat in the front row with her daughter, wearing a gigantic hat with old feathers and lots and lots of shiny stuff sewn or pinned to what she secretly called her pirate hat.

Preach preached. The service continued. When they passed the offering plate, Bird took out a tiny scissors from her purse, golden scissors, the kind fancy women used for their after-dinner needlework, and she cut a jeweled flower off the hat and threw it into the collection plate. Even down to the lake, they had heard about Preach's crazy tithing sermon.

When the service was over, Ada invited her mother and father to stay for lunch. They had to get back to the lake house and make Sunday dinner for the boarders. With more of the space cleaned out, there were more boarders.

"We are the colored division of the retired musicians union," Temple said.

Everyone laughed. Bird got out a big laundry basket she had in the backseat.

"I have not had a drink in twenty-six days. I made these for you."

They were patchwork quilts made out of her old stage gowns. And in the back of their old car sat three old trunks. Bird pointed to them. Then she linked arms with Ada and started talking.

"I cleaned all the best stuff and made a dress-up trunk. One for each of your girls."

"They're too old for dress-up, Mama."

"For their daughters."

"Thank you, Mama."

"Playing pretty-pretty is not the same as whoring."

"Nobody says it is."

"Everybody used to say it. Folks lie. Men cheat. Babies die."

"I know, Mama."

"The difference between a woman and a girl is, a woman finds a way to enjoy herself despite life being lived on a pile of shit. Me, I got to get back home and cook. I'm looking to find some of the pounds you lost. I ain't letting you have none of 'em back."

Bird kissed Ada on the lips. Their lipsticks mingled. Bird thought, If I get killed in a car accident on the way home, I will die happy. For the first time in years, Ada wasn't praying for the Lord to quick come take them. One of the days on her treadmill, Ada had weaned herself off inertia. Moving on, she had stumbled into her mother's remaining sugar tit.

52

MAKE A HEALTH AND
BEAUTY CALENDAR

IT HAD BEEN a bit over a year since Ada had been to her
doctor. She was excited to let the woman see her progress.
She had lost the last pound. Seventy pounds down.

The appointment didn't go as she expected. The doctor had
lost more weight than she had—probably thirty pounds more.
The doctor looked extraordinary. She had lost a hundred pounds.

Willie Angel had had weight-loss surgery.

For a hot minute Ada wondered if she had made the right
decision—not because the work had been too hard, but because her friend had gotten seemingly better results.

But that was only apparently. Where Ada had enjoyed her
year, her doctor friend related that she had experienced her year
as something of a tunnel. She had eaten a narrower and narrower range of food. She had taken something out of her life,
while leaving it almost exactly as it was before. In the end, the
doctor was a woman with a hole in her life. But she was mag-
nificently transformed, and that served to confer a kind of buoyancy, hole or no hole.

She put Ada through the paces: mammogram (she insisted

on digital), colonoscopy (she suggested IV sedation, and recommended a Demerol-Versed mix). In-depth eye exam to check for glaucoma. Full panel of blood work. Skin cancer screen with punch biopsies. The modern midlife black woman works.

The glaucoma tests came back suspicious. She was called back for another test. She sat and looked through goggles at something like a video game screen, squeezing a hand-held device every time she saw a light, indicating the direction it had appeared in. After she got the hang of the device, which wasn't easy because Ada didn't play any computer games, Ada's eyes were cleared. No glaucoma, medicine, or surgery in her immediate future.

Everything else came back great. Willie Angel announced that Ada had taken six years off her life.

Ada reread her food diary. She took another look at the map of her body. She drew a picture of herself standing naked in the mirror of the Seaside house. She needed a life plan.

She wanted it all down on paper so she could stop carrying her beauty calendar in her head.

She started with the simple things, like the daily thirty-minute walk. She put in the yearly big medical tests. In between she put in the mani-pedis, the haircuts, the waxing. She put in changing up the uniforms and reviewing the uniforms. The daily flossing, because flossing is good for the heart. She made a little schedule of all that she needed to do to maintain a bit of shimmer.

And when she had it all laid out, she signed her name to the bottom of the calendar. It was more than a contract; it was a promise to keep. And it was the beginning of her novel. Ada was going to write a novel. The first line was going to be, "I lost seventy pounds writing this book."

She threw out her last box of tampons, then thought better of it and put the box in the twins' bathroom, and slept the sleep of the grown.

53

DO IT FOR YOU

ADA WAS ADA skinny: healthy and happy in her skin. The size-8 tulip dress was packed. With the proper foundations, it looked great. Mainly she wore a 12 but she treasured her one size 8 that fit. All her reunion materials, including the first invitation that had arrived just over a year before, were packed too. In the morning she was flying to Baltimore. A friend—a girlfriend—was picking her up at BWI, and they were driving to Hampton together.

Ada was already in bed and half asleep when Preach sat down on her side of the bed and stroked her arm. She half opened her eyes to see what he wanted.

It wasn't passion, or company; it was the surety she would return. He knew she was going, and he wanted to be sure she would return. He wanted her to be his boomerang. He couldn't say any of that. He was fifty-one years old, but in this place he might lose her, might lose her in the full bloom of autumn roses, because of what he had done, and because of what he had left undone. He was a little boy watching the prettiest creature on earth walk away from him, and he felt too small and too puny to do anything about it. His arms went all over gooseflesh. She felt it and reached for his face with her lips. She kissed him, two pillows to two pillows. He started to sing her a blues song, of his own creation: "Ada stay right there, Ada stay right here, baby turn around, lay your body down, Ada stay right here, don't go to Hampton town, don't make your good man frown, I beg you now."

"Don't beg."

"All night long. Only a fool too proud to beg when he got a woman like you."

"I love you, baby."

"Are there any other Matt Masons?"

"Probably."

"Be serious."

"No."

"Did you get yourself all fixed up for me?"

"No."

"Matt Mason?"

"No."

"Barack Obama?"

"No."

"God."

"No."

"Who?"

"Me. I did it for me."

She kissed him again, and then she fell asleep. He hoped she saw him in her dreams. He would stay up all night and look at her, just in case it was the last night she was his and only his. He didn't want to miss a moment.

Free will. Exquisite design. God's brilliance. She would dally, or she would not. It would be her choice to make, and he would be crowned again with love or he would not be. And he knew he would be. Like he knew he would handle his stuff, and he knew she would never cheat. And he would never cheat again.

There was only one song he needed to sing to Ada, and he sang it: "When a Man Loves a Woman." When he got to the words about loving eyes being blind, for the very first time in the history of his grown life, tears rolled down Preach's face. One fell on Ada.

Her eyes opened, and her arms opened too. Her small but still round shoulders lifted toward him. "Here, I come," she said, and soon she did. With him. At the very same time.

Stubbly gray box and all.

HOW TO USE MY, ADA HOWARD'S, NOVEL AS A DIET BOOK

I lost seventy pounds writing this book. I imagined myself thin. I used what I had to get what I wanted. And you can too. My way, the Ada way.

"Eat less, move more. I know what to do, I just don't do it." Maybe what we're supposed to do doesn't work. And by doesn't work, I don't mean, you do it and you don't lose weight. I mean, girl, you do it and get hungry, grumpy, and less productive—so you stop doing it.

You go back to feeding yourself the way you fed yourself before—to make up for treating yourself so bad in the pursuit of superficial stuff like beauty, and important stuff like health. You tell yourself, "If this is what I have to do to have a long life, I don't want one."

What if there's another way to go? What if we combine folk wisdom with targeted DNA science and then throw in a few new pleasures and old comforts? What if we form superior habits that crowd out the ones that have served us so poorly? What if we stop appealing to our self-discipline and start appealing to our hedonism?

Ada does, and gets skinnier.

What if you reconnect exercise to play, and substitute sex for dessert and prayer for chicken soup? What if you start rewarding yourself with reading a great poem, or listening to a great song, rather than eating ice cream? What if you start treating yourself to a foray into a foreign culture by downloading a zouk song in French, watching a steamy Telemundo melodrama, rewatching *Tampopo*, or taking in a Bollywood extravaganza instead of chowing down on fajitas, or saag aloo, or pancake house crepes, or California roll and tempura and miso and lettuce salad with sweet and fat, orange, never-seen-in-Japan dressing?

If you did any, or all, of that, you'd be living by Ada's Rules.

Ada, me, and Ada, the star of my book, *Ada's Rules*, who is almost exactly like me. Except, for example, my husband's church is called Shiloh Baptist, not Full Love Gospel Tabernacle. And I didn't drop out of divinity school; I graduated from the American Baptist College, but never entered church work. I do work at KidPlay but it's really called KidPlace. This is fiction. With a whole lot of truth in it.

So many people daydream about what their life would be like if it were exactly the same—except thinner. Which is a lot like daydreaming about winning a lottery. What happens if one thing changes out of the blue? Usually not much. Lottery winners who were broke at the get-go are broke five years later. What happens when everything changes? Most everybody.

Finding, adding, and chasing new pleasure changes things.

Ada's Rules pokes us to stop trying to be stoic and start trying to embrace our inner epicurean—our love of all that is delicious and celebrates life—while keeping up with the humdrum daily. And we all got a whole lot of humdrum daily.

Read as a diet book, *Ada's Rules* will lead you to and through creating a healthy liaison with food—and with exercise and body and beauty and youth and age and work and even death—a liaison that will leave you happier when you look into the mirror, more confident when you face a routine blood lab test, more joyful when you close your eyes, no matter what else is going on. And there's always a lot of mess going on.

As you read *Ada's Rules* and root for Ada as she uses what she has to get what she wants, I hope that you will be inspired, as I was inspired writing Ada, to go on your own health and beauty hunt. Seventy pounds later, I'm not a babe and I'm not a blob. I'm good-looking—and that's plenty good enough for me.

This novel will help you lose one to two pounds a week. If you have less than twenty pounds to lose, the fifty-two-day plan repeated should help you get there. If you have twenty to a hundred pounds to lose, try the fifty-two-week plan.

Whether you have seven, or seventy, or a hundred and seven pounds to lose, if you read this book and work Ada's Rules, you're going to be more fit and less fat. And you're going to help balance the national budget.

How's that? Fat is a multibillion-dollar problem for America. That's a lot of money spent on dialysis, heart surgeries, and medicines that would not need to be spent if everybody followed my rules.

So if you don't have weight to lose—read Ada's story anyway.

It will help you create your own little invisible Eden where you eat and exercise with beauty, which, for me and for Ada, means with grace and power. And my very own slogan: *Pitch Your Beauty Revival Tent: Come and Get It—Ada's Rules: 53 Steps to Your BSN—Best Self Now!* One rule for each week of the year and one to grow on—or one to trade out if there's one you can't stand!

Ada's Rules: Fifty-three Perfect Rules for an Imperfect but Excellent Health and Beauty Revival

1. Don't keep doing what you've always been doing.
2. Make a plan: Set clear, multiple, and changing goals.
3. Weigh yourself daily.
4. Be a role model.
5. Don't attack your own team; don't let anyone on your team attack you.
6. Identify and learn from iconic diet books.
7. Walk thirty minutes a day—every day.
8. See your doctor.
9. Do the DNA test.
10. Budget: Plan to afford the feeding, exercising, and dressing of you.
11. Get eight hours of sleep nightly.
12. Eat breakfast.

13. Self-medicate with art: Quash boredom and anxiety.
14. Consider surgery.
15. Keep a food diary and a body journal.
16. Add a second exercise three times a week.
17. Drink eight glasses of water daily.
18. Eat sitting down.
19. Eat slowly.
20. Find a snack you like that likes you.
21. Access the power of quick fixes: poems, fingernail polish, and waxing.
22. Add a Zen exercise: hooping, water jogging, watsu, and yoga.
23. Don't be afraid to look cheap—in restaurants.
24. Manage portion sizes.
25. Eat every three hours.
26. Savor HOT and COLD, the power of herbal teas and flavored ice cubes.
27. Don't initiate change you can't stick with for five years.
28. Find and create DNA-based go-to meals: a home-made and healthy house specialty AND a healthy and palatable frozen dinner.
29. Use consultants: trainers, masseuses, nutrionists, and priests.
30. Massage your own feet.
31. Drink cautiously: no juice, no soft drinks, no food coloring, no corn syrup, no fake sugar; examine alcohol and caffeine intake.

32. Bathe to calm or bathe to excite: recipes for baths.
33. Invent DNA-based care packages that work for you and yours.
34. Don't stay off the wagon when you fall off the wagon—and you will fall off the wagon.
35. Get therapy.
36. Create your own spa day.
37. Get better hair.
38. Fake it till you make it: fine foundations and wide smiles.
39. Update beauty rituals and tools.
40. Shop for your future self.
41. Take ONE bite of anything and never more than TWO bites of anything decadent.
42. Uni up: get yourself a uniform, for day and for night.
43. Front-load: Eat before you go to parties; drink water before meals.
44. Draw a map of your body.
45. Update your goals.
46. Create your own spa week.
47. Get better hair down there.
48. Seize the proper props: scarves, shoes, purses, sunglasses, and respect.
49. Don't stop short of your goal.
50. Celebrate dappled beauty daily: the power of the imperfect and good-enough.
51. Cultivate new interests.

52. Make a health and beauty calendar.

53. Do it for you.

Blessings,

Ada

P.S. You may want send off for the DNA test before you even start reading, so it is there when you finish. And make an appointment to see your internist. Or stop in at a doc-in-a-box. Nobody should start a diet or exercise plan without seeing a doctor first.

P.P.S. *Home Training* is coming. It just didn't come first.

ACKNOWLEDGMENTS

I must begin by thanking Vanderbilt University and Vanderbilt Medical Center. Being located at a university that prizes innovative approaches to creative enterprise and tackling health care disparities provides the fertile ground in which I developed and taught Soul Food as Text in Text, and imagined Ada. I would like to thank all my colleagues at Vanderbilt for cocreating the electric campus I find sustaining. To Dr. Tracy Denean Sharpley-Whiting, director of the Program in African American and Diaspora Studies and dear friend, I owe an especial debt for reading and critiquing early drafts of the *Ada's Rules* manuscript as well as supporting the development of the course Soul Food as Text in Text. I also owe an especial debt to Cecelia Tichi, with whom I developed and co-taught Southern Food.

This book is a work of fiction. Ada's ideas about health, and science, and health care, are hers, and hers alone. They are the ideas of a fictional character. Writing Ada, I was, however, informed by my own experience of weight gain and weight loss as well as by my readings and research into the science related to weight, weight regulation, and nutrition. And I was inspired by the work of a number of dedicated physicians and medical professionals. Some inspired with the power of their research. Others inspired with the compassion and insight of their patient care. And there were still others who inspired by being curious about the possibility of using a novel to help deliver health care information and to help motivate patient compliance. Dr. Kirk Barton, Dr. Frank Boehm, Leslie R. Boone, MPH, Dr. Walter Clair, Dr. Henry Foster, Dr. Chris Lind, Dr. Buzz Martin, Dr. Melinda New, Dr. Kevin Niswender, Dr. William Pao, Dr. James Price, Dr. Judson Randolph, Dr. Wayne Riley, Dr. Dan Roden, Dr. Dave Thombs, Dr. Harold Thompson, Dr. Ellen Shemancik, Dr. William Serafin, Dr. Paul Sternberg, Dr. Edwin Williamson, and Dr. Kelly Wright all taught me something of significance about health care challenges, health care delivery, or medical research. None of these folks endorse all fifty-three of Ada's rules. Some may not endorse any. All of them have a proven track record of service to the health needs of diverse communities.

The diabetes epidemic is a national challenge and a national tragedy with political and economic consequences for all aspects of American life. From the day I first began work on Ada, I have been aided by the fact that I live in Tennessee, where I have been fortunate to be represented by some of the smartest and most well-informed people to serve in the House and in the Senate, including a Rhodes Scholar, a surgeon, and a secretary of education. This project has had the support of my congressman and friend Jim Cooper, acclaimed in the *New York Times* as the conscience of the Congress, and of Congressman Marsha Blackburn, a friend and leader in the Republican Party. Over the years, I have also enjoyed the friendship and support of Senator Lamar Alexander and former Senate majority leader Dr. Bill Frist. I thank them all for encouraging me to think about the politics and economics of health. I also want to thank Representative Lois DeBerry, the second African-American woman elected to the Tennessee House and the first woman to serve as Speaker pro tempore of the House. In the spring of 2010, Representative DeBerry was at the center of Links Day on Capitol Hill, in which Links from all over the state of Tennessee gathered at the Capitol to discuss food deserts, obesity, diabetes, and other matters of pressing concern to do with food quality and health. Representative DeBerry's support of this project and concern for matters of health within the African-American community have been a profound inspiration as I have worked to finish this book.

I want to thank my Link sisters. The Links, Incorporated, is an outstanding social organization of black women who do great things to further the health of all people throughout the world. I am proud to be a Link, and proud to acclaim—Links are green—in all the best ways. Some of the best ways now are standing up against the spread of hypertension and diabetes in communities of color. I owe debts of particular gratitude to Links Dr. Charlene Dewey, Dr. Debra Webster-Clair, and Professor Beverly Moran. I would not be a Link if it were not for my mother-in-law, Florence Kidd, who was brought into the Links by her mother, Corinne Steele of Tuskegee.

I also want to thank Yaddo for giving me five weeks of uninterrupted time, a studio high in the trees, and the Iphigene Ochs Sulzberger Endowed Fellowship. Yaddo shelters and inspires.

This is my second novel with Bloomsbury and my fourth

with my editor Anton Mueller. In a world where many publishing relationships are one deal long, we are happily arguing about whether this is our thirtieth or thirty-first year of a reading and writing friendship. In our Bloomsbury days, Rachel Mannheimer's taste, intelligence, and good cheer have done much to facilitate the publication of these two novels. And I applaud the work of Miranda Ottewell. She is the first copy editor I have ever adored. Helen Garnons-Williams is my UK editor at Bloomsbury. Having a UK editor is my idea of high cotton. In that high cotton I am proud to claim Amy Williams, of McCormick and Williams, as my agent.

My very favorite foodie, and best friend, is Mimi Oka. With her I would like to thank John Egerton, who inspires everyone who thinks about southern food or cares about civil rights. In a delicious twist of fate, Mimi, a Francophile American of Japanese ethnicity, is the reason I first met John more than twenty-five years ago! And through John I have met an organization I love: the Southern Foodways Alliance. If Ada were a real person, I would give her a membership in the SFA.

Writing about the body is an intimate undertaking. Writing with humor and love about the black woman's body is a delicate project. I want to thank all the women I know well enough to talk the triumphs and troubles of the body. They come in all shapes and sizes and colors but these ladies are my kind of brilliantly beautiful: There is power and grace in their hearts, their minds, and their bodies. Allison, Amanda, Becca, Betsy, Caroline C., Edith, Elena, Gail, Gayle, Hortense, Jane, Joan B., Kate, Leatrice, Leslie, Lissa, Martha, Mary Jane, Michelle, Minna, Perian, Siobhan, Thadious, Tracy, and Victoria.

And I want to thank the men who are my brothers who have been sometimes the hands sometimes the heart sometimes the mind of the father I so love and lost: David F., David K., Reggie, Seigenthaler, Steve Earle, and Court. Almost a half century ago, my father took a basketball out of my hands and said, "This is not for you." You put the ball back in my hands. You my Dennis Rodmans. I will never forget that. Nor will I ever forget the men who have been brothers, cousins, godfathers, and other more playful kin: Carter Jun, Neil, Marc, Marq, Matthew, Ray, Ridley, and Steve. And Jerry. He has claimed me as daughter and that makes me proud. As always I thank the godchildren: Kazuma, Charlie, Lucas, Moses, Cynara, Aria, and my play-niece Haviland. I also wish to acknowledge my niece Maddie and nephew Richard. I treasure the steps I have walked with each of you and will walk with each of you.

I want to especially thank my husband, David Steele Ewing, for loving every ounce of me, lost or found.

In the time I was writing this book I was most often fed by Burger-Up, a wonderful farm-to-table restaurant in my neighborhood. I want to thank Miranda and all our bright young friends, musicians, artists, photographers, writers, chefs, and plain joyful livers who have brought so much optimism and so much care to this project. I also want to thank Margot and the staff at my favorite place in the world to eat brunch, Margot Café and Bar. I have been eating at Margot for a decade, almost all my novel-writing life. That is a very good thing. It is also a very good thing that new good places and tastes arrive. For our family, City House has become a well-loved institution. Sitting with Tandy at his chef's bar is a pure food pleasure. Eating in Nashville is nowhere more adventuresome than at the Catbird Seat. Josh and the Goldbergs create exquisite bites that delight the tongue and feed the eye. What to say about Randy Rayburn's Sunset Grill—well, that's where we spent Easter Sunday this year. That tells a lot. Over two decades of dining at Sunset I can't begin to remember all the joys, losses, and new joys I have celebrated and mourned in the shelter of Randy's foodspace. The person who dines out with David and me more often than any other person is Godmommy Lea. Lea is the miracle: a fit black foodie. Lord we all love her so.

While I was writing this book, my daughter was living and teaching down in the Mississippi Delta. We owe a debt of gratitude to our Delta Circle, the people with roots in that place who have been such supportive friends to my sweet girl: Dr. Edwards, Elizabeth, Hiram, Julia, Mary McKay, Maudie, Lang, Melissa, Nick, Ruthie, and Yvette.

And I thank my daughter. Ada's daughters follow Ada to fitland. If I get to fitland it will be because I followed in the strong footsteps of Caroline Randall Williams. She is the sugar in the plum.

Alice Randall was born in Detroit, grew up in Washington, D.C., and graduated from Harvard. She is the author of the *New York Times* bestseller *The Wind Done Gone, Pushkin and the Queen of Spades*, and *Rebel Yell*. She is also an award-winning country songwriter. Randall lives with her husband in Nashville and is currently writer-in-residence at Vanderbilt University. Like Ada, she's done battle with her weight. And, like Ada, she's a proud member of the Links, Incorporated.